Dreamer

Part 2 of the Living Myth Saga

Gabriella Creighton

kindle direct publishing

AMAZON KINDLE DIRECT PUBLISHING

ISBN Information:

Kindle: 979-8-2625785-6-6
eBook: 979-8-9931454-4-0
Print: 979-8-9931454-5-7

About the Author

Gabriella Creighton is a life long lover of the Fantasy and Science Fiction Genres. She has been fascinated by Dragons and other mythical creatures from a young age and grew up dreaming of being a writer. Inspired by great authors like Jane Yolen, Anne McCaffrey, JRR Tolkien and Phillip Pullman, she loves to take an alternative view of myth and weave her own versions. After a long life of working, gaming and enjoying the works of others, she has finally decided to put her nigh on useless Masters Degree in English Literature to work to tell stories of her own.

Growing up in Rural New York and around many of the real life versions of the locations in this book, as well as having been thrown all over the United States, Gabriella has learned she has only three desires. To write until the nail her coffin shut, to never answer the phone and for a cool glass of Salted Caramel Crowne Royal mixed with Cream Soda and Dr Pepper, which she calls a magic elixir. It helps get the writing done.

To the English Department at Buffalo State University

You shaped these books, encouraged me to learn aspects of
the language I never previously understood. You made it okay
for me to write.

For the Future.

Contents

The Garden of Ash

PROLOGUE

I'm a poet, and I like my lies the way my mother
used to make them.

A.C.

THE WIND SIGHED THROUGH the ruins, soft and dry as parchment brushed by ghostly fingers. It stirred the ash that blanketed the ground in a soft, whispering hush, like the rustle of distant silk gowns in a long-forgotten ballroom.

The trees here no longer bore leaves, only twisted limbs that scraped against one another like brittle bones in the breeze. Their bark had long since split and peeled, curling into paper-thin strips the color of old bones and burnt ivory.

This place had once been a garden. You could still see the bones of it beneath the rot: broken marble columns leaned like drunks at a funeral, and shattered statues lay half-buried in soot, their features weathered smooth by time and sin. The sky above held no sun, only a colorless dome of pearlescent grey, pulsing faintly with the memory of light.

No birds sang. No insects chirped. Only the ever-present hush of the falling ash, the restless creak of dead trees, and the quiet breath of something ancient watching from beneath the earth.

Crawly walked through it as if strolling a manicured court-yard, his polished shoes leaving no mark in the cinders. He wore a charcoal-grey suit tailored so finely it caught light like a spider's thread, its silver pinstripe reflecting the strange, low glow of the sky. His tie was loosened, the collar of his white shirt open just enough to suggest ease, but not carelessness.

In one hand, he carried a walking stick carved from twisted yew wood. In the other, he toyed with a single, glossy black apple. It gleamed like obsidian in his palm, too perfect to be real. Unblemished. Unnatural.

He paused beneath the oldest tree. Its roots strangled a for-gotten fountain, and its branches had grown gnarled enough to resemble grasping hands. The fruit had come from this tree, the last one.

Crawly held it up to the lightless sky and smiled with quiet satisfaction.

"It's always the same, isn't it?" His voice broke the silence like a warm knife through butter, low, smooth, with a lilt that was almost musical. "One garden. One rule. One little voice whispering, why not?"

A laugh answered him from the haze. It wasn't loud, but it had weight, like velvet dragged over broken glass.

"You really do love your symbols," drawled the voice, slinking out from behind a ruined archway carved with faded angels.

She moved like smoke made flesh, tall, graceful, and coiled with power. Her skin had the luster of aged bronze, and her eyes burned with the dull glow of coals long banked but never cold. She wore blood-red leather with laces up her arms like barbed vines, and her heels clicked on the stone with a rhythm too precise to be accidental.

Her name had been spoken only once in the old book, and never aloud. Crawly didn't turn to look at her right away. He simply bit into the apple. The flesh gave way with a sickly crunch, and thick, dark juice trickled over his fingers like fresh ink. It dripped onto the roots of the tree, hissing faintly where it touched.

"I prefer archetypes," he said, chewing thoughtfully. "They're more reliable. Last longer."

She arched a brow. "You mean they're easy to manipulate."

He gave a small shrug. "Same difference."

Now he turned, offering her a slow, serpent's smile. No fangs, no threat. Just the kind of charm that made people ignore the cold hand slipping into their pocket, or their soul.

She didn't smile back.

"You've come crawling out of your hole to pick fruit and quote scripture. What's the real play, Crawly?"

"Crowley," he corrected smoothly. "It sounds more refined. Less hissing. Though I confess, Crawly has its charms. Keeps people off balance."

She folded her arms and leaned against a decapitated statue of an angel mid-weeping, now eroded into a blind wail. Her gaze cut through the garden like a razor.

"You think you can succeed where Gomath failed?"

"Gomath was a hammer looking for a nail," Crawly said, tossing the apple core over his shoulder. It landed in the ash with a soft thuff. "Violence is loud. Messy. Predictable."

He began to pace slowly, hands tucked in his pockets. The hem of his coat swept the ash like a priest's robe.

"No. I don't need to burn the world. Just bend it. A whisper here. A crack there. One temptation. One soul."

The demoness tilted her head. "And whose soul are you whispering to this time?"

He stopped. His grin widened, sharklike but somehow still beautiful. "Mia Mason."

For a moment, even the wind seemed to pause. The branches above ceased their skeletal chatter. The name hovered between them like a spell not yet cast. She gave a short, incredulous laugh. "The rebuilt one? Half-demon, half-innocent. That girl's a live wire. You touch her wrong, and she'll explode."

"I'm counting on it," Crawly said simply. "She's fresh. Powerful. Full of guilt and questions. And she's alone, even when she's not."

He reached down and touched the base of the ruined angel statue with reverence. A small crack spread from beneath his fingers.

"All I have to do is make her feel seen. Make her feel heard. People don't betray their friends for power. They do it to matter."

The demoness narrowed her eyes. "You're not doing this for Hell."

He looked up at her, unblinking. "Hell is a pit. I prefer ladders."

There was something ancient in his voice now, older than language. Something snakelike and cold that no longer tried to sound human. She studied him. Then, without warning, she began to laugh, a deep, rich sound that filled the empty air like thunder in a dry canyon.

"Fine," she said at last, shaking her head. "Play your little game. But don't be surprised when the girl breaks you."

With that, she stepped back into the mist. Her form melted away into drifting petals of flame and smoke, leaving behind only the scent of scorched roses.

Crawly stood alone. The wind resumed its whispering. Above, the sky trembled, just once, as if something on the other side of it had stirred. He looked up, his smile returning slowly.

"Come on, Dreamer," he murmured. "Let's see what you're really made of."

Chapter 1

The Farm

The joy of life consists in the exercise of one's energies, continual growth, constant change, the enjoyment of every new experience. To stop means simply to die. The eternal mistake of mankind is to set up an attainable ideal.

A.C.

THE FIRST THING SIA heard was the wind.

Not the hungry howling wind of Hell or the still, breathless hush of the Dreaming, but something softer, earthbound. It stirred tall grass with a dry whisper, brushing through wild sunflowers and broken reeds. Birds sang somewhere, their calls tentative, uncertain, as if even nature had paused to ask: Is it over?

She opened her eyes slowly.

The ceiling above her was old wood, knot-scarred and sun-bleached, crossed with thick beams darkened by age and dust. A fan turned lazily in the center of the room, not to cool but to assure anyone watching that time still moved. Light filtered in through linen curtains, warm, golden, too kind for memory.

Her body ached in strange places. Not sharp pain. Just absence. Like parts of her had burned out and were only now remembering to return.

"Sia?"

The voice cracked with relief.

She turned her head, slowly, as if the motion itself might shatter the peace, and saw her mother sitting beside her bed, clutching her hand in both of hers. Her father stood behind, hands on her mother's shoulders, his face weathered by days without sleep. They looked older. Not by years, but by events.

"Hi," Sia managed, voice a thread.

Her mother smiled. It broke something in the air. "Hi, baby."

The door creaked open. A massive shadow filled the frame.

Domingo ducked as he entered the small farmhouse room, every inch of him too large, too ancient, too mythic to belong anywhere but mountains or thrones. And yet, here he was, in a plaid shirt stretched awkwardly over his shoulders, arms crossed as he tried to pretend he wasn't watching her chest rise and fall like a dragon watching over its hoard.

"She's awake," he said softly, as if announcing a sunrise.

Sia sat up, slowly. Her mother reached to steady her, but she waved her off. Her body remembered how to move, even if her magic didn't yet hum beneath her skin.

"What... happened?" Her voice was dry. Her lips cracked around the syllables.

Domingo stepped forward. His eyes, old as stone and fire, softened.

"After you crossed the threshold with your sister, your body gave out. Too much soul-work. Too much flame." He knelt beside herbed like a knight before a shrine. "But you held the boundary. You lit the path. We found you still glowing."

Sia blinked. "The others?"

Her father answered. "Ella and Tobias are alive, shaken, but they made it. The Hold... we got there just in time."

"We?" she asked.

Domingo gave a small smile, the kind that seemed to shift the world by degrees.

"Your family fought for you," he said. "And not just blood."

Sia let the silence settle around them like ash from a long battle. She closed her eyes. She could still feel the Place

Between in her bones, a silence deeper than death, a light older than stars. Mia had fallen into her arms like a secret returned. The world hadn't ended. Not yet.

But something had changed.

The door opened again.

Mia stood in the doorway like a ghost caught in the act of haunting. Her eyes were shadowed, her posture tense, uncertain. She was wearing a long-sleeved shirt too big for her and jeans that hung loosely on her hips, but her feet were bare, toes curled slightly on the old wood floor like she wasn't sure she was allowed to step further.

Sia didn't say anything.

Neither did Mia.

But their eyes met, and in that long, quiet moment, something deeper than words passed between them. Not apology. Not explanation. Just the raw, aching truth of presence. They were both still here.

Sia scooted aside on the bed, lifting the edge of the blanket.

Mia moved slowly at first, like a wild animal testing the limits of sanctuary, then crossed the floor in two quick steps. She sank beside her sister without hesitation, curling into the offered space like she'd never left. Their bodies folded together, shoulder to shoulder, forehead to temple, breath to breath.

Then came the hug.

Tight. Fierce. Arms around shoulders and necks and backs. Fingers gripping fabric like lifelines. No hesitance. No fear. The kind of hug that doesn't ask permission, because it's what's needed, and what's owed.

Sia pressed her face into Mia's hair, inhaling the faint scent of woodsmoke and something sweet, like burned sugar and regret. Mia clung harder, burying her face into Sia's shoulder as though she could hide there, disappear inside her sister and start over.

And then, finally, the tears came.

Not a storm. Not a sob. Just trembling breaths and warm droplets that soaked into cotton and silence.

"You came back," Sia whispered.

Mia nodded against her. "You pulled me out."

"I didn't do it alone," Sia murmured.

"I know," Mia said. "But you were the one who reached."

They sat there like that, curled in the small bed, a twin flame reignited, not cleanly, not perfectly, but undeniably. No one spoke. No one intruded. Even Domingo bowed his head and stepped out of the room, her parents following behind in reverent silence.

Outside, the wind moved through the fields again, this time with more certainty. A mourning dove cooed. Somewhere distant, a barn door creaked open and then closed with a solid thud, like punctuation at the end of a sentence the world had been holding back for too long.

And at last, the quiet meant peace.

Chapter 2

A Dream Left Open

Having to talk destroys the symphony of silence.

A.C.

The sky above the Farm was impossibly blue.

It wasn't just the color, it was the stillness, the clarity, the way the clouds seemed too soft, too slow, as if the world had paused mid-breath and forgotten how to resume. Sunlight spilled across the golden fields, igniting the tall grass into waves of warm color. A breeze moved through them like fingers through hair, light, gentle, and rhythmically hypnotic.

Sia sat at the edge of the property beneath the tall, rust-rimmed skeleton of the old windmill. Its fan turned with long, lazy creaks, a broken clock marking nothing but memory. Around her, bees drifted through clover and early milkweed, their hum a low, constant vibration in the thick summer air. The scent of sun-warmed wood, fresh hay, and tilled earth clung to everything.

Everything looked… right.
Everything felt… wrong.

She watched a grasshopper leap between stalks near her boots, then vanish. Listened to the faint mechanical buzz of a tractor somewhere beyond the ridge, its movements cutting lines into the earth in patient, looping passes. Life went on here. Predictably. Gently. As though the world hadn't nearly ended two weeks ago.

As though she hadn't stepped through death and fire to reclaim her sister.

Sia shifted, arms resting on her knees, fingers curled around the canteen she hadn't touched since morning. Her boots were untied, laces trailing in the dirt like threads come loose. The light on her skin was soft and warm. Too soft. Too warm.

She hadn't slept the night before. Not truly.

Her dreams, the real ones, the ones that came from somewhere deeper than sleep, had stayed away. All that remained was a presence. A pressure. Like something waiting just beyond the door of her thoughts, breathing slow and steady, not quite stepping in… but not entirely outside.

She hadn't dared to reach for it.

A shadow passed overhead.

Sia's eyes lifted, squinting against the sun.

At first she thought it was a hawk. Then, maybe a cloud. But it wasn't either.

The shape was indistinct, fluid, writhing against the brightness like smoke caught in glass. It moved with no rhythm. No intention. Just drift. Then, as quickly as it had come, it vanished.

The hair on her arms prickled. She stood slowly, brushing bits of grass from her pants, and turned toward the treeline. The windmill creaked behind her like a giant exhaling. There was nothing. No one.

And yet, she felt it. That sense of being watched. Not by eyes. Not by a person. But by the land itself. By the air. As if something old was tasting the edges of her thoughts.

And it wasn't demonic. It was older than that.

She turned toward the far side of the yard, toward the weathered oak that stood near the fenceline, a twisted, massive sentinel that had been there longer than the farmhouse itself. Its limbs creaked softly in the wind, swaying just enough to cast reaching shadows across the earth.

And beneath it stood Marcus.

He leaned against the trunk like he'd grown from the bark itself, tall, still, timeless. A grey shirt clung to his shoulders, sleeves rolled to the elbow, and the sun caught the faint shimmer of bronze scale beneath the collar as he turned.

He didn't speak. Just watched her. She crossed the yard slowly, boots scuffing dry earth, the world sharpening around her with each step.

"You always know where to find me," she said.

Marcus's mouth curved slightly. "I don't find you," he replied. "I wait."

Sia smiled, just barely. "That's very dragon of you."

"It's what we're good at."

She stopped a few feet from him, arms crossing lightly, not guarded, but holding something in. A fragile stillness, maybe. The ache of peace she didn't trust.

"I feel like I never actually woke up," she said.

Marcus tilted his head. "Because you didn't come back the same."

"Did you?"

"Once," he said. "A long time ago."

He pushed off the tree, moving closer. His shadow fell across her like a blanket.

"The Place Between doesn't let you return untouched. It takes something."

"I haven't figured out what it took yet."

"Then it didn't finish."

She blinked at him.

He touched her face softly, just the back of his knuckles along her cheek. "You're still becoming," he said. "And whatever's left... that's who you are."

She leaned into him, letting his arms fold around her like the closing of something old and sacred. His body was warm. His scent clean, salt and smoke and something evergreen. She closed her eyes, not to sleep, just to breathe.

But sleep found her anyway.
And something else.

THE WIND STOPPED.
THE LIGHT vanished.

When Sia opened her eyes again, the world had changed.

She stood in a vast white field that stretched forever in all directions, beneath a sky with no sun, no stars, only an endless pale glow that pulsed softly, like breath.

The ground wasn't grass or stone or snow, but something else. Something soft beneath her boots, like pressed memory. The air was cold and still and full of unspoken thoughts.

Behind her, footsteps echoed. Not crunching or tapping, but sounding, like whispers on stone.

She turned.

Thanatos.

He appeared not like a man arriving, but like a truth being remembered. Robes of ash and smoke lined with faded gold, a circlet of bone on his brow. His face was the same as always: tired, kind, immense.

"You weren't called," he said.

"I wasn't trying to come," Sia answered.

"You didn't. You drifted."

He looked past her, toward the edge of the field where the light began to... shudder. A shadow was forming. Not approaching. Not chasing. Just appearing, like a bruise rising beneath the skin of reality.

"The door was left open," he said. "And something has begun to dream its way in."

"Crawly?"

"Not yet. But the Dream remembers him. And so does someone near you."

Sia stared into the darkness. "Mia."

Thanatos didn't answer immediately.

"She's trying," Sia said. "She wants to be here."

"She is here," Thanatos replied. "But she is not alone."

The shadow rippled, just once. Like a breath held too long.

Thanatos turned back to her, and in his eyes she saw something new.

Worry.

"Watch. Listen. Do not run. And do not wake her too soon."

Sia nodded.

And the light cracked.

SHE GASPED AWAKE IN Marcus's arms, heart pounding. His grip steadied her.

"It's okay," he whispered. "You're here."

But Sia looked to the sky.

And above the Farm, the first cloud of the day had formed, black at the edges.

Still. Watching.

CHAPTER 3

Broken Mirrors

Every one interprets everything in terms of his own experience. If you say anything which does not touch a precisely similar spot in another man's brain, he either misunderstands you, or doesn't understand you at all.

A.C.

THE FARMHOUSE BREATHED DIFFERENTLY before dawn.

Its walls held on to the night, creaking softly like they were still deciding whether to wake. Somewhere in the distance, a rooster crowed half-heartedly, as if remembering its job mid-dream. The wind outside was still and heavy, carrying the scent of earth and distant rain not yet fallen.

Sia padded barefoot through the narrow hallway, each step quiet on the worn wooden floor. The door to the bathroom groaned softly as she pushed it open, the sound oddly loud in the hush.

Inside, the world was pale.

Muted lavender light spilled through the small, crooked window above the sink. Dust floated in it, weightless, turning slowly like thoughts unspoken. The mirror was old, framed in tarnished brass, its corners flaked with silvering that peeled like dried leaves. The glass was foggy in the middle, not from breath or steam, but from age. As if it had seen too many faces and grown tired of remembering them all.

Sia stepped closer and looked at herself.

Her face stared back. Still hers. Still the same cheekbones, same mouth, same soft freckle near her left eye.

But the eyes.

The eyes had changed.

They were no longer warm brown, no longer plain or forgettable. Now they shimmered in a way that felt unnatural in morning light. Gold, molten and deep, ringed with radiant blue, like the heart of a flame that refused to die. Her pupils still held their human shape, but everything around them told another story. One of fire, and choice, and something older than prophecy.

She blinked, slowly, and the colors shimmered. They didn't look fierce, they didn't even look strong. They looked… tired.

Like the eyes of someone who had seen something she shouldn't, and hadn't yet decided whether to speak of it.

Sia leaned forward, resting her hands on the porcelain sink, palms cold against its chill. She exhaled. Fog bloomed across the mirror, brief and faint.

It should have stayed longer. It should have clung, warmed by her breath, softened the hard edges of her reflection. But the condensation faded almost instantly. Gone. Erased. As if her warmth no longer belonged here.

She didn't pull away. Instead, she studied the mirror, not her reflection, but the frame, the imperfections. A small crack ran along the lower edge, spiderwebbing just enough to catch the light. She'd never noticed it before. Had it always been there? Her fingertips moved unconsciously, brushing the glass. And for one moment, only one.

Her reflection moved after her. But slower. As though something inside the mirror had to think before it mimicked her motion.

Sia's breath caught. She took a step back. The mirror began to fog again, faint and patchy this time. Shapes formed. Lines. A face…

No. Her face. But not quite. The reflection standing where she had just been looked older. Leaner. She wore a long, high-collared coat the color of blood and storm clouds. Her hair was longer, windswept. Her eyes were the same gold-blue, but brighter, too bright. Like they didn't blink.

And she was smiling.

Not kindly.
Not cruelly.
Just... knowingly.

As if she'd waited for Sia to see her. Sia blinked, and the image was gone. Only herself again. Barefoot. Bleary. Breathing too fast. The mirror was blank, save for her reflection.

But the silence that followed felt like someone else had left the room.

BACK IN HER ROOM, Sia moved automatically.

The door clicked shut behind her, the light barely shifting through the gauzy curtains. She crossed to the small desk in the corner, scuffed wood, one crooked leg, the surface scattered with half-used pens, loose paper, and a worn leather-bound notebook.

She sat down and opened it.

Page after page greeted her, some filled with idle doodles, others with dream fragments half-captured in frantic strokes.

The first drawing she'd done after waking up at the Farm was of Mia's eyes, wild and violet, haunted and alive. Below that, in uneven script: *She was real. I didn't imagine it.*

Now she turned to a blank page.

Her fingers didn't hesitate.

They moved like she was remembering something more than drawing it, shapes flowing into place, lines forming the high collar of the red coat, the longer hair swept back like wind had carved it, and the face... almost hers.

Almost.

She didn't draw the eyes yet.

She paused with the pencil resting just above where they should be. For a moment, she couldn't remember their shape, only their intensity. Like they weren't hers. Not anymore.

Instead, she wrote a single word beneath the image.

Version?

And closed the book.

THE LIBRARY INSIDE THE Farm wasn't large, but Eric had claimed it with the intensity of someone taming wild ground. The walls were lined with books, some leather-bound, others spiral-spined, one that looked suspiciously like it had been stitched shut with actual thread. Glowing runes drifted lazily across the spines, shifting with mood or moonlight. Papers and charms were strewn across the desk like fallen leaves.

Sia stood just inside the door, the sketchbook cradled in her arms.

Eric didn't look up at first. He was bent over an array of dream charts pinned to the wall with brass tacks and broken bits of rune-glass, a piece of chalk dancing between his fingers. He traced an invisible curve in the air, muttering softly in Latin, then tapped the wall with the chalk.

The diagram flared briefly, then died.

"Still collapsing inward," he said to no one. "It's folding space without breaking boundary. Like the dream is... bruising."

"Eric," Sia said.

He turned, blinking once before softening. "Ah. You're up early."

"Couldn't sleep."

"Should I be worried, or is that just poetic?"

She walked in and placed the sketchbook gently on his desk, flipping to the page.

Eric studied the drawing in silence.

He didn't speak right away, which unnerved her more than if he'd launched into a lecture. His brow furrowed as he took in the shape of the coat, the lines around the eyes, the faint glimmer she'd shaded into the hair.

"Did you see this in a dream?" he asked.

She nodded. "After I looked in the mirror. She was me. But older. And... not just older."

He nodded once, a tiny movement. "Mirrors in dreams aren't reflections. They're invitations. Sometimes warnings."

"She felt like both."

He reached into a drawer and pulled out a small, flat charm etched with a spiral and pressed metal ridges, a dream anchor.

"This will keep you from slipping too far. It won't stop dreams, but it will help you remember that you're not only the person you become inside them."

Sia hesitated. "But what if the person I become in the dream... is just another version of me?"

Eric met her gaze.

"Then you get to decide which version of you comes back."

She took the charm, clutching it tightly.

He closed the sketchbook gently, resting his palm on the cover. "This is good work," he said. "Keep drawing. Even if it hurts. Especially if it hurts."

She smiled faintly. "I didn't think you were the artistic type."

"I'm not," he said. "But I've learned to listen when the Dreamer leaves messages for herself."

SLEEP DID NOT TAKE Sia so much as open around her, like a mouth she had unknowingly stepped into.

One moment she was lying in bed, fingers curled loosely around the dream anchor Eric had given her. The next, the world stretched sideways, her breath folding inward, her skin lightening, her bones no longer anchored in gravity. She didn't fall. There was no descent, no rush.

Only stillness.
And then, arrival.

She stood barefoot on a floor of cold stone, smooth as glass, dark as ink diluted through silver. The air tasted faintly of smoke and metal and the brittle sweetness of something long buried. It was the scent of old fire and forgotten memories, the breath of a dream that had never woken.

The chamber was vast and circular, but not like a room.

It felt like a heartbeat made real.

All around her, towering mirrors curved inward like a ribcage of glass and metal. Each one stood taller than a door-frame, framed in wrought-black iron that seemed to twist and breathe ever so faintly, as if alive beneath the stillness. The walls pulsed with soft illumination, not from any source, but from the mirrors themselves. They glowed faintly from within, like embers struggling not to die.

And none of them showed her reflection.

Not exactly.

She approached the nearest mirror. The surface shimmered as she drew close, resisting clarity until she was inches away, then flaring into definition.

It was her. But not her.

Sia stood inside the mirror, yes, but older. Her hair was pulled back in a braid, her eyes burned like twin suns, and flames licked across her shoulders like living armor. Another mirror showed her kneeling, robed in white, mouth sewn shut with thread made of light. Another still revealed her laughing, too wide, too sharp, hands covered in black fire and ash.

They were her.
And they weren't.

Her footsteps echoed hollowly as she moved deeper into the chamber. The sound wasn't quite right—it echoed once, then again, then whispered backwards, as if the room couldn't quite remember what a step sounded like.

She turned to a mirror on her right. This time, she saw herself younger, barely twelve. Crying. Holding Mia's hand in a storm of smoke. Her mouth moved, but no sound came through the glass.

Each mirror whispered something different.

Not in words.
In emotions. Echoes. Regret that hadn't been spoken yet. Futures she hadn't dared to imagine. Burdens she hadn't chosen but still carried.

And then she saw it:

At the far end of the chamber, a single circular mirror, larger than the rest, rimmed in deep bronze carved with the script of the old tongue. It shimmered like still water beneath moonlight, silent and unyielding.

Sia stepped toward it, breath shallowing.

This one reflected two figures.

On the left: herself. Barefoot, pale, trembling.
On the right: Mia.

But Mia's image flickered with every heartbeat.

She stood there one moment, tall, defiant, whole. Then she shifted, wings outstretched, horns gleaming, eyes bottomless with shadow. Then again, a child, crying. A demon, snarling. A corpse with burned hands. A crowned woman, sitting alone on a throne of thorns. The flickers weren't transitions, they were collisions, identities smashing against one another behind a fragile wall.

A crack split the mirror's surface down the middle.

Thin. Clean. A single line.

Then another.

A *tink* sound broke the silence, soft, sharp, like a teacup fracturing in a still kitchen.

Sia stepped closer, pulse rising.

And the mirrors around the chamber shuddered.

Reflections blurred. The glass rippled like wind across water. Faces twisted, stretched, folded into themselves. One screamed. One shattered. One, hers, stepped toward her with eyes of endless white.

She froze.

And from every mirror, from every broken image, a voice emerged, layered, resonant, ancient.

Thanatos.

But not whole.

The voice came fractured, as if heard through water, through glass, through bone.

"Each choice you make," he said, "etches a line."

The mirrors pulsed.

"Each line divides you."

Another crack echoed, this time louder. The central mirror veined with fractures.

"But it also shapes you."

Sia reached out, breath held, and pressed her fingers to the cool surface.

From the other side, Mia reached back.

Her hand met Sia's, palm to palm, glass between them.

And for one moment, everything stilled.

The flickering stopped. The shadows froze.

Mia's face became whole.

Tears tracked her cheeks, silent and slow. Her eyes shimmered violet, not with fury, not with corruption. Just need.

The mirror pulsed.

And Sia stepped forward.

The glass did not resist. It yielded like water warmed by memory. The boundary dissolved.

Warmth bloomed through Sia's chest, a rush of spice and fire and the bitter tang of salt. Her breath caught.

And then...

Darkness.

DARKNESS HELD HER, BUT it wasn't empty.

It was warm. Heavy. Laced with the scent of ash, myrrh, and burning parchment. Sounds came next, slowly at first. The cracking of embers. The whisper of turning pages. Footsteps on stone that did not echo.

Then, light.

A faint glow ignited beneath her, like ink bleeding through paper from the other side. Sia opened her eyes to find herself standing on a narrow platform that stretched into nothingness, suspended in a vast and hollow chamber of shifting color. The floor was parchment. The walls were smoke. The air itself felt like breath that hadn't been released.

Ahead, a robed figure stood with their back to her.

Thanatos.

But this was not the version she'd seen in the white fields, calm and distant. This form was taller. His robes flowed like river-water, stitched with gold veins that pulsed faintly in rhythm with something older than time. His circlet now gleamed like fire-forged bone, and his shadow stretched unnaturally long behind him, curling at the edges like torn vellum in a dream too long kept secret.

He turned, slowly, hands folded before him.

"Why did you reach for her?" he asked.

Sia blinked. Her voice didn't want to come, but she forced it forward.

"Because she needed me."

He nodded once, as though that were expected.

"But did you need her?" he asked again.

The question struck deeper than it should have.

Sia didn't answer.

The air around them shimmered, and the world shifted.

Suddenly, the space expanded. Platforms unfolded in all directions, lined with mirrors. Each one was dark at first, then flickered to life, showing her. Not just versions of her. Not reflections. Moments.

One mirror showed her cradling Mia in the Place Between, weeping into her twin's hair.

Another showed her hurling fire through the gates of Hell, eyes wild, skin cracking with divine energy.

A third showed her standing beside Marcus, hand in his, a faint crown hovering behind her head like a threat.

Each mirror held a future or a past or a possibility. Some showed triumph. Some showed ruin.

One showed her burning everything to save one person.
One showed her doing nothing, and everyone surviving without her.

Thanatos walked between the mirrors, trailing his fingers along their edges.

"These are not punishments," he said. "They are questions. Every Dreamer is judged not for what they see, but for what they believe they must become."

He stopped before a mirror that showed her kneeling, hands over her ears, weeping while the world burned behind her.

"What do you fear most, Sia?"

She turned away.

He stepped in front of her.

"What do you fear?"

"That I'm not enough," she snapped. "That I'm not what they think I am. That I'll break trying to protect everyone, and that it still won't be enough."

Silence.

The mirrors around them dimmed, but one flared brighter.

The central one. The circular one.

Mia's image returned, but now, it was clear.

She was kneeling, just like Sia had been in that other vision. Alone. Wings folded, eyes dull. As if something in her had collapsed inward.

Thanatos turned back to her.

"You are bound," he said. "To your sister. To your choices. To this world. That is your trial."

He raised a hand.

The world cracked again.

And the ground beneath Sia's feet gave way.

She fell, not fast, not screaming, but drifting. Spiraling down into light that blurred at the edges, like ink in water.

And just before the dream released her-

Thanatos's voice followed her down.

"You have reached once.
You will be asked to let go.
And that will be the true test."

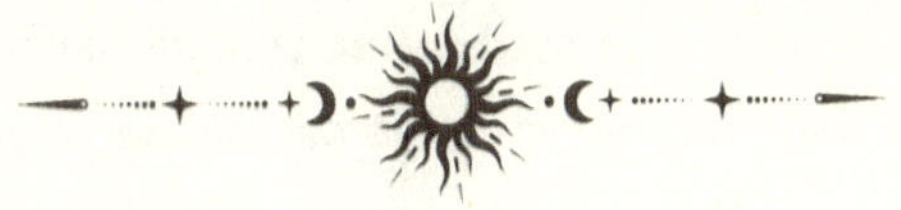

SHE SURFACED SLOWLY.

Not like waking from a nap, but like breaking through ice.

The first thing she noticed was the stillness. Heavy. Absolute. The silence of a place that had held its breath too long.

Then came sound, muffled, distant, as if the world were just beyond a glass wall. The creak of wood in the walls. The groan of old plumbing somewhere downstairs. The rhythmic flapping of laundry on a line outside, caught in a lazy breeze. A bird called once, low, hesitant, and was answered a moment later.

Her skin tingled.

The air in the room was cool, touched with the faintest edge of autumn. It carried the scent of old wood, wild mint, and something more subtle; ozone, like the ghost of a storm that hadn't happened yet.

Sia opened her eyes.

Dust floated in the air above her, spinning like constellations in the sunbeam slicing through the window. The ceiling loomed overhead, painted an uneven white that had yellowed gently with age. Tiny cracks spiderwebbed from the corners. In one, a spider had spun a single silk thread, just one, catching the light like a hair-thin blade.

She lay atop the quilt, half-twisted in the blankets. Her clothes clung to her skin with cold sweat, though her body didn't remember the heat. Her breath emerged slowly, steady, but shallow.

Her fingers ached.

They were still closed around something.

The dream anchor.

Or what was left of it.

The charm had blackened to a dull, burnt charcoal. The spiral that once shimmered with silver threading had warped into a jagged coil, the edges flaking away like overbaked sugar. It left faint soot marks on her palm.

She sat up, slowly.

The quilt rustled beneath her, fabric rasping like dry paper. Her pillow slipped sideways with the motion, and something under it glinted.

She pulled it away.
And froze.

Scattered beneath were tiny glass shards. Not from a window. Not from anything physical. They shimmered faintly with rainbow edges, too delicate to have belonged in this world. Dream-glass. The kind that cut memory, not skin.

Sia didn't touch them. Not yet.

She swung her legs off the bed and stood.

The floor was cold, farmhouse cold, deep-set into the bones of the house. Every board beneath her foot creaked with familiarity. Outside, wind moved through the trees like a whisper passed from branch to branch. She crossed to the desk in three steps.

The sketchbook waited, exactly where she had left it.

She flipped it open to the drawing, herself in red, eyes too bright, smiling like she knew something she shouldn't.

Only now, a crack had formed beneath the eyes. A fine, uneven line. Not drawn, not inked. Etched.

It hadn't been there before.

She stared for a long moment.

Then, behind her, the floorboard just outside the door creaked. Not loud, but definite.

Sia turned as Marcus stepped into the doorway.

His shirt clung to his chest, damp from training. He smelled faintly of smoke and morning dew, like someone who belonged to older seasons. His brow furrowed as he took in her posture, the anchor in her hand, the sketchbook still trembling on the desk.

"You're awake," he said softly.

Sia nodded, but didn't speak.

He walked in slowly, letting the door click shut behind him. His steps were quiet, respectful. Careful, like approaching a wounded animal who trusted you, but still remembered pain.

"I heard you moving," he said. "Then I felt the air change."

Sia let out a breath she hadn't realized she was holding.

"I didn't dream," she whispered. "I... arrived somewhere. And then fell through it."

He moved beside her, eyes scanning the desk, the pillow, the blackened charm in her hand.

His gaze caught on the sketchbook.

She tried to close it.

He reached out, gently, and covered her hand with his.

"I won't look if you don't want me to," he said.

She hesitated. Then let her fingers fall away.

Marcus looked.

He studied the image for a long time, longer than she expected. His brow furrowed not with confusion, but recognition, like he'd seen this before in another dream, another war, another girl with too much fire in her soul.

Then he spoke, his voice low. Thoughtful. Careful.

"She's afraid of you."

Sia blinked. "What?"

He didn't look away from the sketch. Instead, he traced a hand just above the paper, hovering over the fine crack etched below the eyes. His fingers didn't touch the page, but the air above it trembled like it remembered being broken.

"Not because you're dangerous," he said. "But because you still believe she's worth saving."

The words hit her harder than she expected.

She opened her mouth to argue, but nothing came. Because it was true. Because that belief, quiet, stubborn, desperate, was still the one thing holding everything in place. Not certainty. Not power. Just love.

And love, lately, felt like standing on a rope bridge over fire.

Outside, a gust of wind stirred the trees again, stronger this time. The branches scraped gently against the windowsill with dry fingers. The curtain lifted slightly, brushing against her arm like a ghost too tired to haunt.

"I don't want her to break," Sia murmured.

Marcus turned to her, his eyes soft but steady. He didn't offer the false comfort others might have. He didn't say Mia wouldn't break. He didn't say it was all going to be okay.

Instead, he said the truth.

"She already is."

He took a step closer, his presence grounding, heat radiating from him like a banked fire.

"But you're what keeps the pieces from drifting apart."

Sia looked down at her hands. They were steady now, but she could still feel the imprint of the dream in her fingers. The warmth of Mia's hand pressed to hers. The echo of that terrible moment of stillness before the fall. The line between prophecy and madness felt razor-thin.

"I don't know how long I can keep doing that," she admitted, voice barely above a breath.

She felt like glass herself, etched and refired too many times. She hadn't cracked yet, but the strain... it was there.

Marcus reached up slowly, letting her see his hand, giving her every chance to move away. When she didn't, he brushed a loose strand of hair from her face and tucked it gently behind her ear. His fingers lingered just long enough to tell her he was real, and then dropped.

"Then I'll hold the rest," he said.

Not a promise.
A vow.

The silence that followed wasn't empty. It was filled with breath and tension and quiet, painful hope. It was filled with the scent of ash and morning wind, the sound of birds just beginning to reclaim the morning, and the shared understanding that they were standing together not at the end, but at the edge.

And that edge was watching them back.

CHAPTER 4

First Lessons

Magick is the science and art of causing change
to occur in conformity with the Will.

A.C.

THE MORNING SUN SPILLED across the farmhouse kitchen in long golden slats, broken by the dancing of curtain lace in the open windows. It wasn't warm yet, spring still held its breath in the hills, but the light suggested it might try later. Outside, birds argued noisily from the gutter, their high, rapid chirps weaving between the creaking of wind-tossed branches and the low hum of a tractor starting somewhere down the road.

Inside, the kitchen was a strange harmony of motion and stillness. Steam rose lazily from the kettle on the stove. The scent of toasted bread and wildflower honey lingered in the air. A half-washed bowl sat tilted in the sink, catching light like a basin of memory.

Sia sat at the corner of the wide pine table, cradling a chipped ceramic mug. The tea inside had gone lukewarm, but she didn't move. Her fingers curled around the handle like it was an anchor, like maybe if she held still long enough, the moment would too.

Across from her, Ella was packing the last of her supplies into a weather-soft satchel, careful, methodical. A sheathed dagger tucked beneath a folded tunic. A string of prayer beads wrapped once, twice, around a bundle of dried sage. She moved with a kind of reverence, each item touched like a blessing.

On the hearth bench, Eric was sprawled with theatrical despair, eating toast like it owed him money. He wore a navy bathrobe over yesterday's jeans, one sock on, one sock missing, and his hair stuck out in three separate directions like he'd slept on a lightning bolt.

"I just think," he said, gesturing with his toast, "if we're going to send two glorified squires up a mountain to get spiritually slapped around, we could at least give them matching helmets. Or, I don't know, certificates. A divine permission slip signed by God."

Ella didn't look up. "Eric."

He raised both hands in mock surrender, a few crumbs falling to the floor. "Sorry. You're right. You're both very stab-resistant."

Sia smiled, just barely. It came and went like a flicker behind her eyes.

The side door creaked open, and Tobias stepped in with the cold. Morning dew clung to his boots, his breath still visible in the air behind him. He slung his travel pack onto the bench and dusted off his gloves with a thud. A crow called distantly as the door clicked shut.

"Car's ready," he said simply.

Ella nodded once. She closed the satchel with a leather strap and stood. Her eyes flicked to Sia.

"I left something in your room," she said softly. "In the top drawer."

"What is it?" Sia asked.

Ella offered the faintest smile. "You'll know when you need it."

There was a pause, long and gentle.

Behind them, quiet steps brushed down the stairs, bare feet on old wood, cautious, almost weightless. Mia paused in the doorway, wrapped in a loose grey sweater that hung off one shoulder. Her skin still bore a faint lavender tone in the morning light, her horns cropped short and unobtrusive, her wings tightly folded against her back. She didn't speak.

But she watched.

Ella turned slightly, nodding to her, not quite a greeting, not quite farewell. Mia dipped her head in return, arms folded over her ribs, eyes unreadable.

Eric broke the silence with a cough and a stretch, reaching for another slice of toast. "Well, I, for one, will be staying right here. Where the cereal lives. And where I am not expected to commune with glowing apparitions or climb a mountain to be judged."

"You'd never make it past the gate," Tobias said.

Eric smiled. "Because I'm too holy?"

"Because you'd flirt with the gatekeeper."

Sia laughed. It was small and sudden, but real.

Ella leaned over and kissed her cheek, her hand lingering briefly on Sia's shoulder. Then she turned to the door.

Tobias paused. His gaze moved over the room, not just to Sia or Marcus, but to Mia as well. His expression remained unreadable.

Then he nodded.

Marcus, standing silently by the kitchen doorway, returned the gesture. It was not warm, but not cold either. Just true.

The car engine turned over a moment later, the rumble distant but steady. Tires crunched gravel. The sound faded.

And then it was quiet again.

Only the wind brushing the curtains, the birdsong ebbing, and the soft creak of a floorboard as Mia stepped further into the room. A distant rooster crowed, late and lonely.

She didn't sit. She just hovered, caught between the kitchen's warmth and the hallway's shadow.

Sia looked at her and offered the still-warm mug.

Mia blinked, startled. Then took it in both hands and wrapped her fingers around it like she was trying to remember what comfort felt like.

No one spoke. The light moved slowly across the floor.

Eric cleared his throat.

"So," he said, stretching out one leg dramatically and staring into the middle distance like a bard about to recite an epic, "we've got one holy twin headed to Greece, one demonic twin brooding in a sweater, one reluctant chosen one sketching future trauma, and me, who just burned the toast again."

He held up the blackened slice like it was a relic.

"Truly," he added, solemn as a priest, "we are the greatest magical team of our generation."

Mia snorted. Actually snorted.

Sia laughed.

Even Marcus gave the smallest shake of his head.

Eric grinned, victorious. "You're welcome."

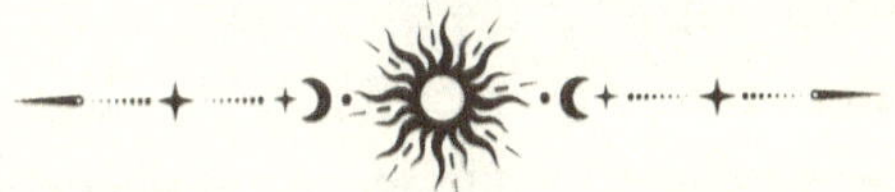

THE TERMINAL AT THE regional airport was almost laughably small. A single strip of tarmac stretched into the treeline like a forgotten trail, and the waiting area smelled faintly of old coffee and pine-sol. The ceilings were low, the vinyl chairs cracked, and the fluorescent lights flickered like they resented still being alive.

Ella sat near the window with her knees drawn up and her bag tucked between her feet, watching a robin hop across the concrete outside. It looked just as lost as she felt.

Tobias was at the vending machine. He returned with a bottle of water and two protein bars, offering one without comment. She took it and turned it over in her hands, not hungry.

The short flight downstate had been quiet. The layover at JFK passed in weary silence, filled only by the distant rumble of suitcase wheels, muttered boarding calls, and the smell of hot grease from overworked terminals. The transatlantic leg was worse, eight hours in a dim cabin filled with restless children, glowing seat-back screens, and the ambient ache of unspoken thoughts. Ella had drifted in and out of shallow, breathless sleep. Dreams came, but left no meaning, only impressions. Flame. Wings. A hand reaching upward into shadow.

Now, the ferry rocked gently beneath their feet.

The deck smelled of salt and rust. Seagulls wheeled above in slow spirals, crying out in the language of hunger and wind. The Greek coastline curved behind them, all green slopes and whitewashed walls, while ahead the mountain rose, not tall, but ancient. Its summit was crowned in mist, its lower cliffs split with weatherworn paths and forgotten chapels.

Ella stood at the railing, the ocean wind tugging strands of her hair loose from her braid. The water slapped gently at the hull below, rhythmic as a heartbeat. Tourists clustered near the stern, murmuring in French, English, and Greek, quiet now, as if something about the place hushed even the most tired among them.

Tobias stood a few paces behind her, hands in his coat pockets, his duffel slung over one shoulder like it had grown there.

"Looks like the kind of place that either kills you or gives you a revelation," he said.

"Maybe both," Ella murmured.

She didn't turn. Her eyes stayed fixed on the mountain.

She could feel it, not magic, not pressure. A pull. Like a thread strung taut between her bones and something waiting on that slope.

"I left it in her drawer," she said softly.

Tobias didn't reply, but the wind shifted, carrying her words away like smoke.

"It was my mother's," she went on. "A firebird. Carved wood. I used to keep it under my pillow when I was little. I'd rub the wings when I had bad dreams."

"You think it'll help her?"

"No," Ella said, "but I think it'll remind her that she can survive them."

The ferry groaned softly beneath them, adjusting to a deeper current. A bell clanged once from the upper deck. Ahead, the dock waited, small, stone-walled, silent. The seafoam brushed its base like a whisper.

"Do you feel it?" Tobias asked.

She nodded. "Like the mountain remembers me."

"Do you think it's Uriel?"

"I think it's the part of me that's already said yes."

Tobias finally stepped up beside her, silent for a long beat. Then, quietly: "We'll find out soon."

And as the ferry cut toward the mountain's shadow, neither of them looked back.

THE FARMHOUSE WAS QUIET in the way only old buildings could be, wood settling, pipes whispering, silence woven into the grain of the floorboards. Mia sat alone at the edge of the upstairs hallway, back against the wall beneath a half-curtained window. The glass was fogged at one corner, faint with breath or condensation, and the old curtain stirred gently with each pass of the wind through a cracked windowpane.

Morning light spilled across the floor in pale stripes, cutting through the dust like blade-thin memories. The air was still, warm from the sun, but underneath it hung the faint scent of ash, something imagined, perhaps, or remembered.

She didn't remember sitting down.

She only remembered waking up with her hands clenched, breath caught, and the feeling that her skin didn't fit quite right.

Her wings were out again.

Not fully, not fanned or spread, but there. Tucked against her back like broken limbs trying to remember how to hide. She had wrapped herself in one of Sia's sweaters, oversized and soft, the collar wide enough to slip down and cover the base of her horns. But it didn't help.

She could still feel the heat in her bones.

She pulled the sleeves down over her fingers and stared at the floor. Her toenails were dark now, just slightly. Not painted. Shifted. Like her blood had decided color on its own.

A fly buzzed somewhere near the ceiling, trapped between the window and the screen, throwing itself repeatedly at the light. The hum of the house felt off-balance, like something beneath the floorboards was exhaling too slow.

She had only been alive again for two weeks.
And yet, everything had changed.

A mirror sat just across the hall, leaned against the wall at an angle. She could see part of herself in it if she moved her head just right.

She didn't.

Downstairs, a chair scraped. The kettle hissed. Marcus's voice murmured low and firm, probably speaking to Sia or Eric. The words didn't reach her, but the tone did. Measured. Calm. The voice of someone used to commanding dragons or defusing explosives with a touch.

She wanted to scream into it.

Mia drew her knees to her chest and rested her forehead against them. Her pulse thudded in her ears. Beneath her skin, something shifted, a shiver, a twitch, a spark that wanted out.

She breathed.
In. Out.

It didn't help.

She remembered fire. And velvet. And the sound of chains too far away to see.

A memory flashed unbidden, someone whispering to her, coaxing her, *You could be more if you stopped trying to be less.*

She swallowed it down.

The stairs creaked.
Mia didn't move.

Sia stood halfway down the hall, frozen in the shadows. She hadn't spoken, hadn't stepped closer. She just watched.

Mia looked like someone halfway through turning into a statue. Still. Folded. Fragile in a way that had nothing to do with weakness.

The morning light kissed her cheekbones and cast her wings in shadow across the wall behind her.

Sia's throat tightened.

She took one quiet step forward.
"Hey."

Mia flinched.

Then blinked up at her sister, eyes clearing like storm clouds momentarily pushed aside.

She didn't speak.

Sia sat down across from her, back to the opposite wall, leaving space between them like a bridge yet to be crossed.

"Rough morning?" she asked gently.

Mia gave a short, dry laugh. "Do I look like I'm thriving?"

"You look like someone who tried to win a fight with their own reflection."

Mia shrugged without lifting her head. "It's losing that gets me."

The silence stretched again, but not as sharp as before. Sia let it breathe.

"They're not gone forever," Sia said. "Tobias and Ella."

"I know. Doesn't stop it from feeling like they took the sun with them."

Sia traced a pattern in the dust with her finger. "You've still got me."

Mia's voice dropped low. "Yeah. And that's what scares me."

Sia looked up.

Mia's eyes shimmered violet, rimmed with exhaustion. "I don't want to mess this up. I don't want to hurt you. Or them. Or... me."

Sia leaned forward slightly. "Then don't disappear. Not again. Don't vanish into guilt. We already did that story."

Mia let out a slow breath. "It's not that easy. It still feels like I'm wearing someone else's skin."

Sia smiled faintly. "Maybe. But it looks better on you than you think."

She paused, drawing a long breath through her nose.

"You know," she added softly, "Ella would've just hugged me. No questions. No speeches. Just... wrapped me up until I believed I deserved it."

Mia didn't move.

Sia shifted, scooting forward on the old wood floor until the space between them was gone. She opened her arms without fanfare and waited.

Mia hesitated.

Then she leaned in.

She folded into the embrace like someone who hadn't realized they were cold until warmth reached them. Sia's arms came around her fully, anchoring her. The sweater bunched between them. Mia's horns pressed lightly against her sister's temple, but Sia didn't flinch.

For a moment, they just breathed together.

The house was still. Outside, a wind moved through the trees like breath through lungs, rattling the windowpanes gently, affirming that the world, and the girls within it, were still turning forward.

But even as the warmth of the hug lingered, Mia's eyes stayed open.

She watched the sunlight drift across the floorboards like time escaping. The guilt didn't fade, it merely curled deeper into her ribs, quieter now, but coiled.

She didn't deserve this. Not really.

And even wrapped in her sister's arms, part of her was already bracing for when the warmth would leave.

THE WOODS BEHIND THE Farm were still damp from morning dew, the scent of moss and turned soil thick in the air. Long beams of sunlight filtered through the canopy in soft, golden shafts, breaking across the underbrush in scattered lines. Somewhere far off, a woodpecker drummed against a tree, rhythmic and relentless. The hush here was different than the silence in the house, this was older, fuller. The kind of quiet that listened back.

Mia stood in the center of a shallow clearing, her boots rooted in damp mulch and shadow. Her wings were gone now, tucked beneath illusion, or suppression, neither of which sat comfortably on her frame. The edges of her sweater fluttered with each breath, though the air around her was still.

Across from her, Marcus circled slowly. Not predatory. Not cautious. Just present. Watching her like one might observe a campfire, not afraid it would leap, but ready in case it did.

He said nothing at first.
She didn't either.

Birdsong warbled in the canopy above. Leaves rustled overhead. A squirrel barked somewhere nearby and fled.

Finally, Marcus spoke.

"You're running hot."

Mia's jaw tensed. "Is that your professional opinion?"

"It's not professional. It's ancestral."

He stopped, standing a few paces from her. The earth beneath his boots seemed to accept him, like it knew him.

"There's a rhythm to power," he continued. "Yours is misaligned. Out of step. Not wild, not yet. But close."

Mia crossed her arms, more to steady herself than to defy him. "And you think I can just meditate it away?"

Marcus shook his head. "No. But I think you can learn to listen."

He raised one hand, not toward her, but upward, fingers splayed. The air shimmered faintly around him. A pulse moved through the clearing, not wind, not heat. Just pressure.

Something inside Mia flinched.

"Again," he said. "Breathe."

She inhaled.

The scent of bark and ash filled her chest.

She exhaled.

The light around her shifted. A flicker of dark fire danced at her fingertips, only for a moment, then vanished.

Marcus didn't react. He simply nodded. "There. You felt it."

"What was that?"

"A resonance," he said. "Between your soul and the blood that's still arguing with it."

She looked at her hands. They weren't shaking. But they didn't feel still.

"You mean demon blood."

Marcus took a slow breath through his nose.

"I mean shared blood."

Mia looked up.

His eyes weren't harsh. They were steady. Older than the forest, somehow.

Then, almost imperceptibly, Marcus shifted.

The weight of him changed, not in body, but in presence. The trees around them stilled. The wind paused. Even the birds seemed to hush, as if some invisible veil had been pulled back and something far older had stepped forward.

Mia's breath caught.

It wasn't heat. It wasn't light. It was gravity, like standing in the orbit of a great star, knowing you were small and yet chosen to witness it.

The clearing stretched and shrank in the same breath, as though it, too, remembered the forge Marcus spoke of.

"The dragons and the demons came from the same forge," he said. "One chose destruction. One chose guardianship. But they both remember fire."

A breeze stirred the clearing, lifting a few leaves into the air.

Mia's heartbeat slowed.

And for the first time since her return, her breath didn't feel like it might burn her from the inside. Not entirely, anyway.

She looked up at him again, something softer in her gaze now, wary, but no longer on the edge of breaking.

"So," she said, voice low, "what now?"

Marcus let the weight of his presence fade, the stillness of the forest returning in gentle increments—birds chirping again, leaves stirring as though they'd forgotten to rustle.

He turned slightly, eyes flicking toward the path back to the farmhouse. "Now we teach you how not to flinch when it answers."

Mia blinked. "When what answers?"

He glanced over his shoulder with the hint of a grin, thin, sharp, old as mountains.

"The fire."

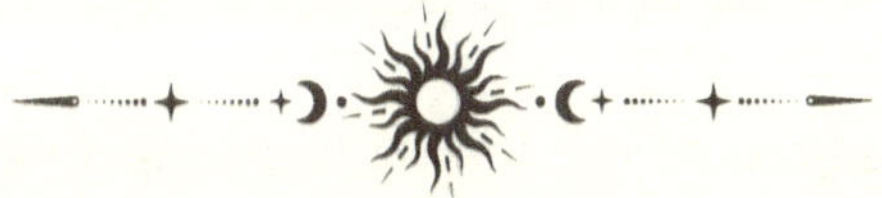

ERIC HAD COMMANDEERED THE wide back porch as his classroom. A rug had been rolled out over the boards, covered in chalk marks and half-finished runes. The wood beneath it still held the scent of morning dew and old sun-bleached varnish. A pitcher of lemonade sat sweating on the rail, catching the light like a lazy jewel, and a stack of magical theory books teetered precariously on a crooked chair that looked like it hadn't been stable since the Reagan administration.

Sia arrived to find him humming to himself, barefoot, and wearing sunglasses despite the mild cloud cover. He had somehow managed to look both scholarly and like someone who had just rolled out of bed and into a sarcastic version of a yoga retreat.

"Welcome to basic magical conditioning," Eric said grandly, sweeping one arm like a game show host. "Where the spells are made up and the focus doesn't matter—until it explodes in your face."

Sia crossed her arms. "You're not going to make me chant in Latin while standing on one foot, are you?"

Eric gasped in mock offense. "You wound me. That's intermediate work."

Despite herself, she smiled.

"Sit," he said. "Let's see where your balance is."

She lowered herself onto the rug, legs crossed, palms on her knees. The boards beneath her were warm from the sun, the breeze soft but constant. Birds called somewhere in the trees, a liquid trill, a chattering caw. The world was alive, but in a quiet, watching sort of way.

Eric circled her once, slow and deliberate, then dropped directly in front of her with theatrical clumsiness, folding himself like a marionette that had surrendered to the floor.

"You've got a lot of tension in your shoulders," he said, voice softer now. "You keep it there because you think if you relax, you'll drop everything."

Sia's lips pressed into a line. "It's not that easy."

"I know. But we're not doing easy. We're doing possible."

He reached over and tapped her forehead gently. "Now, close your eyes and breathe before I make you recite spell structures backward while doing jumping jacks."

She chuckled. Then did as he said.

The air moved gently through her lungs. The porch creaked in time with the shifting wind, the sound like an old ship listing at sea. Something in her chest loosened, just a notch. The silence here wasn't empty; it was filled with the whisper of pine trees, the distant crackle of leaves, the fizz of something not-quite-there in the space between breaths.

Eric didn't push. He didn't dig.

He just sat.

And in that space, Sia didn't feel like she was being watched or tested.

She just felt... here. And for now, that was enough.

After a minute or two of quiet, Eric cracked one eye open. "Alright, theory time," he said. "Let's talk fundamentals. What do you know about the nature of magic?"

Sia peeked at him. "That it's finicky, dangerous, and likes to turn on you at the worst possible time."

"Accurate," Eric said, nodding. "But let's go deeper. Magic, in our world, is about resonance. Energy follows intent. But intent has to ride on focus, and focus has to ride on stability. Think of it like a tuning fork. You can't get a clean note if your hand's shaking."

Sia frowned slightly. "So what happens when I dream something? I'm not focusing in those moments."

Eric grinned. "Exactly. Dreaming is raw signal. Unfiltered magic, tied straight to your subconscious. That's why Dreamers are terrifying, and kind of awesome. You're pulling from the source without asking nicely."

She opened both eyes, interest sharpening. The chalk symbols around her feet caught the corner of her gaze, humming faintly in the corner of perception.

"So how do I keep from leaking it everywhere?"

"By learning how to build a proper circuit," Eric replied. He grabbed a stick of chalk and began drawing a sigil in the air, simple, flowing, like cursive on invisible parchment. "You build pathways in your mind. Rituals. Anchors. Routines. Things that tell your magic where it's allowed to go. Otherwise, it gets… curious. And hungry."

Sia raised a brow. "Magic gets hungry?"

"Oh yeah," he said, wiping off the chalk with a dramatic flick of his wrist. "Magic loves attention. It feeds on awareness. The more you feed it, the more it wants to show off. Which is why grounding is the first thing we teach."

He pointed to the chalk marks at her feet. "You're sitting in a field of runes. Old ones. They help redirect excess energy so you don't accidentally summon a weather pattern or blow out a light bulb while meditating."

Sia blinked. "Is that what happened in the kitchen yesterday?"

Eric put a hand to his chest. "One hundred percent. And also, maybe I was trying to toast bread with my mind. But yes."

She laughed again. Fully this time.

"There she is," Eric said, leaning back on his elbows, a grin creeping into his voice. "Our resident Dreamer. Not a menace. Yet."

Sia shook her head and looked back down at the chalk lines, more curious than afraid now. The runes seemed to ripple subtly, like ink floating on water.

"Okay," she said. "Teach me how to build the circuit."

"With pleasure," he said. "And also snacks. This kind of work demands carbs."

"I knew it," she muttered. "Magic is just wizard sports."

"We take our snacks very seriously," Eric replied solemnly. "You'll fit in fine."

EVENING SETTLED OVER THE Farm in gentle strokes of gold and lavender, the sky a canvas of retreating color. The porch creaked softly under Sia's weight as she sat alone at the edge, her sketchbook balanced on one knee. A pencil moved lightly in her hand, tracing lines that she didn't fully understand until they were already on the page.

She wasn't drawing from memory.

She was drawing from somewhere distant, somewhere real. A place her eyes hadn't seen, but her dreams had.

On the page, a jagged mountain took shape, dark stone veined with light, a halo of wings hovering above it. A monastery clung to its edge, half in ruin, half in prayer. Above, the sky shimmered with strange clouds, and in the center of it all, a faint outline of a sword embedded in flame.

It was Mount Athos. She was certain of it, though no one had shown her a picture. No one had spoken its name in hours.

Somewhere across the world, Ella stood beneath that sky. Tobias walked that path.

And through her sketch, through the half-trance of pencil on paper, Sia followed them.

The wind stirred through the fields, carrying the scent of grass and distant ash. A dog barked once far off. The trees rustled like an old man turning over in sleep.

She looked up at the sky. Stars had begun to appear, first one, then another, timid lights testing the deepening dusk.

Behind her, the farmhouse murmured with the faint sounds of movement—Eric shuffling through books, Marcus sharpening a blade, Mia pacing just above. Life continuing. Uneasy, but intact.

Sia touched the edge of the drawing lightly, her fingertip brushing the sword.

It felt warm. Or maybe that was her. She closed the sketchbook slowly, letting the hush of twilight settle around her like a cloak.

For now, things were still.

But the Dream was never far.

But the Dream was never far.

CHAPTER 5

Two Paths

The Way of Mastery is to break all the rules—but you have to know them perfectly before you can do this; otherwise you are not in a position to transcend them.

A.C.

THE PATH UP MOUNT Athos was carved from centuries of silence. It wound through groves of cypress and olive, flanked by weathered stones inscribed with prayers in ancient Greek. Mist hugged the ground like breath from a sleeping god, curling around Ella's boots with every step. The air was sharp with pine and salt, carrying with it the faint, distant sound of bells that might have rung hours ago, or not at all.

She didn't speak. Neither did Tobias.

Their guide, a monk draped in simple black robes, moved ahead without turning. His staff tapped rhythmically against the stone, a soft metronome that measured the slow rise of tension in her chest. Around them, the world felt held in a breath, like the mountain itself was watching.

The monastery came into view slowly, as if the cliffside parted reluctantly to reveal it. Built directly into the stone, its walls bore the same pale gray as the mountain itself, streaked with age and lichen. Bells hung from a crooked tower, unmoving despite the wind that whispered through the pines like a prayer half-remembered.

They stopped at the base of a narrow stair carved into the rock. The monk turned.

"Only the chosen pass beyond this step," he said, voice low and grave. It felt like stone tumbling through quiet water. "Your companion may wait here."

Ella looked at Tobias. He didn't argue. His eyes searched hers for something—certainty, maybe—but she gave him only a nod. He stepped back, folding his arms, eyes scanning the landscape but always circling back to her.

She climbed.

Each stair was worn smooth by the passage of generations, and her boots found purchase with practiced care. As she rose, the world below fell away into shadow and haze. The sea far below was a dull smear of silver beneath the overcast sky, and clouds clung to the mountain like it refused to be seen in full.

At the summit, a chapel waited. Small. Stone-walled. Silent.

Its archway was framed with ivy and worn carvings—a lamb, a flame, an eye. She stepped inside, and her breath caught. It was cold, but not with the chill of air, cold like stepping into memory.

Seven monks stood in a circle, robed and hooded, faces shadowed by candlelight. The air smelled of smoke and cedar. The flame from the candles danced slowly, giving no warmth, only shape to the dark.

Ella stepped into the circle without being told.

No one moved. No one spoke.

Time became a still thing. A held breath.

Her heartbeat filled the silence like a drum beneath her ribs.

She closed her eyes.

A weight settled over her shoulders, not heavy, not crushing. More like presence. Like she was being seen.

A soundless pulse rippled through the chapel. Not air. Not vibration. Just... awareness.

Light bloomed beneath her feet. A sigil, one she had never seen and somehow always known, etched itself into the stone in radiant white lines. Wings outstretched. A sword flanked by a crown of stars. Flames in perfect symmetry.

The monks bowed their heads.

One stepped forward. He raised a hand, slow and reverent, and pressed his fingers to her brow.

And the voice came, not from him. Not from the air.
From within.

Uriel.

"You walk in flame and do not burn. I have waited long enough."

The warmth spread from her forehead through her chest like wildfire made of clarity. A soft glow began to rise from her skin, subtle at first, like the shimmer of heat on pavement, then brighter, wrapping her in a halo of golden-white light. It pulsed in rhythm with her breath, not harsh or blinding, but radiant, a silent declaration that something divine was stirring inside her. It didn't comfort. It commanded. It filled the corners of her spirit that had been quiet too long.

In that moment, she remembered every fire she had survived. Every wall she had stood between. Every prayer she never thought she had spoken.

When her eyes opened, the chapel was empty.

The monks had vanished.

Only the sigil remained, still glowing faintly on the stone floor, like a promise carved in the first language ever spoken: light.

THE DREAM BEGAN IN warmth.

Mia stood in a room that felt like memory and illusion wrapped around one another. Dim lanterns swung from wooden beams overhead, their glow amber and low. Velvet curtains framed tall windows that opened onto nothing, just blackness, deep and unyielding. The air carried a scent of spice, incense, and old smoke. Jazz curled from a gramophone in the corner, lazy and smooth, its melody slinking through the shadows like a well-fed cat.

She wore a silk dress she didn't own. It clung to her like breath, black as oil and cut low across her back. Her wings were bare, draped behind her like folded velvet, and her horns glinted with a soft gold sheen. A slender, spade-tipped tail swayed lazily behind her, flicking once like a feline's as she moved, more instinct than thought, a part of her she didn't think to hide. She didn't flinch at the sight of any of it. Here, in this place, they felt less like marks of damnation and more like a crown.

The floor beneath her was polished mahogany, warm against her bare feet one moment, cold the next. Every surface in the room held a reflection—windows, brass fixtures, the high-gloss bar—and they all showed slightly different versions of her. One smiled. One wept. One turned away.

A voice, smooth as velvet and threaded with mirth, curled into her ear before she saw him.

"There she is. The real Mia."

She turned.

Crawly stood at the far end of the room, leaning against the bar like he'd never left it. His suit was charcoal grey, his tie deep crimson, his grin framed by eyes that gleamed like polished mercury. The firelight danced across his features, softening the edges of something ancient.

He didn't approach. He simply raised a glass and motioned to the space beside him.

"Come. Sit. No one's judging here. Not tonight."

Mia hesitated, but only a little. Something in her chest warned her, but the warmth of the dream world made everything feel distant. Weightless. Her defenses melted like wax.

She crossed the room. Her heels—when had she put those on?—clicked softly against the lacquered floor. The rhythm echoed strangely, as though each step landed a second time in some distant chamber. She sat on the stool beside him and accepted the offered glass without a word.

He studied her.

"You wear this better than the act you put on for them."

She didn't answer. But his words landed. A flicker of guilt tugged at the corner of her thoughts.

"You know what I like about you, Mia? You were honest, once. When you burned. When you took what you needed. When you lived."

Her throat tightened. She remembered those moments. Not with pride, not entirely, but with power. With clarity. There had been no room for doubt in Hell. No space for masks.

The drink burned like velvet and smoke. She took another sip. The liquid slid down her throat like liquid dusk, heavy and sweet.

"They don't want you strong," he said casually. "They want you sweet. Soft. Safe. You think Marcus trains you because he believes in your goodness? He's terrified of your potential."

Her jaw clenched.

Was he wrong?

"And Sia," he said, smiling like a secret, "she wants her sister back. Not you. The you who survived Hell. The you who made it out with power, teeth, purpose."

It hit her like a wave.

The image of her sister, eyes soft and forgiving, always trying to pull her closer—was that love? Or a wish to restore what she had lost?

She looked down at her reflection in the glass: horns, wings, shadowed eyes. And for a heartbeat, she didn't know which version was real.

He leaned in.

"But I see you."

The gramophone hissed. The tune distorted briefly, as though warped by heat.

The shadows in the windows deepened. They no longer showed the night, just the room reflected again and again, endless copies folding into each other like a spiral staircase of mirrors.

Mia's heart pounded, but not from fear. From recognition. From the echo of something that wanted to be let loose.

Crawly clinked his glass against hers, silver eyes glowing brighter.

"What would happen, I wonder," he murmured, "if you stopped apologizing?"

Mia didn't reply.

But the glass in her hand didn't tremble.

And deep in her chest, something whispered back: *I want to know.*

THE FIRE CRACKLED LOW in the hearth, burning a knot of pine that hissed like a quiet warning. The den was cloaked in shadow, save for the amber flicker of flame licking against stone. Marcus sat in the high-backed chair closest to the blaze, posture still, hands steepled like a man preparing to deliver a verdict. The firelight painted gold into the hollows of his cheeks, catching in the deep lines around his eyes—eyes that looked older than the rest of him by centuries.

Across from him, sprawled on a couch like he owned the place and owed it nothing, Eric held a half-empty glass of something amber and smelled faintly of citrus and arrogance. His socks were mismatched. His hair had declared rebellion sometime after dinner. He didn't care.

"You ever notice how the world only gives us peace when it's planning something deeply stupid?" he asked the ceiling.

Marcus didn't blink. "The world does not plan. But forces do."

Eric gestured broadly, nearly spilling his drink. "Ah yes, the eternal wisdom of the walking anachronism. Tell me, were you always this poetic, or is it just the firelight bringing out your inner philosopher-warrior?"

"It comes with time," Marcus said calmly. "And blood. Usually more of the latter."

Eric sighed and rolled to a sit, glass dangling between his knees. "Well, I've got both in questionable supply. And I'm telling you, those girls are going to come apart if someone doesn't help them glue down the edges."

Marcus shifted his gaze to the fire. "They're not children."

"No, but they're raw," Eric replied. "Sia's trying to outrun whatever fate strapped wings to her back, and Mia's walking around like a house with the lights off. One spark and—poof. Demonic barbecue."

"They're balancing on a blade," Marcus said quietly. "And neither has seen the edge."

Eric took a long sip and pointed at him. "There it is. Now we're talking in cryptic forge-myth again. I love this part. Next you'll tell me we need to find the hammer that forged the universe."

Marcus raised an eyebrow. "Do you think that would help?"

"I think I'd make a great universe-smith," Eric said, grinning. "Custom planets. Bespoke moons. Occasional sentient raccoons."

The fire popped.

Silence fell again, more comfortable than before.

"They need to be prepared," Marcus said at last. "For what's coming. For what's already begun."

Eric leaned back, some of the levity draining from his face. "And if we lose them?"

Marcus stared into the fire like it owed him answers. "Then we teach the world to mourn properly. And begin again."

Eric let that sit for a moment. Then, without looking up, he said, "You know she's in love with you, right?"

Marcus was quiet for a long moment. The firelight danced in his eyes, reflecting something older than emotion. "I know."

"And you?" Eric pressed, swirling his drink. "You planning on riding off on a noble dragon horse the moment this is over, or are you going to let yourself want something?"

Marcus didn't answer immediately. "I've buried more than I've held. But she..." He paused, searching for the right word. "She sees through the smoke. And still stays."

Eric exhaled, softening. "Well. Damn. That's almost romantic."

There was a beat.

Eric's voice dropped, quieter. "I think I'm starting to see her, too. Mia. Not the demon. Not the twin. Just... her."

Marcus turned slightly. "That scares you."

"Yeah," Eric said, laughing once. "Because I joke when I'm terrified. And I think she's still trying to figure out if she's allowed to be loved, or if she'll bite the hand that dares offer it."

Marcus gave the smallest of nods. "She might do both."

Eric lifted his glass. "To women who can destroy us. May we be lucky enough to be worth sparing."

Marcus raised an imaginary glass in return. "And brave enough to try."

The fire popped again. The silence that followed was warmer.

"And you," Marcus said, rising slowly with the grace of a man carved from older stories, "are necessary."

THE DREAMING WAS UNSETTLED tonight.

Sia knew it the moment her feet touched the ground—a ground that didn't look like earth at all, but glassy water reflecting a violet sky bruised with streaks of crimson and gold. The surface rippled like the skin of a lake caught mid-breath. Beneath it, shifting lights swam, phantom memories flickering like fish in deep currents.

The air shimmered with silver mist, cool and dry, tasting faintly of ozone and lavender. The wind didn't blow; it hummed, a sound pitched somewhere between a whisper and the sigh of an ancient book being opened.

Above her, constellations formed and unformed in rhythmic pulses: birds taking flight, shattered crowns, an eye that blinked once and vanished. Stars dropped in slow spirals, burning without heat, shedding feathers of light.

She didn't walk. She moved. Floated. Her steps left rings in the water-glass ground that echoed into the horizon, warping the world for a breath before fading.

Then came the sound.

Not footsteps. Not breathing.
A bell.

Low. Hollow. Resonant as a cathedral buried under the sea. It tolled once, and the sky above twisted gold at the edges, like fire licking at the corners of parchment.

He stepped from the mist a moment later, tall, draped in a black mantle threaded with constellations and ash, his presence bending the horizon like gravity. Thanatos. His eyes glowed like moons obscured by storm.

"Dreams run too deep tonight," he said, his voice a hush layered over thunder.

Sia turned toward him. "It's not just me, is it?"

"No," he replied. "The Dreaming is fraying at the seams. A thread has been pulled. A sister's guilt. A whisper in the dark."

Sia frowned. "You're talking about Mia."

Thanatos inclined his head. "And the serpent who watches her."

The air pressed inward, dense and vibrating. The sky churned slowly above them, the stars rearranging into a spiral that bled downward like ink dropped in water.

Sia looked down. The glass under her feet flared with color, now showing a girl curled in shadow, flames licking the edges of her silhouette. A bar draped in velvet. A serpent with silver eyes hidden behind laughter.

"I can feel her," Sia whispered. "Even here."

Thanatos stepped beside her, his cloak dragging shadow across the surface, but never breaking it.

"The Dreamer's burden is not merely to see," he said. "It is to carry. To bind what unravels."

Sia clenched her fists. The air around her buzzed, and distant thunder rolled despite the star-filled sky.

"Then tell me how to stop it."

"You don't."

The word hung like a sword.

"You weather it," Thanatos said, turning toward her now. "You survive it. The threads will stretch. Some will snap. But others will hold, if you choose to hold them."

She looked up at him, the fire in her chest flaring against the chill. "And what about you? Are you just going to watch while it all burns?"

The corner of his mouth curved, not a smile, but an acknowledgment of the weight she carried.

"No. I am not just watching."

He raised one hand.

The stars above convulsed into order, forming a vast sigil, wings braced behind a luminous shield, its center marked with a symbol she had drawn a dozen times in waking sketches without knowing why. It was the same sigil Ella had seen carved in light during her own initiation, the same celestial brand that had flared beneath her feet as Uriel's voice spoke from within. Recognition hit Sia not as memory, but as instinct, as if the Dream itself were weaving their fates together in mirrored strands of flame and grace.

"I will meet them when the veil breaks," he said. "But until then, you must learn. Not from me. From within."

The sky shattered into a hush of falling light, starfeathers tumbling like snow across a soundless void.

Sia looked down again.

This time the reflection showed her alone, surrounded by mirrors, each cracked and flickering with scenes she couldn't name.

She blinked.

And woke up with a gasp, her heart racing, breath sharp, the ghost of starlight still clinging to her skin. The sigil glowed faintly over her sternum, fading slowly like a promise not yet due.

THE FARMHOUSE WAS QUIET **again.**

Morning sun filtered in through gauzy curtains, painting long golden bars across the floorboards. The scent of brewed coffee lingered in the air, layered with something subtler: graphite and paper, the perfume of dreams captured before they could escape.

Sia sat at the dining table, still in her sleep shirt, sketchbook open before her. Her pencil moved without conscious thought, guided by the echo of what she'd seen. Constellations. A sigil. The silhouette of a shield cradled by flame.

She didn't look up. Didn't need to.

The image coming together beneath her hands wasn't hers alone—it felt borrowed, channeled from some deeper well. The lines pulsed faintly even in the lamplight. Her fingers trembled, but she didn't stop. She couldn't.

When she finally leaned back, exhaling, she saw what she'd drawn.

A mountaintop haloed in light. Ruins folded into its face. A narrow stair etched with runes. And at the summit, a chapel with a door of fire and wings made of light.

She didn't know the place.

And yet... she did.

Somewhere across the sea, Ella stood beneath that same sky. Tobias walked beside her. The image in Sia's book was no fantasy, it was a window, a pulse of magic binding them across miles of distance and silence.

The back door creaked open.

Marcus stepped in, boots lightly dusted with dirt. He paused when he saw her at the table, then crossed the room quietly, glancing at the sketch.

"She's there," Sia said, her voice soft.

Marcus looked again. "Yes."

He didn't ask how she knew. They were past that now.

"Did you sleep?" he asked.

Sia nodded, then hesitated. "Sort of."

He reached out, resting a hand gently on her shoulder. "That's something."

She turned her face into his touch, letting the quiet wrap around them.

Then, in a breath, she stood.

She stepped closer to him, her sketchbook forgotten on the table. Her eyes found his, questioning, vulnerable, strong.

Marcus didn't speak. He just cupped her cheek with his hand, thumb brushing a loose strand of hair away.

She rose onto her toes and kissed him.

It wasn't urgent. It wasn't desperate.

It was slow. Gentle. Real.

And in that moment, the room held only them.

On the stairs above, Mia stood watching through the banister, unseen.

Her eyes fell to the open sketchbook, narrowing slightly. The image stared back at her like a memory she had never lived but always carried, lines too familiar, shapes echoing the sigil from her sister's dream, and now echoed in this waking page. Reflections shimmered faintly on the glossy pencil lines, like mirrored versions of herself—Mia as she was, Mia as she had been, and something else entirely, veiled in flame and shadow. And now, this.

She felt it stir in her chest, a twist of envy, of longing, of distance that widened just a little more.

She didn't move. Not yet. Below, she heard a shift in Sia's breath, a catch, maybe, as if the kiss had stirred something more than just emotion. And for a fleeting instant, Mia wondered if her sister sensed her absence, the way light senses where shadow falls.

The world kept turning downstairs. Safe. Soft. Steady.

And Mia, standing in shadow, wasn't sure she belonged in it.

She lingered, unseen, fingers curled around the banister rail as if it were the only thing tethering her to the moment. The sound of their breath, shared, soft, drifted upward through the hush of the house. The creak of a floorboard as Marcus stepped closer. The faint rustle of fabric as Sia leaned into him, the sound of something quiet and intimate and earned.

Mia's wings prickled beneath her sweater. Her tail curled tightly around her ankle, unnoticed and reflexive. She didn't resent them, not really. Not yet. But she resented the distance between the world at the table and the one at the stairs.

The smell of coffee and graphite didn't reach her where she stood. Only the cold iron tinge of memory. Of fire. Of ash.

She backed away, one step at a time, careful not to make a sound. The wood beneath her feet was familiar but felt foreign, like it belonged to someone else's life.

And as she turned toward her room, the echo of the kiss—silent, invisible, searing—followed her down the hall like a ghost.

CHAPTER 6

To Dream Is to Divide

Balance every thought with its opposition. Because the marriage of them is the destruction of illusion.

A.C.

THE DREAM BEGAN WITH silence.

Not emptiness, not absence, but the kind of stillness that feels like being watched. Sia stood barefoot on damp moss, its cushion cool beneath her toes, the softness a welcome reprieve from the weight in her chest. Trees rose around her like cathedral columns, their trunks pale and smooth, bark flecked with veins of silver that pulsed softly, like veins filled with light instead of blood. The air was still and heavy, humming faintly like the inside of a bell just after it's been struck. There were no sounds of birds, no rustling leaves, only her own breath and the slow rhythm of her heartbeat.

No leaves adorned the branches above. Instead, the trees bore mirrors.

They hung like fruit in a forgotten orchard, oval, circular, jagged, crystalline. Some mirrors were no larger than a pendant; others were as tall as doors. They dangled from fine silver chains, swaying gently even though there was no breeze. The movement gave them voice, a soft chiming chorus that whispered around her in a language just beyond understanding.

Sia moved forward with careful steps. Each footfall rippled through the moss like she were walking across a living memory. Her reflections flickered in the mirrors, dozens of Sias, each fragmented and distorted. One reflection smiled when she didn't. One had no eyes. One was still cloaked in flame from the final battle. One turned away, ashamed. The variety unsettled her, but she did not turn back.

She had learned better than that.

Above her, the sky was a watercolor of deep violet and bruised gold, the stars spiraling slowly like a galaxy trying to remember its shape. Her hand drifted to her sternum, where the sigil pulsed beneath her skin, not glowing now, but not gone either. It felt like a scar that hummed with warmth, a symbol waiting to be triggered again.

A low, rasping caw echoed from the woods ahead.

Sia turned.

Thanatos stood at the edge of the grove, beneath the largest mirror of them all, twice her height, framed in twisted gold that writhed like snakes frozen mid-slither. His cloak was made of midnight and stardust, every fold of it catching light that didn't exist.

He didn't speak.

He only gestured.

She walked toward him. Each step sent a quiet resonance through the dream, like the air was singing her name back to her in pieces. She reached the mirror, breath held, and stared.

It showed Mia.

First as she had been, laughing, alive, whole. Then it shifted. Her horns curled elegantly from her head. Her wings unfurled, vast and shadowed. Her smile became something older, colder. Then again it changed, Mia standing alone, lost between shadows, her hand outstretched to something Sia couldn't see.

Sia reached for the mirror.

It shattered.

A soundless implosion, like a vacuum sucking the breath from the forest. The mirror didn't crack or fall, it folded inward with a suddenness that stole the air from Sia's lungs. The surface collapsed in on itself like a reflection doused in black ink. For a beat, everything held its breath. Then the shards burst out in all directions, silent, slow-moving, suspended in the air like snow caught in amber light.

Light fractured across the clearing, beams bending and re-fracting through the floating glass like a kaleidoscope made of futures. Each shard spun lazily, catching stars and dreamlight and memories as they turned. The mirrors above groaned on their chains. One snapped, crashing to the moss with a heavy, wet thud. The others began to sway more violently, their melodic chimes rising into a dissonant crescendo.

Sia flinched as a shard passed in front of her face, its edge glinting with crimson. Not her blood, yet.

Each shard held a vision.

Sia saw herself, burned and broken, lying in ash. She saw Mia, standing beside Crawly, her eyes empty. She saw a tower falling. A field of bones. The earth splitting open in flame. One shard just showed her own eyes, wide and afraid.

Her hands trembled.

Thanatos was suddenly beside her. She hadn't seen him move. He didn't speak. He only looked, at the shards, at her, at her hands.

Blood trickled from her fingers, unnoticed until it patterned the moss. The blood shimmered as it hit the dream-soaked ground, turning to motes of silver light.

She looked at Thanatos, a question already forming.

"Why did it break?"

"Because you looked," he said.

The dream spasmed.

The sky twisted, stars flaring bright white, then red. The mirrors began to swing violently, clashing like wind chimes in a storm. The forest groaned.

Sia gasped and awoke.

The room was quiet. Her sheets were soaked through. Her nose was bleeding. The sketchbook was already open in her lap. She didn't remember reaching for it. But her fingers were already moving.

She drew a mirror. A girl with her hand reaching into fire.

THE OLD FARMHOUSE BATHROOM still had a medicine cabinet with a mirror that didn't quite shut. The corners of the glass were silvered with age, giving the reflection a ghostly halo that never went away. A spider had built a web in the corner of the ceiling, and morning dew sparkled in its threads like stars suspended in a galaxy of still air. The window was open a crack, letting in a cool draft that smelled faintly of earth, coffee, and pine.

The light above the mirror buzzed intermittently, flickering with a kind of exhausted rhythm. It threw long shadows against the tile walls, making the room feel deeper than it was, like the mirror wasn't the only thing that could reflect.

Mia stood before the sink, toothbrush in one hand, the bristles unused and damp. Her eyes stared into the mirror as if trying to recognize the person within. Her skin held a warmth it never used to, a sunlit bronze that hadn't come from sunbathing. It was something more internal, like heat stored beneath her bones. The horns were gone for now, but her eyes still flickered red in certain lights, like coals not ready to die.

Her tail was curled under the hem of her sweatshirt, pressing tight against the back of her calf. She hadn't meant to hide it, but the instinct lingered. Old habits. Mortal habits.

She leaned forward. Fog crept up the corners of the mirror. Her breath left a slow haze over the glass. Her own eyes met hers. Hard. Searching.

And then the mirror blinked. The surface shuddered, just once. A ripple passed through it like wind across a pond. Mia froze. Her reflection smiled at her—but not with her mouth. But with his.

"Good morning, little storm," Crawly's voice coiled through the glass like smoke through a keyhole. Sweet. Smoky. Dangerous.

Mia staggered back a step, one foot skidding on the cold tile. The toothbrush clattered into the sink with a dry ceramic clink.

"Don't be so dramatic," Crawly's tone oozed out, smooth as oil. "You knew we weren't finished."

Mia's breath caught in her throat. Her pulse thudded against her ribs. "You're not real."

"Oh, I'm quite real. Just considerate enough to stay on the other side, for now."

His hand rose within the mirror, elegant fingers tapping once on the inside of the glass. The tap echoed, not in the air, but in her skull, like a flick just behind the eyes.

"You came back incomplete," he said. "Tell me you haven't felt it. The way your shadow pulls wrong. The way your voice tastes like ash when you lie to them."

The mirror's surface rippled with each word. His reflection stepped closer, impossibly tall, silver eyes glowing like a promise and a threat. He filled the glass as though the mirror had become a window, and the world behind it more real than the one Mia stood in.

"You don't belong here," she said, voice hard but trembling.

"No," he agreed. "But neither do you."

Mia's jaw clenched. Her fists balled at her sides. The hum of the bathroom light grew louder, louder, until it felt like a scream wrapped in silence.

"You're afraid," Crawly said. "Not of me. Of them. Of her."

The mirror shifted. Now it showed Sia, bright, human, holy. Her arms stretched out, reaching for Mia. But her face was shadowed. Faintly disappointed. Softly accusing.

Mia looked away.

"Even Marcus watches you," Crawly said, voice softer now. "He counts your breaths. Times your silences. He wonders if today is the day you slip."

A heartbeat of stillness.

The image changed again. Mia, her full demonic form, stood proud, regal. Her wings swept wide, shadows laced with flame. Her eyes blazed. She wasn't monstrous.

She was magnificent.
And she was alone.

Mia's fingers reached for the glass. It was cool. Smooth. Inviting.

"Say the word," Crawly whispered, voice no longer seductive but reverent. "And I will make them see you. The real you."

Her lips parted—

And there was a knock on the bathroom door. Three short taps. Marcus.

"Mia? You alright?"

The mirror stilled. Crawly's image faded, his smile the last thing to vanish. Only her reflection remained, eyes wide, lips pale, breath fogging the glass.

"Yeah," she said, barely above a whisper. "I'm fine."

She didn't believe it. And the heat that lingered on the glass beneath her fingertips said Crawly didn't either.

THE RUINS WERE OLDER than the stones suggested. Time had weathered the edges, smoothed carvings into whispers, and sunk half the foundation beneath moss and twisted roots, but something deeper still lingered, something unspoken, waiting. Ella walked across broken flagstones that pulsed faintly with residual energy, as if the earth beneath remembered what had once been summoned here. The air felt thicker the farther in they walked, like the humidity of a storm held in abeyance. The trees grew gnarled and watchful around the perimeter, and light filtered through them in narrow golden shafts, speckling the ground like scattered gold leaf.

Tobias walked beside her, silent but coiled. His steps were measured, boots crunching over loose stone and brittle leaves, eyes constantly scanning. His fingers twitched near his hip where his weapons would have been. It wasn't that he felt unsafe, he simply couldn't stop measuring threat.

"This place feels... wrong," Ella said quietly.

"Divine places always do," Tobias murmured. "Especially the old ones. They're shaped by what we believed. Not always what we knew."

They reached what might once have been a courtyard, though only half the walls still stood. A broken arch framed the rising sun, casting long shadows like blades across the altar stones. A sigil remained carved into the center floor, burned in rather than etched, darkened with ancient char. Ella knelt beside it, fingers brushing its edges. The symbol wasn't just holy. It was familiar. She had seen it in her dreams. In firelight. And again on Sia's sketches, drawn before she had ever known it existed.

"She left this for us," Ella whispered.

Tobias didn't answer. He was watching her, arms crossed. There was something guarded in his posture, something unsure. She was changing. He could feel it as much as he could see it, the way she moved, the way she breathed in this space, as if it resonated with something hidden inside her.

She stood slowly and turned to face him. "You're worried."

"I'm watching," he replied.

"Same thing," she said, half-smiling.

He hesitated, then walked over and placed a hand on her shoulder. "You're growing faster than I expected. Stronger. Uriel is... awake in you now. I don't know what that means for the rest of us."

"I'm still me, Toby," she said, softer. "I still need you."

He gave a faint nod, but his eyes never quite relaxed. "Then show me. Let's see what the Archangel taught you."

She didn't hesitate.

Her sword, plain before, now shimmered faintly in her hand. When she moved, light trailed from the edge like the blur of a sunrise caught mid-stroke. The blade wasn't enchanted. It was simply responding to her. To Uriel.

They circled. No real aggression, just the slow build of rhythm. Tobias moved like a shadow, precise, efficient, brutal in restraint. Ella moved like something learning its own grace. Her strikes were lighter but rang with force, each contact echoing against the broken stone like a bell struck in some long-abandoned chapel. Wind stirred around them, catching the loose dust and dry leaves. There was no need for words. Their rhythm became language.

Tobias dropped low, sweeping wide, and Ella met him with a parry that rang through her bones. Sparks scattered. Her counterblow was not wild but instinctive, and he dodged it by inches, grinning now.

"You're thinking faster," he said between breaths.

"You're holding back," she shot back, stepping in with a quick feint.

He laughed, ducked under her swing, and spun. Their blades locked again. "Maybe. Or maybe I'm trying to remember when my baby sister learned to move like a war hymn."

"Uriel sings loud," she said, teeth bared in a smile.

They broke apart. Breathed. Then clashed again. This time they moved across the whole courtyard, past shattered stone benches and the remnants of statuary worn faceless with time. The echoes of battle seemed to awaken the place. The wind grew restless. The leaves hissed overhead.

When at last they stopped, sweat streaked their faces and their chests heaved in unison. They stood across from each other, not as teacher and student, not as protector and protected, but as equals forged by the same fire.

Ella's eyes glowed faintly now, touched by something divine. Tobias saw it, and something in him cracked, not with fear, but pride. The kind that burned.

"You're not a paladin," he said.

"No," she agreed. "Uriel didn't choose a sword. He chose a flame."

Tobias grinned and finally let himself relax, shoulders lowering. "Then let's keep the world from burning before you learn how to bank it."

THE FARMHOUSE WAS QUIET again, the kind of quiet that had weight. Wind rustled gently outside, and somewhere in the distance, an old wooden shutter creaked like a memory trying to escape.

The morning light slanted through the kitchen windows in long, golden bars, dust motes floating lazily through them like suspended thoughts.

Sia sat at the table, a steaming mug untouched by her elbow and her sketchbook spread open across three pages. The pencil in her hand moved with unconscious certainty, dancing across the page as if it had a will of its own. The lines weren't just drawings, they were impressions, echoes, reflections of something deeper than memory.

She drew the courtyard where Ella had trained, but she hadn't seen it in person. The broken arch, the sigil burned into the stone, Tobias's silhouette beside her. It came together in graphite with unnerving accuracy. On the next page, the dream, a thousand mirror shards suspended in a forest of silver trees, each one holding a sliver of possible truth.

And on the final page, Mia. Not just her face, but the feeling of her. The struggle. The separation. Her twin, drawn not as a demon or a girl, but something in between, caught mid-transformation, fire haloed around one half of her body and shadow cloaking the other.

She didn't know what it meant. Only that it had to be recorded.

Eric leaned against the doorway, half-shadowed by the frame, arms crossed over his chest. He watched her for a moment in silence, his usual smirk tempered by thought.

"You know," he said eventually, "for someone who claims to be overwhelmed, you sure draw with purpose."

Sia startled slightly, then looked up, the corners of her mouth tugging into a soft, tired smile. "I don't think it's me drawing anymore."

Eric stepped into the light, glancing down at the pages. His brow furrowed. "You weren't at the ruins. This is exact. Down to the chipped corner of the altar stone."

She didn't answer. Her hand kept moving, sketching in the sky above the arch, constellations that didn't match any known star map. He reached down and flipped back to the image of Mia.

"This one feels… heavier," he said.

"She's different," Sia whispered. "She's still trying, but it's like something's pulling her toward a version of herself I don't recognize. Or maybe I do, and that's the problem."

Eric didn't joke. Not now. Instead, he lowered himself into the chair opposite her and studied her face.

"You're seeing things none of us can," he said. "You're not just dreaming anymore, Sia. You're tethered. You're bridging something."

She nodded slowly. "I think it's them. Tobias. Ella. Mia. Even you. I can feel where you all are. Like threads connecting us. And every time I draw, the thread gets clearer."

Eric leaned forward, voice softer now. "So what do you see coming?"

Her pencil hesitated. For just a second.

Then she sketched the outline of a city. But it wasn't just a skyline, it was a vision unraveling itself through her hand. Spires rose like ribs, curved inward toward a central tower that pierced the clouds like a needle through flesh. The buildings weren't straight or stable, they leaned at unnatural angles, some melting at their tops into curling smoke, others covered in what looked like hundreds of tiny watching eyes. Bridges connected rooftops in looping, chaotic patterns, like a spider had drawn the city's blueprints during a nightmare.

At the base of the tower, she drew a procession of featureless figures in chains, some crawling, some being dragged. Their limbs blurred and incomplete, as if the graphite didn't want to fully commit to their suffering. Great cracks split the earth between buildings, and within those fissures were smaller scenes: fires consuming rooms full of furniture, schools turned to prisons, altars buried under ash. Above it all loomed the eye at the tower's summit, veined, swollen, and alive. It pulsed with something terrible, and the lines around it distorted as if the paper itself recoiled.

Even the sky above the city was wrong. She shaded in layers of concentric black circles, like ripples formed in smoke. Stars bled at the edges, and a thin white arc like a crescent grin split the sky in half. The horizon curved up instead of down, enclosing the city like a dome. The very air around it looked as though it howled.

"I don't know," she said, "but I think it's waking up."

THE DINING ROOM AT the Farm had once been a stable, long ago, its high ceilings and worn beams still carried the scent of hay and horses if the wind was right. A wide farmhouse table stretched the length of the room, its surface marked with knife scratches, burn rings, and old ink stains that refused to come out. Mismatched chairs ringed it like a council in waiting. Morning light spilled through the open windows, warm and golden, painting the space in gentle strokes of calm.

Sia sat with her fingers curled around a ceramic mug, not drinking, just holding it. Across from her, Peter Mason stood at the stove with the quiet focus of a man who'd spent decades wrangling code and logic rather than people. His mind still worked in loops and conditionals, always anticipating the next problem before it arose. He flipped pancakes like he was debugging a system, quick and decisive, every motion efficient. Though long retired from the office, he wore his IBM hoodie over flannel like a badge, sleeves rolled up to his elbows. The habit of always being half on call never left him, there was still a Bluetooth headset in his pocket, just in case some old system pinged him from a server graveyard.

Mariah Mason, by contrast, moved with the fluid command of a school nurse who had long ago mastered the balance of empathy and sternness. Her footsteps were soft but firm, every action deliberate. She knew how to read children, especially her own, like open books they were trying desperately to keep closed. She'd faced down crying kindergartners, overconfident teens, and a few belligerent adults, and she brought that same calm precision to the breakfast table. Her blonde curls had been tied back, but wisps escaped at her temples as if even her hair refused to stay subdued. Her eyes, usually soft, were sharp today, scanning each face for symptoms no thermometer could catch. She kissed Sia's forehead on her way past, then paused briefly at Mia's chair. Mia stiffened under the touch, her smile brittle. Mariah didn't comment. She just moved on.

Marcus, sitting beside Sia, kept one hand resting near hers on the table, fingers occasionally brushing against her knuckles. Across from him, Eric shoveled scrambled eggs with the appetite of someone who thought the world might end again by lunch. He cracked a joke about burned toast and got a weary smile from Peter in response.

Then Mia spoke, her voice low but cutting through the gentle clatter of breakfast like a knife through soft fruit. "Why are we pretending this is normal?"

Silence fell like a dropped curtain. Even the eggs on the skillet had stopped their sizzle. Peter turned off the stove with a slow, deliberate movement. Mariah froze mid-step, one hand still outstretched with a fresh glass of juice. Eric, who had just been about to deliver another quip, closed his mouth without a sound.

Mia didn't look up. Her gaze was fixed on her plate like she might burn through it with sheer will. "Look at me. Look at us.

We're not a family having breakfast. We're a time bomb dressed in hand-me-down normalcy."

Mariah set the juice down and moved to Mia's side, lowering herself with practiced grace to a crouch. She reached for Mia's hand, resting her fingers lightly on top. "Sweetheart, we're trying. That's what this is. Trying to hold on to the part of us that's still family."

Mia pulled her hand back, not harshly, but with the quiet withdrawal of someone who had grown used to isolation. "I don't know if I'm still that. You all keep looking at me like I'm going to break. Or worse, like I'm not supposed to be here at all."

"No one thinks that," Peter said, turning from the stove and crossing his arms, his voice measured but firm.

"I do," Mia replied without hesitation. "I think it every time I catch myself flinching when someone raises their voice. Every time I wake up and feel like my bones are still on fire. Every time I walk into a room and the conversation gets just a little quieter."

Sia reached across the table, palm open, but Mia didn't take it. She stared at it for a heartbeat, then looked away. Her silence spoke volumes.

Marcus shifted slightly, as if about to speak, but the weight of the moment held him still. Even Eric, usually a wellspring of levity, kept his head down, his fork slowly turning circles in what remained of his eggs.

After a beat of silence too long to be comfortable, Mia stood. She didn't shove her chair or make a dramatic exit. She simply stood with grace and finality. "Thanks for breakfast," she said, though it sounded more like a concession than gratitude.

She walked out with the composure of someone who had cried all her tears in advance. The space she left behind filled slowly with silence. It was the kind that didn't just settle, it echoed.

Sia stood next, more hesitant. She collected her sketchbook from the windowsill, clutching it like a lifeline. No one stopped her as she left.

Mia found the sketch already on her bed, carefully placed between the folds of her blanket. A quiet offering.

It depicted two girls standing beneath a sky full of stars, their hands clasped between them like a single thread of light holding the heavens together. But the stars weren't dots or symbols, they were eyes. Watching. Waiting. Witnessing.

Mia sat on the edge of the bed and stared. Her hands trembled around the drawing's edges. She didn't cry.

She didn't smile.

But she didn't throw it away.

CHAPTER 7

Garden of Crystal & Flame

It is the mark of the mind untrained to take its own processes as valid for all men, and its own judgments for absolute truth.

A.C.

THE FARMHOUSE WAS WRAPPED in midnight quiet, the kind that made even the floorboards seem to breathe slower. Outside, the wind stirred the trees in long, sighing waves, and branches tapped the windows like restless fingers. A moth bumped against the glass once, twice, before vanishing into the dark again.

Mia lay awake in the small guest room she'd claimed, the blanket twisted around her legs and one wing half-unfurled over her shoulder like a shield she didn't remember deploying. The faint blue glow of the moon spilled across the floor in thin ribbons, casting everything in a dreamlike silver haze. The sketch Sia had left her, two girls beneath a sky of watching stars, rested beside her pillow. She hadn't been able to put it away. Not even under it. It remained where she could see it.

She'd traced the line of her own drawn face a dozen times with her finger. The charcoal lines were gentle, but there was something solid in them. Belief. That was what made it worse.

Mia swung her legs over the side of the bed and stood, bare feet brushing the creaky floor. The wood was cold, grounding. She padded quietly to the window and opened it, letting in the sharper scent of pine and dew. The wind kissed her face, and her hair lifted slightly in the breeze. She felt the presence then, not a sound, not even a whisper, just the curling sensation of being noticed.

"Not now," she said under her breath.

But nothing answered. Nothing needed to. Crawly wasn't always so direct. Sometimes he was the quiet between sentences, the pause in the middle of a laugh, the flicker at the edge of a mirror. Tonight he was the space beneath her ribs that wouldn't fill.

She looked up at the moon, huge and pale and too distant to matter. Her wings rustled once before settling.

"If I break again," she murmured to the night, "I don't think they'll try to fix me."

No one responded.
She didn't expect them to.

But the shadows outside the window shifted slightly, as if something in the dark had nodded.

In the hush that followed, Mia didn't move. The silence settled again, not peaceful, but waiting, as if the world itself had paused to listen. Somewhere beyond the trees, a low breeze whispered through the branches, and the stars above held their breath.

THE RUINS DIDN'T SLEEP. Even in the dark, they breathed with a hush that sounded like prayer. Tobias moved through the half-lit arches with practiced grace, his boots skimming the gravel and broken stone, the rhythm of his steps measured and precise. He didn't need light. He knew this place by now, the way a blade knows its sheath.

Ella was already there, seated on a fallen column, her sword laid across her lap. The moonlight silvered her hair and armor, giving her an otherworldly glow. She didn't look up as Tobias approached.

"You're late," she said.

"You're early," he replied. "We balance."

A ghost of a smile flickered at her lips. She stood, stretching her limbs with a slow roll of her shoulders. "I couldn't sleep. Thought maybe the ground would tell me something if I sat still long enough."

"Did it?"

"Not yet."

Tobias stepped into the clearing and drew his short sword in one smooth motion. The edge caught the moonlight like a whispered promise.

"Let's see if it prefers motion."

Their first clash was ceremonial, just enough contact to wake the air between them. Steel met steel with a clean, bright ring, and the sound echoed through the broken stone like a memory. They moved in a slow spiral, testing each other, finding breath and rhythm, slipping back into a pattern that had once been brotherly routine.

But Ella was different now.

Each strike she gave off sparks, not just of metal but of something deeper. Light trailed her blade in faint arcs, like halos drawn in motion. The sigil beneath her skin pulsed once as she advanced, and Tobias saw it, felt it, in the bones of his arms as he blocked her next swing.

"You're pushing harder," he grunted, stepping aside.

"I'm not sure it's me," she replied, breath quickening.

The tempo built. Their blades moved faster, footwork more aggressive. Tobias dropped low and swept toward her knees, and she jumped, turning midair and landing behind him with divine agility. He spun, expecting a follow-up strike, but she paused instead, blade leveled at his chest, waiting for his move.

"You hesitated," he said.

"I was gauging the weight," she answered. "My sword feels lighter here. Or maybe I do."

He narrowed his eyes, stepping in close, blades locking again. "Too light and you'll get thrown off balance. Grace without grounding isn't control."

She shoved him back and adjusted her stance. "So teach me."

Tobias nodded. "Anchor in your hips, not your shoulders. You're leading with spirit, not structure. Let your feet remember you're still flesh."

They resumed, slower now, each motion deliberate. She took his corrections and folded them into her rhythm, refining her arcs, shaping her strikes to land true with less force and more intention. The light from her blade steadied, no longer flaring wildly with every movement but trailing like moonlight caught on wind.

"You're learning to temper it," Tobias said approvingly. "Good. Now again. But close your eyes."

She hesitated. "Why?"

"Because you won't always see your enemy. Sometimes you'll only feel them. Listen with your body."

Ella exhaled slowly, closed her eyes, and lifted her sword.

He moved. Quick. Sharp. The kind of feint he would never use on a true novice. But Ella spun, pivoted, struck, not perfectly, but clean enough to knock his blade wide. Her eyes flew open in surprise.

Tobias smiled. "Now you're fighting like someone who believes in herself."

The words struck deeper than his blade ever could.

They stood across from each other, not as teacher and student, not as protector and protected, but as equals forged by the same fire. Ella's eyes glowed faintly now, touched by something divine. Tobias saw it, and something in him cracked, not with fear, but pride. The kind that burned.

"You're not a paladin," he said.

"No," she agreed. "Uriel didn't choose a sword. He chose a flame."

Tobias grinned and finally let himself relax, shoulders lowering. "Then let's keep the world from burning before you learn how to bank it.

As they stood there, breathing in the stillness between them, the divine heat that had flared in Ella's chest began to cool, but it didn't fade. Somewhere in the stone beneath their feet, a low hum pulsed like a heartbeat. Uriel, it seemed, was still listening.

SIA STOOD IN THE clearing, boots pressed into frost-stiff grass, the early light catching on each blade like tiny daggers of silver. Breath fogged the air before her, not just from cold, but the quiet panic simmering just beneath her skin. Her hands hovered at her sides, fingers twitching like they were trying to remember the shape of something they'd once known, some forgotten spell etched into muscle memory. Each breath felt borrowed. Each moment strained.

Across from her, Eric leaned lazily against a mossy fence post, arms crossed, his posture relaxed but eyes sharply attentive. A twig hung from the corner of his mouth like a mock cigarette, chewing on it with the kind of nonchalance that only made his focus more obvious.

"You're thinking again," he said, voice dry. "That's your first mistake."

"That's not helpful," Sia muttered, glaring at the air in front of her where her last conjuration had collapsed. A flaming sword had warped into something between a glider and a rotary saw before dissolving into blue smoke and glittering dust. It hadn't exploded. But it had laughed. That was worse.

Eric spat the twig into the grass. "Dream magic isn't about control. It's about shape. Emotion. Pattern. You're trying to logic your way through it like a Blue Circle initiate. You're not one of us."

"Wow. Thanks. I feel so supported."

He stepped forward, expression serious now. "No, listen. You're bigger than us. That's what makes it dangerous. Your power doesn't come with rails. It listens to your feelings, not formulas. If you're scared, you get chaos. If you're angry, you get fire. If you're anxious—"

"You get a flying sock puppet screaming about taxes," she said, flat.

Eric barked a laugh, caught off guard. "That thing? That was... uniquely horrifying."

"It chased me around the barn yelling about property codes."

"In Latin."

"In Klingon."

They both broke. Laughter rolled out, unexpected and sharp-edged. It cut through the morning fog and the heavy cloud of tension hanging between them. For a brief moment, it felt like old times, before the war, before hell, before the Dreaming had taken root in her spine.

Eric wiped his eyes, still grinning. "Okay, okay. Let's try something smaller. Forget constructs. Forget weapons. Just conjure a shape. A symbol. One emotion made visible."

Sia nodded, but there was hesitation in her breath. She closed her eyes. Dug deep.

Fear. Uncertainty. The tight coil in her chest, like grief wrapped in hope and pressed too tight to breathe. She focused on that pressure, not to fix it, but to give it a name.

The air snapped.

Magic surged from her in a pulse of heat and light, and then it coalesced.

A horse-sized rubber duck in a crimson velvet cape and ornate golden crown now stood where the shimmer had been. It blinked at them with large, soulful eyes and gave a royal-sounding quack that echoed too loud in the clearing.

Eric stared. "... Okay. I did not see that coming."

Sia opened one eye. Then the other. Her entire face dropped. "Seriously?"

"I mean, it's regal. Clearly, you have unresolved authority issues."

She couldn't help it. She laughed again. But it was shorter this time. Sharper. Her shoulders sank with the weight that didn't leave.

"This isn't funny," she said, voice low.

Eric's grin faded. "I know."

"I keep seeing things. Places that aren't real yet. Drawing them. Dreaming them. I don't know what's real anymore. I conjure nonsense when I'm trying to do something meaningful. I don't feel stable."

He took a step closer, eyes earnest. "Then stop trying to win the war today. Just take the next step."

"And if it's wrong?" she asked. "If it leads someone into danger again?"

"Then it's wrong. And you learn. That's the only way forward."

Sia's fists clenched, sparks crackling between her fingers. "You say that like you're not scared. Like you understand what it's like to be made of prophecy and guesswork."

Eric's face hardened. "Don't put that on me. I've buried friends over single-word mistakes in rituals. I've seen fire eat through people I was supposed to protect. You're not special for drowning, Sia. You're just not alone in it."

She flinched. The sparks dimmed. Her breathing shallow.

Eric winced. "That was too far." He stepped back, running a hand through his hair. "I'm sorry. I don't always know how to talk to people when it counts. I just know what it's like to hate the thing in you that's supposed to be your gift." He looked at her, more carefully this time. "And I know I don't want you to hate it too."

The rubber duck exploded with a quiet pop, releasing a puff of golden glitter and a crown that tumbled to the grass like a discarded joke.

Sia turned and walked away, sketchbook tucked under one arm, wind catching the pages as she moved.

Eric didn't follow. He just stood in the clearing, alone again, watching the glitter settle.

The crown lay there, noble and ridiculous, gleaming in the morning light.

Far off, past the trees, the wind picked up again. A single page from Sia's sketchbook stirred and flipped open where she had dropped it. The drawing that faced the sky now wasn't the duck or the sword, it was a jagged spiral of light wrapped around a keyhole.

THE MORNING FOG HADN'T yet lifted when Mia found herself wandering again. She wasn't sure what she'd been looking for, a breath that didn't taste like ash, maybe, or a moment that didn't feel borrowed. Her thoughts looped endlessly, tangled and slippery. Every step she took made her more aware of the weight she was carrying, not just in her shoulders or back, but deeper, in the marrow.

Marcus found her behind the old barn, sitting on a half-rotten fence post with her knees pulled to her chest, tail flicking absently in the dirt. Her wings were half-folded, hunched around her like she wasn't sure if they were for shielding or for hiding. He said nothing at first, just approached with the slow certainty of someone who never needed to ask permission to exist in a space.

"You're up early," he said.

"I never slept."

Marcus didn't reply. He sat on a nearby stump, posture straight but unthreatening. He looked like a man carved from patience.

"You want to talk about it?"

"No," Mia answered too quickly. Then softer, "Maybe."

The wind moved around them, tugging at stray leaves and carrying the distant scent of woodsmoke. It should've been comforting. It wasn't.

"I don't know who I am," she said, staring at the ground. "I'm not human. I'm not a demon. I'm not what they remember. Every time someone looks at me, I can see them wondering if I'm going to slip."

"You feel like a stranger in your own skin," Marcus said. "Like you were written into a story someone else started, and they forgot to give you a voice."

Mia looked up, eyes narrowing. "That's... disturbingly accurate."

He smiled, faint and knowing. "I know the feeling."

For a moment, silence settled between them. Not awkward, reverent.

Marcus reached into his coat and pulled out a thin length of blackened steel, a twisted shard that shimmered faintly in the light.

"This came from the forge where I was born. Not the literal fire, though that too, but the one where things are shaped to survive. The kind that burns away everything that doesn't matter."

She tilted her head. "You think I came from a forge?"

"I think someone made you," he said. "Not like a puppet. Not like a pawn. Like a purpose. Dragons and demons aren't so different in that. We're forged. Called into being with a reason, even if we don't understand it at first."

Mia didn't speak. Her hands were clenched in her lap, claws half-drawn without realizing it. There was a tightness in her throat she couldn't name.

"I'm tired of trying to be what they want," she whispered.

"Then don't," Marcus said. "Be what you are. Figure out what that means. And if you fall along the way..."

"I'm afraid no one will catch me."

Marcus looked at her, really looked. "Then we teach you to land."

For a long moment, neither of them moved. But something in the air shifted, the sense of being watched from afar, not with judgment, but with ancient expectation. As if their words had been recorded by something older than gods.

THE DREAM BEGAN WITH silence. Not the gentle quiet of sleep or the hush of distant wind, but a vacuum, a silence so deep it pressed inward, wrapping around her bones like the inside of a bell jar. Mia stood barefoot on a floor of obsidian glass that stretched endlessly in all directions. Each step made no sound, but every breath she took echoed, not through the air, but in her skin, her spine, her skull. Above, there was no sky. Only a ceiling of constellations turning in slow, deliberate circles, each star blinking like an eye pretending not to watch.

She didn't remember falling asleep. She never did when he was coming.

Her wings twitched. She was aware of every part of her body in that space, painfully so. The dream held her too tightly, as if even her subconscious couldn't forget what she had become. Her reflection formed in the mirror-like floor beneath her: human, almost. But with streaks of shadow and flickers of flame curling along her skin like tattoos alive and breathing.

"You always dream in such lonely places," said the voice, liquid, warm, and venomous.

Crawly emerged from the darkness without drama. There was no flourish. He simply was, like a truth someone had tried to forget. He wore a tailored suit of deepest black, its threads stitched in a pattern that looked different every time Mia blinked. A red pocket square winked like fresh blood. His silver hair was perfectly slicked, and his eyes... those eyes weren't silver anymore. They were mirrors.

"You're early," Mia said. Her voice didn't echo. It fell, like a pebble into a well too deep to hear the splash.

"Time is flexible here," Crawly said, circling. "And so is consent. You think of me, and the door opens."

"I didn't call you."

"You missed me." He grinned. "That's worse."

She didn't deny it. Her silence said enough.

He continued walking around her, hands folded behind his back like a professor touring a student's poorly constructed thesis. "They say you're healing. That you're getting better. But you know what they mean, don't you? They mean becoming less. Less of what frightens them. Less of what you are."

"I'm trying to be good," Mia said.

"Good," Crawly echoed, stopping in front of her. "The cage word."

She met his gaze. "You don't know me."

"I know every woman who's been told to smile through pain. Every girl who was told she should be grateful for being saved from her own fire."

He held out his hand. A key rested there, blackened bone wrapped in coiled gold. Its teeth were jagged, and its head was carved in the shape of a mouth open mid-scream.

"What is it?" Mia asked, heart fluttering.

"A choice," he said. "One you won't need now. But later, when the dream ends and the real world forgets to be kind, you'll want it."

She didn't move.

"Why me?" she whispered.

He stepped closer, his voice a velvet blade. "Because I remember Lilith. I remember what Adam did to her. I remember the price of silence. And you, dear girl, are loud. Even when you don't speak."

The stars above pulsed once, and the floor flickered. Mia's reflection stared back at her, this time in full demonic form. Proud. Beautiful. Alone.

"You are the storm they tried to name into stillness," Crawly whispered. "And storms do not obey. They are invited. Or unleashed."

He opened his palm. The key hovered, its glow dancing across her cheek.

"Take it, or don't. I'll keep it close either way."

The space pulsed again. Red. Heavy.

Mia woke with a gasp, lungs aching like they'd been held underwater. Her hand was clenched tight around something warm and metallic.

When she opened it, there was nothing.

Only the faint scent of smoke, and the impression of a key's teeth pressed into her skin.

She stared at the marks a moment longer, then closed her hand around the emptiness. The lines glowed faintly, just for a second, as if something unseen had acknowledged her hesitation. Somewhere in the back of her mind, she felt the storm shift.

Whatever came next, the key would remember.

CHAPTER 8

The Warden of Fire

For pure will, unassuaged of purpose, delivered
from the lust of result, is every way perfect.

A.C.

THE SCENT OF COFFEE curled through the farmhouse like a warm
hand, softening the edges of morning. Sunlight streamed
through the kitchen window in long golden stripes, catching
on dust motes and flickering gently across the worn wooden
table. The place felt lived in now, scattered notebooks, a pair
of boots by the door, a half-finished mug of tea forgotten on
the counter. This was not a battleground. Not yet.

Sia sat at the table, pencil in hand, sketchbook open to a
clean page. Her eyes were distant as the pencil moved, not in
sweeping gestures but short, certain lines. She wasn't drawing

from memory. She was drawing from instinct, like she'd woken with the image already waiting behind her eyes.

Across from her, Mia picked at a piece of toast, her expression unreadable. The horns had receded some, faded into the illusion Marcus had taught her to maintain, but her skin still held that deeper hue, a bronze undertone that shimmered faintly where the sunlight hit. Her wings were hidden. Her tail wasn't.

"You're getting faster," Mia said, not quite looking.

Sia didn't respond at first. She was shading something, an archway? A door? The details were still emerging, but they had weight. Age. She paused only when she noticed the silence stretching too long.

"I think I'm not drawing anymore," she murmured. "I think I'm remembering."

Mia looked up. Her fingers stilled on the toast. "From a dream?"

She wanted to ask more. She wanted to believe this was just like before, Sia scribbling strange things in the margins of her school notes, whispering about weird dreams with that same breathless awe. But this wasn't that girl anymore. And Mia… Mia wasn't the sister who used to laugh at it.

She watched the pencil glide across the page and felt the same helpless distance she'd felt since waking up in this world. Since being dragged back into the light.

'I'm not part of this,' she thought. 'Not the same way she is. Not anymore.'

Sia shook her head. "No. From something else. Like a memory that hasn't happened yet."

The toast cracked in Mia's fingers. Her grip had tightened without her noticing. Her body still reacted like it belonged to something else, something coiled and ready, even now.

She set the toast down gently, like it might turn to ash if she held on too long.

"I keep seeing a city," Sia said softly. "Tall towers like ribs. Windows like eyes. People chained to nothing, just... held in place. And above it all, a sky that watches back."

Mia swallowed hard. Something in the description made her chest tighten.

"Sounds like Hell."

But it didn't. Not exactly. Hell, for all its torment, had purpose. This... this sounded like something worse. A prison without locks. A sentence without a crime.

"I don't think it is. I think it's somewhere worse."

Mia said nothing, but her tail twitched once, sharply. She hated that it gave her away so easily, every flick a betrayal.

She looked at Sia, really looked. Her twin had changed. There was power in her now, something raw and unfinished. Mia could see it like an outline burning through her skin.

And for just a moment, she wondered who would still be standing at the end of this. Her, or the girl with the open door.

The silence that followed wasn't unfriendly, but it wasn't comfortable. It was the silence of two people sharing the same fire but not the same warmth.

Sia looked up at her twin. "You okay?"

Mia gave a half-smile. "Getting there."

They let that sit between them, like an offering they didn't know how to unwrap.

Outside, the wind moved through the trees in a slow, whispering hush. Sia's pencil moved again, tracing a line down the center of the page, an open door, this time. Something just beginning.

And behind it, in the sketch's shadow, something was watching back.

THE PORCH CREAKED UNDER Peter Mason's weight as he stepped out into the morning. He carried two mugs of coffee, the dark liquid steaming faintly in the crisp air. The sky was clear, blue as polished glass, and the trees surrounding the farmhouse swayed like slow dancers, whispering secrets to the breeze. There was an old stillness to the land, the kind that came after storms but before the world remembered how to breathe again.

Domingo stood at the edge of the yard, his back to the house. Even when still, there was something monumental about him, as if the ground itself leaned toward his presence. His coat fluttered around his legs like wings barely folded, and his long silver hair gleamed in the sunlight with the sheen of ancient metal. He looked less like a man and more like a carving weathered by centuries. A monument still waiting for its purpose.

Peter offered one of the mugs without a word. Domingo accepted it with a small nod, holding the cup like a gesture rather than a need.

For a while, they stood in silence, one forged in heat, the other in time. Two men who had already watched too much of the world bend and break.

"She's changed," Peter said eventually. "They both have."

Domingo didn't look at him. "Change is the first truth of becoming. And becoming always costs."

Peter sipped his coffee, brow furrowed, the steam curling around his jaw like ghost-breath. "I keep trying to see my daughters in them. Keep thinking if I squint hard enough, I'll see twelve-year-olds in Halloween costumes. But all I get are strangers who look like them. Talk like them. Sometimes even smile like them."

"They are still your daughters," Domingo said. "But they are also something more. And less. That is the nature of those chosen."

Peter let out a dry breath that might have once been a laugh. "You're talking prophecy again."

"I am speaking of patterns. Your people call it myth. My people call it memory."

Peter turned to look at him. "So what memory are we walking into, then?"

Domingo's gaze drifted toward the horizon, as if searching for something he'd buried long ago. "A familiar one. The cycle of the Hero. A mantle passed from soul to soul, through wars and empires and collapses. They rise. They carry the weight of fate. And they fall."

Peter's fingers tightened on the mug. "You're saying Sia's not the first."

"No. She is only the latest. Heracles. Rostam. Gilgamesh. Urduja. Heroes, all. Each given the same choice: shape the destiny of humanity, or let it burn."

"And they failed?"

Domingo's nod was slow, heavy with remembrance. "Or were made to fail."

The silence returned, deeper now, laced with ghosts.

Peter stared into his coffee, as if it might offer a prophecy of its own. "Then why let her walk it? Why let any of them?"

"Because one must. And because someday, perhaps, one will not fall."

Peter chuckled, but there was no humor in it. "You sound like you've been saying that a long time."

Domingo turned his head slightly, the closest thing he gave to a smile. "I have. Longer than most would believe."

The wind shifted, rustling the grass in a slow ripple. Birds chirped without joy in the trees. Far off, a dog barked once, as if reminding the world that life was still trying.

Peter raised his mug in a tired salute. "Here's to daughters who don't break."

Domingo's voice was low, but resolute. "Here's to daughters who endure."

They stood there, drinking to ghosts and futures, and to a hope that had not yet failed them.

THE BARN HAD BEEN cleared for the morning session, its old hay lofts empty, the floor swept, the sun slanting in through high windows like shafts of golden judgment. Dust hung in the light, catching on the edges of breath and motion. It felt holy, somehow, in the way all quiet places did when you knew something powerful was about to happen.

Eric stood at the center, arms crossed, watching Sia with a guarded kind of curiosity. He had drawn a faint circle on the floor with chalk, runes etched into its edges in both Latin and a language older than paper. The scent of old cedar mixed with something sharper, ozone and char, like the aftertaste of lightning.

Sia stepped into the circle with deliberate care. Her bare feet pressed into the cool wood, and she felt the magic settle against her skin like a blanket soaked in memory. Familiar, but not safe.

"You said this was safe," she said.

"It is," Eric replied. "Mostly."

She shot him a look.

He grinned. "Look, worst case scenario, we lose the barn. Again."

She didn't laugh, and he softened.

"This is called anchorpointing. You pull something internal out, memory, fear, love, and we give it form. A symbol. Something the dream magic can grab onto. It teaches you to shape, not just react."

Sia nodded. "And if I can't control it?"

Eric tilted his head. "Then we learn what it wants."

She took a breath and let it out slowly, eyes closing.

At first, there was nothing. Then the breath rushed from her lungs, not exhaled, but stolen, and the barn dissolved. Her body remained, but the world had shifted around it. She stood now in a different place entirely.

Stone beneath her feet. Blackened, broken. The air carried the stench of something old burned too long: ash, blood, oil. A hush lived here, not silence, something waiting to scream.

She turned slowly. Ruin greeted her. The building had once been sacred, a cathedral maybe, but now the stained glass lay like melted confetti across the scorched altar steps. Ash drifted through the air like fake snow in a forgotten nativity scene.

At the far end, a figure loomed.

Wings of coal-black smoke. A face she couldn't see, only its eyes, blazing twin suns, veined with threads of crimson rage. It opened its mouth, and the sound tore through her like thunder made personal.

"SIA."

The word wasn't just a call. It was a claim.

She stumbled backward, arms raised, breath ragged. The dream cracked like a mirror underfoot. In an instant, she was back in the barn. The circle flared with blue fire, then white. Smoke curled from the runes etched around her. She dropped to her knees, heart racing.

Eric was beside her in an instant, his voice low but urgent. "Hey. Breathe. You're alright. You're back."

"I saw... a cathedral. It was gone. Burned. And that thing, it screamed my name."

Eric placed his hands on her shoulders, grounding her. "What did you try to anchor?"

"I didn't. I wasn't trying anything. It just... it found me."

He glanced toward the circle, now blackened and cracked. "That's new."

Then the air changed.

No wind. No spark. Just a shift, as though gravity remembered something.

Thanatos stood in the doorway. He wasn't shimmering or cloaked in flame. He simply was. Still and silent, a punctuation mark between thoughts.

He met Sia's eyes. His voice was almost kind.

"He's close now."

And then, he was gone. Not vanished, unwritten. Like the barn had never known he'd been there.

Sia stared at the space he left behind, pulse hammering.

Eric sat back, stunned. "What the hell does that mean?"

Sia didn't answer. She was already reaching for her sketchbook, fingers moving before thought returned.

Lines formed. Shapes. The cathedral. The figure.

She didn't know what it was. Not yet.

But deep in her chest, something opened, a door she hadn't known existed.
And it was no longer locked.

She looked down at the page, the charcoal smudging under her fingertips. The image wasn't complete, it never was, but it felt like something true. Something that didn't come from her, but through her.

Her sketchbook had once been a comfort. A journal of the unreal. Now, it felt like a divining rod pointed at the heart of something ancient and unfinished.

Whatever was coming, it was watching.
And it knew her name.

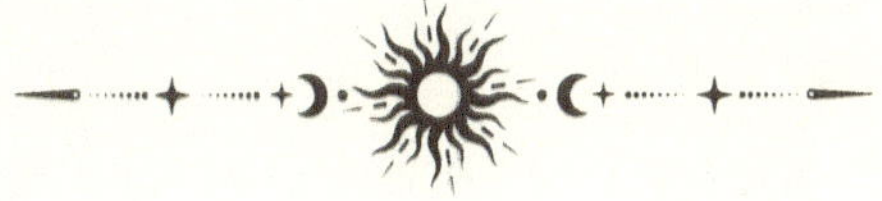

THE DREAMING WAS QUIETER at the edges.

A wind that wasn't wind brushed across the endless fields of thought, ruffling the pale reeds of memory that grew where dreams came to die. Far off, something howled, not in fear or hunger, but in recognition. The noise didn't carry far. Nothing did here. But it stirred the edge of the void, like breath fogging a cold window.

Thanatos stood alone beneath a sky that did not hold stars, but ideas of stars, flickering constellations drawn in thought and memory rather than light. Here, at the farthest fringe of the realm he guarded, the fabric of reality frayed like a cloak worn thin. It was not a place most dared visit. It was a place for watchers, and for endings.

He did not breathe. He did not blink. He simply watched. A tear had opened in the Dreaming.

It wasn't large, yet. A jagged line, pulsing red and gold, veined like a wound across a seam in the world. But it throbbed with meaning. With hunger. Crawly's presence oozed from the fissure like smoke from a sealed grave.

Thanatos knelt. His fingers touched the edge of the rift, and it recoiled, not in fear, but recognition. He felt its memory, its weight. It had been here before. Ages ago. Long before the name Crawly. Long before Sia. Long before he had chosen to stay.

The Hero always drew the rift. It was not coincidence. It was pattern. The kind baked into myth and written into bones. He closed his eyes.

"Heracles," he murmured. "Rostam. Gilgamesh. Urduja. All of you stood here, once. All of you saw the wound."

He rose slowly, like mountains remembering how to move. His cloak of black and pale blue flickered in unseen wind.

"You were brave," he said into the nothing. "You were bright. And still, you broke."

He turned his gaze back toward the distant threads of Sia's dreamscape, toward the girl who would now bear their mantle. The Hero reborn.

"I will not let her fall alone."

The rift pulsed. It did not answer. But it listened.

Thanatos stepped back and whispered to it, not a warning, but a promise.

"So the garden splits again," he said, voice nearly reverent. "And still they pick from the tree."

CHAPTER 9

Shifting Currents

I slept with faith and found a corpse in my arms
on awakening; I drank and danced all night with
doubt and found her a virgin in the morning.

A.C.

THE SUN CREPT OVER the treetops, painting the training field in long, uneven strokes of amber and shadow. The dew hadn't yet burned off, clinging to the blades of grass like a thousand tiny mirrors. Every breath drawn in that crisp morning air felt charged; not with peace, but with anticipation, like the air before a storm that refused to break.

Mia stood at the edge of the field, arms crossed, posture tense. Her wings remained hidden beneath the illusion Marcus had taught her, but her tail betrayed her, flicking with restless irritation behind her. She was dressed for combat, like the others, but her silence wrapped around her like a second skin; thick and impenetrable.

She didn't laugh when Tobias and Ella clashed swords in the sparring ring. Ella's movements were tighter than usual, driven by something focused, internal. Tobias tested her with precision, pushing her to learn, to adapt. Sia stood nearby, winded but attentive, her staff lowered at her side as she observed the bout with a mix of curiosity and envy.

On the edge of the ring, Eric leaned on a fence post, chewing a twig and offering commentary with lazy sarcasm. "Well, that was almost graceful. Try not to decapitate each other before breakfast."

Mia didn't speak. She watched her sister laugh at something Tobias muttered, saw the lightness in her face that hadn't existed weeks ago, and felt her stomach twist. Sia was healing. Moving forward. And she was... standing still. Or worse, being left behind.

"You're holding your breath again," Marcus's voice came from behind her, low and even.

She turned slightly. "Didn't realize I needed to breathe to watch."

He moved to stand beside her, hands clasped behind his back. "You're not here to watch."

Mia's lips thinned. "I don't want to hurt anyone."

"You won't," he said simply. "Not unless you let your fear swing the blow."

There was something in his tone that left no room for pity, only truth. Mia sighed and stepped toward the circle, eyes on her sister.

Sia straightened as she approached, offering a small, tentative smile. It wasn't forced. But it wasn't steady either.

They took positions across from one another. Sia's staff raised again, splintered from age and repaired more than once. Mia lowered into a stance, claws glinting faintly beneath her gloves.

No one called for the spar to begin. It just did.

Mia moved first.

Her speed outpaced thought. A single flash of motion, a swipe meant to test boundaries; but her claws caught the staff dead center. The wood didn't creak. It cracked. A clean, brutal snap that echoed through the field like a shot.

Sia hit the ground hard, more from surprise than injury.

Mia's breath caught as she stepped back, hands half-raised.

"I didn't mean—"

Eric was already at Sia's side, helping her up with a concerned but practiced ease. "Well. That escalated quickly."

"I'm fine," Sia said, brushing herself off and managing a tight smile. "Seriously."

The group remained still, unsure whether to continue or retreat.

Mia turned away before she could see the looks. She didn't want to see pity or even worse, fear.

She didn't want confirmation of what she already felt.

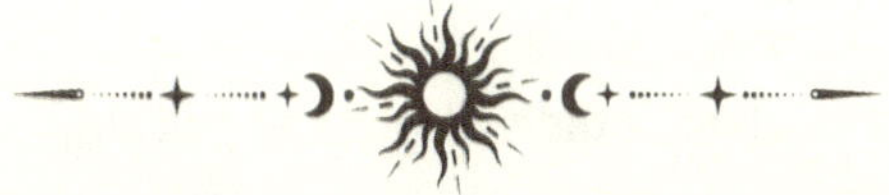

THE BARN GROANED SOFTLY as Mia slipped inside, the old wood bending and creaking like it remembered other visitors, older sins. The darkness welcomed her; it was not oppressive, but close, like the hush of a breath held too long. She didn't bring a lantern. Didn't need one. Shadows recognized her now. They made space.

She paused in the center of the floor, letting her eyes adjust. Dust swirled in the beams of moonlight cutting through the slats, catching on motes like stars trapped in wood grain. Above her, something shifted.

"Rough day?" Crawly's voice dripped from the rafters, smooth as oil. He lounged in a makeshift throne cobbled from hay bales and forgotten farm tools, the perfect crown of rusted debris perched like a halo behind his head.

Mia didn't flinch. She'd stopped reacting to his theatrics. What was the point? The devil never needed a second entrance.

"They're afraid of me," she said. Her voice was low, steady. "They don't say it, but it's there. I can feel it. In the way they hesitate before touching me. In how they watch me spar."

"Of course they are." Crawly stood slowly, fluid as smoke, landing on the floor with barely a sound. "You've been to Hell and brought back pieces. That scent clings. Mortals have long memories for things that smell like damnation."

Mia's jaw clenched. "I didn't ask for any of this."

"None of us do," he said, circling her now. "The real trick is what you do once it's yours."

She turned to face him. His features were sharp, unfairly handsome in the way masks sometimes are beautiful until you realize they were never meant to move. And when he smiled, it was with teeth too perfect, too patient.

"They think I'm going to turn," she said. "That I'm still that thing I became down there."

"Because you could be," he answered softly. "And isn't that the fun part?"

He opened his hand between them. Resting on his palm was a ring; small, silver, and unadorned. It shimmered faintly in the moonlight, and yet somehow cast no shadow.

"Choice," he said. "It's all about choice. Not what you were. Not what they fear. What *you* become. This..." He gestured with the ring. "...isn't a promise or a curse. It's a reminder. You don't belong to them. You don't belong to me. You decide what power means."

Her tail curled tighter around her leg, a reflex she didn't notice. Her voice, when it came, cracked slightly. "I don't want to hurt them."

Crawly tilted his head. "Then don't. But don't let them mold you into something breakable just to feel safe. You've already walked through fire. Why return to ash?"

Mia said nothing. The shadows stretched longer around her, and the ring in his hand gleamed like a sliver of memory she wasn't ready to claim.

And still, she didn't look away."

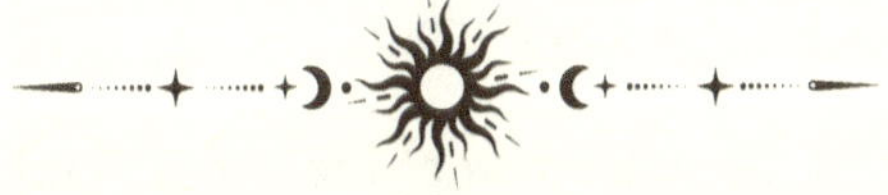

THE WIND WHISPERED THROUGH the high rafters of the loft, tugging gently at the curtains and stirring the pages of Sia's sketchbook even before her fingers moved. Moonlight pooled through the single window, turning the wooden floor silver and shadowed, casting her in a world somewhere between sleep and waking.

She didn't remember picking up the pencil. Didn't remember turning to a new page. Her hand moved with a rhythm that didn't feel like hers, it was an instinct born of something ancient scratching through the veil.

She drew.

Rough lines became terrain. A jagged peak of some forgotten mountain. Weathered stones forming a perfect circle at its summit, like ancient sentinels waiting for judgment. In the center, a sword. Not gleaming. Not triumphant. It stood like a warning; wedged in earth, humming with something older than steel.

Every detail came with certainty. She shaded the cracks in the stone, not because she imagined them, but because she remembered them. The sky above the scene was full of ash instead of clouds and the light that bled through it was the color of a bruised wound. It didn't make sense. None of it did. But it felt *true*.

She blinked. The image was there.

Far away, on the other side of the world, Tobias and Ella stepped cautiously through the rising fog of twilight. The wind had teeth, but it didn't bite, the air blew but it did not impede, it just watched. The summit of the mountain rose before them. The same stones. The same sword. The same tension, like air right before a storm confesses itself.

Ella stopped first. Her breath caught in her throat. "You feel that?"

Tobias scanned the horizon, his stance half-coiled, ever-ready. "Yeah. Like being measured."

They stepped closer. The circle of stones thrummed beneath their feet. The ground wasn't shaking, no it was vibrating, organically moving as though it was *breathing*. Slow, ancient. Like the world was holding something beneath its surface and had yet to decide if it wanted to share it.

The sword stood motionless, but it pulsed faintly with hidden light, not gold, but the color of old flame. Worn and waiting.

Back in the loft, Sia's pencil snapped in half between her fingers. The sound cracked the quiet like a hymn undone. She gasped, breath catching in her throat as if something in her own chest had broken with it.

She stared down at the sketch, her pulse quickened. It was exact. Down to the tilt of each stone, the weight of the mist. The arch of the wind.

She reached for the corner of the page. Her fingers trembled as she read the date.

Tomorrow's.

The sketch had arrived before the memory. Before the moment had even happened.

Her gaze lingered on the blade in the center of the image. It wasn't just symbolic, it was a *signal*. A marker planted in time. Her gift was changing. The Dreaming wasn't just showing her possibilities. It was reaching out through her. Mapping futures.

And somewhere behind her eyes, the Dreaming stirred.

It was not finished with her yet.

THE FARMHOUSE HAD QUIETED under the weight of night. Its old wooden bones creaked softly as it settled into the dark, and the only light that remained came from the hearth. The fire was low but steady, coals glowing like dragon eyes beneath the soft flicker of flame. It was the kind of silence that could only be found in places where truth might accidentally slip free.

Marcus moved with care, placing another log into the fire with the kind of deliberate stillness he wore like armor. He stood for a moment, letting the warmth touch his face, eyes reflecting the amber light. Shadows danced across the stone and wood, cast by the flicker of fire and thought.

Eric sat nearby in a sagging armchair that had seen better decades, one leg thrown over the other, a glass of something strong cradled in his palm. He swirled it once, watching the contents catch the firelight. The smell of cedar smoke mingled with the faint scent of citrus and spellwork lingering on his coat.

"She's changing," Marcus said, breaking the silence without turning.

Eric looked up. "They both are." He took a long sip. "You think it's supposed to go like this?"

Marcus's shoulders shifted, but he didn't answer immediately. The fire popped, sending a spray of sparks up the chimney like lost stars.

"Nothing ever goes how it's supposed to," he said at last. "That's how you know it's real."

Eric gave a tired laugh. "Deep for a guy who teaches sword forms like a boot camp drill sergeant."

Another beat passed. Eric's gaze returned to the flames. "I'm scared for her. For both of them. They're being pulled in opposite directions, and I don't think either of them can see it. Not fully."

Marcus finally turned, folding his arms. "It's not that they don't see. It's that they can't *stop*. Sia's being pulled by prophecy. Mia's being pushed by fear. Both are moving faster than they're ready for."

"They'll need anchors," Eric murmured.

Marcus nodded once. "And people who don't look at them like ticking clocks."

Eric raised his glass. "Then let's be those people."

Marcus allowed himself a faint smile, just enough to ease the tension in his jaw. "They'll hate us for it."

"That's what makes it love."

Outside, the wind pushed against the farmhouse with a long, keening whistle, like the night itself had teeth but hadn't decided what to bite.

CHAPTER 10

Faultlines

The sin which is unpardonable is knowingly and wilfully to reject truth, to fear knowledge lest that knowledge pander not to thy prejudices.

A.C.

THE SKY BURNED.

Not in shades of red or gold, but in bleeding whites and grays, the color of ash caught in lightning. It churned overhead in ragged spirals, screaming without sound. Thunder cracked, not in the sky, but beneath it, as if the world's bones were being broken one by one.

Sia stood in the center of a blackened field where nothing should have survived. The grass had melted into glass. The trees were nothing but skeletal shadows, their limbs twisted skyward in silent agony. Smoke rose in thick coils, not gray but the color of bruises, purple, blue, and sickly green. It clung to her skin. It tasted of iron and ruin.

The heat pulsed outward in waves, each breath harder than the last. It wasn't fire in the usual sense. It was like standing in the presence of rage made physical. Every gust of wind felt like it might peel the skin from her bones. The air itself was blistered.

Around her, figures moved, or tried to. Blurred silhouettes staggered through the smoke, half-formed and falling apart. Faces she should have known blurred into charcoal smudges. Someone reached for her, a hand stretching from the haze, and as she stepped toward it, they turned to ash. Another screamed, and she felt it inside her ribs, though no sound escaped their mouth.

And then she saw Mia.

She stood at the edge of the carnage, untouched. Her skin glowed faintly, the bronze sheen catching the firelight like polished armor. Her wings unfurled slowly, vast and oil-dark, stirring the rising smoke in gentle waves. Her tail curled behind her like a question mark carved in flame. Her eyes were open, but they did not blink. Did not see.

"Mia?" Sia's voice broke on the smoke.

Mia didn't move. Didn't speak. Behind her, the inferno crept higher, licking the sky, crowned with lightning. Yet none of it touched her. She turned, slow and sure, and began walking into the deeper smoke. Away.

Sia's feet refused to follow. The ground fractured beneath her, splitting in long veins of molten light, like cracks in a stained-glass window made of fire. Her voice caught in her throat. Her arms refused to reach. She was bound, not by chains, but by inevitability.

Then the field melted away.

She stood in a hallway of white stone, cold and silent. The air was damp with something old. Moss grew in the cracks between the stones, glowing faintly blue. The walls wept water in slow trickles that echoed with each drop, a heartbeat of silence broken only by breath.

At the far end, a door glowed. Not with light, but with memory. It pulsed like something alive. It called to her, wordless and ancient. She moved toward it, not by choice, but because she had always been moving toward it.

Her fingers reached for the handle.

A hand caught her wrist.

Cold. Firm.

Thanatos.

He stood there, eyes like extinguished stars, shadows clinging to him like fabric soaked in sorrow.

"You have to choose," he said. Not a threat. Not a command. A truth.

Then the dream shattered.

Sia woke with a gasp, tangled in sweat-soaked sheets. Her breath came in shallow bursts, chest heaving like she'd run a mile uphill. Moonlight painted stripes across the room, cool and sterile against the storm still pulsing behind her eyes.

Her sketchbook lay open in her lap. Her pencil, she didn't remember grabbing it, was still warm in her fingers. The page was half-filled. Blackened trees. A cracked sky. A lone figure walking into fire.

Mia.

THE MORNING BROKE SLOWLY, its golden light filtered through a thin veil of mist that clung to the ground like a second skin. The farmhouse breathed quietly around it, timbers settling with gentle creaks, walls humming faintly with the memory of laughter now held in reserve. Outside, dew collected in pearled beads along the wooden rails of the porch, and the wind carried the faint scent of rain not yet fallen.

Inside, the kitchen felt suspended in that hush before words form. The low gurgle of the coffee pot and the occasional tick of cooling metal were the only companions to the hush that had settled deep into the bones of the old home.

Sia sat at the end of the kitchen table, elbows braced, head lowered over her sketchbook. The worn wood beneath her arms was cool to the touch, the grain faintly warped by years of spilled tea and late-night talks. Her eyes were rimmed red from sleep she hadn't truly found. She flipped the pages slowly, her fingers trailing charcoal smudges, each image a fragment of something more, something unfinished.

The newest page remained untouched save for its beginnings: flame curling around a figure with no face, wings half-sketched in jagged arcs, smoke coiled like fingers around the edges of the frame.

A chair scraped softly against the floor.

Mia entered like a shadow loosed from the wall. Her steps were cautious but not soft, her weight carried differently than it once had, more grounded, heavier, like each footstep remembered chains that had since been broken but not forgotten. Her tail flicked once behind her, then went still, a living question mark.

She crossed to the counter without speaking. The coffeepot hissed softly as she poured a cup, its steam rising in thin tendrils that curled toward the ceiling beams like smoke from an old fire. She sat at the opposite end of the table, her eyes downcast but aware, listening without seeming to.

The silence between them stretched, neither hostile nor comforting. It simply was. Like the air before a thunderclap.

Eric stumbled in next, his hair askew, hoodie sagging off one shoulder. He paused mid-yawn when he saw them, blinking as if he'd stepped into a pressure chamber. "Morning," he said, a feeble attempt at humor. "Or something that wants to be morning when it grows up."

No laughter. Just the hiss of the kettle.

He busied himself at the stove, movements gentler than usual. Even his mug clinked more softly when he set it down.

Marcus arrived last, and with him came a pause, a stilling. He lingered in the doorway for a moment, reading the room with eyes honed on wars fought in more than just armor. He took a place near the far wall, arms crossed, one boot propped against the baseboard.

No one spoke. Not at first.

Sia's voice came quiet and unsure, but it cut the stillness like a blade drawn too early. "I had a dream."

Mia looked up.

Sia swallowed. "Not like before. This one was... heavier. It didn't feel like mine."

She flipped the sketchbook around, showing the half-finished image. The others leaned in, subtly, cautiously.

"It was fire. And shadows. You were walking away. And I couldn't follow."

Mia's hand tightened around her coffee cup. Her face didn't shift, but her body said enough.

"Do you think I'm going to betray you?" she asked, her voice level, but low.

"No," Sia said, her grip on the sketchbook white-knuckled. "But I think something's pulling us apart."

The kettle shrieked behind them, high and insistent.

No one moved to silence it.

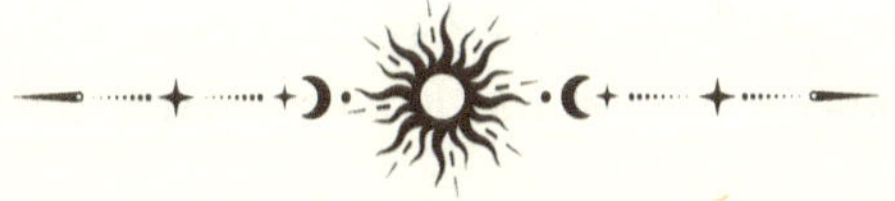

Mount Athos rose like a silent sentinel above the Aegean, wrapped in fog and old prayers. The wind that whispered along its cliffs carried no warmth, only the salt-slick breath of the sea and the heavy hush of sacred things too old to forget themselves. Clouds moved sluggishly through the sky, like ghosts with nowhere left to haunt.

Ella's boots scraped over worn stones as she followed Tobias up the narrow path toward the monastery. The stones beneath her feet were ancient, smoothed by centuries of passage and pilgrimage. She could feel the reverence etched into every step, though it sat uncomfortably on her shoulders now. Like a robe she wasn't sure she had earned.

The main structure loomed ahead, modest, weathered, and clinging to the mountain with a quiet stubbornness. Vines threaded through its outer walls, curling like veins along sun-bleached brick. A bell tolled in the distance, low and slow, like a heartbeat filtered through stone.

Inside, the monastery was all cold air and candlelight. The scent of beeswax and incense drifted through the halls, layered with the faintest trace of olive oil and parchment. Shadows clung to the high ceilings like smoke that refused to rise.

They were led to a side cloister where several of the monks waited, seated in a semicircle beneath a fresco of Saint Michael casting down the Dragon. The Archangel's face was faded by time, but his sword still gleamed with painted flame.

Brother Anastasios spoke first, his voice a gravel path. "We welcome you, Daughter of Light, and her chosen blade." His eyes lingered on Ella, narrowing slightly. "But your request troubles us."

Tobias shifted his weight, arms crossed. "Troubles you, or threatens you?"

The monk gave no answer, but the tension in the room thickened.

Ella stepped forward. Her voice didn't rise, but it filled the space. "We don't ask for Templars to invade this place. We ask for protection. For reverence. You've guarded the chamber this long, but the world outside is changing. You felt it when we arrived."

There was a murmur among the monks, brief and brittle.

Another monk, older still, leaned forward. "We feel what stirs beneath this mountain. We feel the sword calling. But it is not your place to call its guardians."

Ella met his gaze. "I'm not asking for permission. I'm trying not to let the next war begin with a tomb being torn open."

Tobias placed a hand on her shoulder, steady, but not stopping her. "You saw what happened in New York," he said to the room. "You know the Hold wouldn't send us lightly."

The monks said nothing, but their silence was not consent. It was caution. Suspicion.

Ella turned back toward the fresco of Michael. The dragon's eyes had faded into shadow, but the flame in the sword still burned. She touched the pendant beneath her shirt, a warmth that pulsed faintly against her palm.

Uriel had chosen her.

But that didn't mean the world would follow.

THE BARN STOOD HALF-EMPTIED, its rafters tall and solemn as a cathedral left to time. Dust hung in the air like suspended breath, turning golden where the late sun caught it through a crooked windowpane. The boards creaked under even the stillness of the air, warped with age and use. The smell of hay, old wood, and rusted chain oil clung thick in the air, layered with something deeper, like the scent of long-held sorrow.

Mia sat in the corner beneath a dangling chain, knees drawn to her chest, arms looped tightly around them. The illusion that cloaked her horns and wings had long since faded, melted away like fog under scrutiny. Her skin bore a faint heat beneath its surface, like coals that would never quite die. She didn't try to hide the tail that curled listlessly in the straw beside her. Here, in the half-light and shadow, there was no point pretending.

She breathed shallowly. Each inhale dragged against her ribs, laced with the scent of old leather, dust, and the ghost of ozone, memories of fire not yet lived.

The others didn't know. Not really. They saw her restraint and mistook it for strength. But it was fear. Fear that if she moved too fast, laughed too hard, felt too much, she would slip. And when she slipped, something ancient beneath her skin might take the wheel.

She wasn't sure if she was a person trying to stay good, or a thing trying to look human.

The sound came softly, grain shifting under weight. She didn't flinch.

Crawly stepped from the gloom at the far end of the barn. He moved like he'd always belonged there, like the dust and the scent of oil had whispered a welcome. His shirt was half unbuttoned, sleeves rolled, feet bare on the boards. He radiated calm like a trickle of warm honey, slow, sweet, and a little too easy.

"Hard day?" he asked, voice gentle, touched with mock concern.

Mia didn't answer.

He leaned against a post, arms loosely folded, letting the silence settle like fog. Then, after a beat: "They don't trust you."

"I know," she said. Her voice was dry. Sandpaper and smoke.

"They want to. But you scare them." His voice caressed the room like a confession. "You scare yourself."

She looked up at him, eyes glowing faintly in the twilight. Gold overlaid with ember.

"You think I don't know what I could become?" she said.

"I think you know exactly," Crawly replied, his tone soft, reverent almost. "And that terrifies them more than it ever will you."

Mia looked at her hands. They were still, but the memory of them coated in hellfire, clutching a demon's throat, never quite left her. She remembered what it felt like to crave destruction, not because she wanted to, but because it had wanted her back.

"I'm tired," she said, and it wasn't a complaint. It was a surrender.

"Then let me help," he murmured.

She closed her eyes. The barn breathed around her, wood ticking, chains swaying slightly as a breeze slipped through the slats. The air smelled of thunder that hadn't yet arrived.

"Help always comes with a price."

Crawly stepped forward, but not too close. "Not always. Sometimes, help just comes from someone who sees you. Not the risk. Not the myth. Just you."

Her tail curled tighter around her leg. Her throat closed.

"I don't want to hurt them," she said again, her voice shaking now. "I just... I don't want to be alone in this."

"You won't be," he said, softer than before. "Not if you stop letting them define you by what they fear. You've carried enough."

She opened her eyes slowly, breath shaky. There were tears. They didn't fall, but they shimmered.

Crawly said nothing more. He didn't need to.

And Mia... didn't send him away.

IT STARTED WITH SPARKS.

The training yard behind the farmhouse had been still, just the wind in the trees and the scuff of boots on dirt as Mia tried to control her breathing. She had asked to be alone. Marcus had hesitated but relented, promising to stay nearby. She needed to feel her own center again without eyes judging her every twitch.

She was trying. God, she was trying.

The energy pulsed beneath her skin like a storm waiting for a reason. The lesson earlier had been simple, summon a flame without feeding it. Contain the fire. Will, not instinct.

But the wind picked up.

Her hand trembled, and the heat surged. A flicker of light bloomed in her palm, curling upward like a flame made of shadow and gold.

She held it there, sweat gathering along her hairline.

Control it. Just breathe.

A branch snapped in the woods. Her head jerked toward the sound. Her focus shattered.

The flame exploded.

It wasn't large, not at first. But it caught the grass, then the dry straw bundled near the barn wall. Fire leapt like it had been waiting. The explosion cracked like thunder, and suddenly the yard was bathed in red and orange.

Mia screamed, not from fear, but fury. At herself. At the flame. She threw her arms forward and tried to pull it back, but her power surged in response, wild and frantic.

By the time Marcus and Eric came running, she was already backing away, eyes wide, breath coming in ragged gasps. The fire hissed, curling higher with every second.

Eric yelled something, Marcus threw his arms wide, calling wind to smother the flames. The air roared as magic collided, scattering embers and choking smoke.

And Mia ran.

She didn't wait to hear what they said. She didn't want to see their faces. She fled toward the house, up the stairs, and vanished into the attic.

She didn't come out for the rest of the day.

THE NIGHT HAD DEEPENED by the time Sia found Marcus, standing alone beneath the warped porch light that flickered like a heartbeat on the verge of giving out. The bulb buzzed softly, a nervous hum in the silence between them. Crickets called from the edge of the treeline. Somewhere far off, a barn owl gave one sharp cry and fell quiet.

She hadn't meant to wander. Her feet had taken her here.

Marcus turned his head slightly, sensing her before she spoke. "She's not back."

Sia nodded, though he hadn't asked.

He gestured to the step beside him, and she sat. The wood was warm from the day's heat, but her arms felt cold.

"I saw her," she said. "In the dream. She walked into the fire, Marcus. She didn't even look back."

He didn't answer right away. Just stood there, arms folded, watching the dark horizon.

"She's scared," he finally said. "You both are."

Sia exhaled. "Everyone's scared. But they still look at me like I'm supposed to lead. Like I'm supposed to have the answers. And I don't."

"No one ever does," he said. "Not before it matters."

She looked at him then, really looked, at the way his shoulders bore an invisible weight, at the way his jaw stayed clenched even when he tried to speak gently. He wasn't just a warrior. He was someone trying to keep people from breaking while quietly breaking himself.

"Eric thinks she's a danger," she whispered.

"He's not wrong," Marcus replied. "But that doesn't mean she's the enemy."

"I can't lose her again," Sia said, voice low. "I already did once. If she falls, if Crawly turns her, I don't know if I can fight her."

He knelt beside her, one hand resting on her shoulder.

"Then don't fight her," he said. "Stand for her. Stand for who she was before the fire, and who she could still be after."

Sia's eyes stung.

"She's still my sister."

"I know."

They sat in silence for a long time, the wind rising and falling like the breath of the land itself. And somewhere, beyond the trees and beneath the stars, Mia walked the border between salvation and surrender.

CHAPTER 11

Widening Rifts

Ordinary morality is only for ordinary people.

A.C.

THE KITCHEN SMELLED OF rain and old wood, of coffee long gone cold and the faintest sting of ozone from a storm still hovering somewhere on the edge of memory. The windows were open to the overcast morning, letting in a dull gray light and the sound of wet leaves rustling in the breeze. The house felt heavier than usual, as if it too was waiting to see which way the wind would shift.

Sia sat at the head of the table, her body hunched over like she was bracing for impact. Her fingers curled tightly around a chipped mug of tea she hadn't touched in half an hour, the steam long gone. Her dreams still clung to her ribs like moss, damp and dense and hard to shake. Every breath reminded her of the fire she'd seen. Of Mia walking into it, glowing and distant and utterly unreachable.

Across from her, Marcus and Eric mirrored each other in opposite tones, one calm and composed like stone under pressure, the other taut with frustration, sparks curling beneath his voice.

Mia remained absent, her chair conspicuously empty. That absence spoke more than any word could.

Eric was the first to speak, his fingers drumming a slow, impatient rhythm on the tabletop. "So, what are we actually doing here? Pretending this isn't getting worse?"

Marcus didn't move, but the line of his shoulders stiffened. "It's a discussion, not a trial."

Eric scoffed. "Feels like one."

Silence settled between them. Sia didn't lift her gaze. The ticking of the clock on the wall stretched between beats like it was holding its breath.

"She hasn't hurt anyone," she said at last, voice rough. "And she's trying."

"Trying doesn't stop accidents," Eric replied. "You didn't see her face yesterday. You didn't see what she looked like in the field. That wasn't your sister, that was something else."

Sia swallowed. Her heart thudded in her chest, a deep and aching rhythm.

Marcus leaned forward, speaking with quiet steel. "And what, exactly, do you think she'll do? Burn down the barn? Possess a chicken?"

"I think she's a walking question mark," Eric said. "And I think we're pretending she's still the same girl who played violin in your garden when she was twelve."

Sia's knuckles whitened on the mug in her hands. She remembered that day, the late summer breeze, the sound of bow against string, Mia laughing with her eyes closed, a song for no one but the wind. That girl had felt untouchable, full of light.

"She is still that girl," Sia said, barely above a whisper. "She's also more. But she hasn't given up."

Eric looked like he wanted to argue. Instead, he shook his head and looked away.

Marcus pulled out his phone and tapped in a code. "Let's get a second opinion."

He turned on the speaker just as Tobias's voice crackled through. "Hey. Connection's weak up here. Ella's meditating, so I've got a minute."

"Tobias," Sia said, her voice steadier now. "We're talking about Mia. About whether she's safe to keep here."

There was a pause. Static rustled like wind in dead leaves. Then: "She's dangerous. We all are. But she's not the enemy. If you start treating her like she is, you'll lose her faster than Crawly ever could."

Eric clenched his jaw but didn't speak.

"Thanks," Sia murmured.

Tobias's tone softened. "Just... remind her she's not alone. That'll do more than any ward or sword can."

The line went dead.

For a long moment, no one moved. The silence felt like a closing door.

Finally, Marcus stood. "No more questions today. We let her rest. We all do."

Eric didn't object, but his expression said the conversation wasn't over.

Sia stayed behind as the others left the kitchen, her hands still wrapped around the cooling mug. She looked down into it, watching the surface tremble faintly with every beat of her heart.

Outside, the wind picked up. The world waited to see what they would become.

THE AIR BENEATH MOUNT Athos was thick with age. Every breath Ella drew tasted of stone and salt, like secrets ground into dust over centuries. The narrow staircase spiraling downward was carved directly into the rock, slick in places where generations of pilgrims had worn it smooth. Each step echoed with a low, distant hum that made the bones in her chest vibrate.

The torch Tobias carried flickered as they descended deeper, the flame catching on the damp walls and casting long, crooked shadows. Moss glowed faintly in the seams between the stones, an ethereal blue that lit their path more softly than the fire.

Ella walked in silence, her boots making almost no sound on the stone. Her hand remained lightly pressed to her chest, just above the pendant. It pulsed with warmth, slow and steady. She wasn't sure if it was responding to the chamber ahead, or to her.

"This is deeper than last time," Tobias murmured.

She nodded. "The closer we get, the more... I feel it."

"What does it feel like?"

Ella hesitated. "Like I'm being seen. Not watched, seen. Every scar, every truth, every lie I've told myself. It's all just... laid bare."

They reached the bottom of the stairwell and stepped into a circular chamber. The ceiling arched high above them, vaulted like a cathedral. At the center of the floor, a sigil burned softly in gold and silver, pulsing like a heartbeat beneath ancient runes.

Before it stood a sealed door, plain stone, cracked down the middle, yet bound by light that hummed faintly like a low chant heard through water.

Ella stepped forward, one hand hovering near the center of the sigil. Her breath caught.

A whisper rose in her ears. Not in a voice, but in light. It flooded her chest with pressure, not pain, not fear. Purpose.

She staggered slightly, and Tobias caught her elbow.

"You alright?"

She nodded slowly, lips parted. "He's here. Uriel. Or... what's left of him."

She didn't mean dead. She meant present. She could feel it, not as a sound, not as a word. As a weight of expectation. A warmth like standing too close to a star. Something divine that had once burned with perfect justice, now echoing down into her bones.

The sigil flared brighter for a heartbeat, then dimmed.

She didn't cry. But something inside her twisted, sharp and bright. A knowledge she hadn't asked for, but now carried. This place wasn't just sacred.

It was hungry for something holy.

Tobias spoke quietly. "Do you want to go further?"

Ella shook her head. "Not today. Not without the Templars. It feels... fragile. Like something's listening back."

They turned together and made their way slowly back up the stairs, each step a whisper into the mountain's waiting heart.

THE ATTIC WAS QUIET, save for the faint ticking of the old grandfather clock downstairs, its voice muffled by walls and distance. Dust drifted lazily through the slanted shafts of late afternoon light, catching on cobwebs in the rafters and turning the air gold and grainy. A single moth fluttered near the windowpane, its wings tapping gently against the glass.

Mia sat cross-legged on an old quilt, her back against a beam, the dream-key cupped in her palms like something sacred, or dangerous. It was a small thing. Cool to the touch. Silver-black, like a crescent moon caught mid-bruise. It pulsed faintly with an inner light, the rhythm too slow to be a heartbeat, too steady to be random.

She hadn't meant to use it.

But silence was unbearable. The house had too many eyes now. Too many silences loaded with fear and judgment. She could feel the weight of it pressing against the walls like water against glass, aching to crack.

She pressed the key to her chest.

It didn't burn. It didn't glow. It simply... opened.

The world shifted, not a fall, not a blink. More like the attic peeled away, layer by layer, revealing something beneath it that had always been there.

She stood in the Dreaming.

Not the soft surrealism she remembered from when Sia brought her here, not the calm drift of visions or strange landscapes unfolding like pages from a storybook. This was different. This place hummed. It was darker, heavier. A version of the Dream filtered through her fears.

The trees were too tall. Their branches twisted like veins above her. The sky pulsed with slow-moving clouds, all colored in bruised purples and golds, like spilled oil over a dying fire. The air smelled of jasmine and ash.

And in the clearing ahead, Sia stood.

Or something like her.

Her twin was barefoot, dressed in white. But her skin shimmered like moonlight on water, and her eyes were solid gold. She was fighting, something black and shape-shifting, tendrils of shadow lashing from the ground, rising like broken thoughts given form.

The false-Sia moved beautifully. Powerfully. Too much so.

She struck with light, but it was merciless. Surgical. The kind of light that didn't warm, it cauterized. Mia stepped forward, her voice catching in her throat.

The golden-eyed Sia turned toward her and smiled. It wasn't a cruel smile. But it wasn't kind, either. It was the smile of someone who had already chosen their path and didn't expect anyone else to follow.

The Dream lurched. The clearing blurred. Mia stumbled back, the air seizing like a vacuum.

Then she was alone again, in the attic, heart hammering like she'd run for miles.

The dream-key lay beside her, still pulsing faintly, cold as guilt.

SIA'S PENCIL SNAPPED MID-LINE.

The sketchbook trembled on her lap, the page already half-covered in twisting trees and a figure in white, unfinished, eyes blank. She hadn't drawn for more than a few minutes, just trying to catch the shape of a feeling that wouldn't leave her since waking. But now, the page was changing. Not just through her hand. The charcoal moved.

Not like ink bleeding or graphite smudging, but shifting. Rewriting. Lines warped, branches curling inward like fingers. The figure's smile lengthened. The shadows in the corners of the paper deepened to pitch, swallowing the margins.

She gasped, dropping the book. It hit the floor with a slap, its pages flaring like wings.

And then she wasn't in the room anymore.

The world fell inward.

The Dream took her without permission.

She stood in a field of cracked glass and fog. No horizon. No sky. The stars above were still, like painted holes in a dark ceiling. Wind moved through her hair, slow and cold, carrying a scent like burnt myrrh.

Her breath came sharp, shallow. Her fingers curled unconsciously at her sides. Every inch of her skin prickled with static. Not fear, forewarning.

Thanatos stepped from behind a broken pillar, his robe catching no dust, his form heavier than shadow and more solid than time.

"You were pulled," he said, not angry. Not surprised. Just... there.

Sia steadied herself, legs shaky beneath her. "It was Mia. She used something."

"The key." He walked toward her, every footfall echoing like it struck memory, not stone. "Crawly gave her a way in. It's small now, but it will grow."

She turned slowly in place, trying to grasp the geometry of the Dream. It was warped around her, curving, breathing. Her presence here was causing ripples. She could feel them in her teeth.

"I didn't summon the vision," she whispered. "But it still came. That's what you are now. You don't see the Dream, you shape it."

She went still. Her hands trembled. The fear wasn't loud. It was quiet. Surgical. It sliced beneath the surface, whispering of things she might not mean but might make real.

Thanatos stepped closer, gaze lowering to her hands. Her fingertips were still stained from charcoal, but now there was something else beneath the skin, a faint glow, subtle and opalescent, like moonlight drowned in deep water.

"You're evolving," he said gently. "Faster than I hoped. The boundary between vision and creation is thinning. Soon... there may not be one."

"I don't want to make anything," she said. Her voice cracked. "I just want to understand it."

"But you will make it," Thanatos said. "The Dream responds to your truths, even the ones you're not ready to admit."

Sia looked down, and the field beneath her fractured. Little cracks branched out with every throb of her chest, fragile truths made visible.

Thanatos reached out, his touch resting lightly against her temple. His hand was cold, grounding, real.

"I can't hold the door forever," he said. "If she opens it again, you must be ready. Next time, she won't just look."

Then the Dream shuddered and Sia woke, sprawled on the floor of her room, the sketchbook closed beside her. Her heart slammed in her ribs like a war drum. She sat up slowly, her head heavy, the scent of charcoal and paper thick in her nose. Her hands were shaking. The image on the last page was new. She hadn't drawn it.

And it was looking at her.

Chapter 12

Fracture Lines

Modern morality and manners suppress all natural instincts, keep people ignorant of the facts of nature and make them fighting drunk on bogey tales.

A.C.

THE FARMHOUSE WAS STILL in the hour before dawn. The kind of stillness that hung heavy over the fields and made every creak of old wood sound like a confession. Outside, mist clung low over the grass like a ghost unsure of where to go. The air smelled faintly of ash and damp earth, yesterday's storm still lingering in the bones of the land.

Sia sat on the back porch wrapped in a flannel blanket, sketchbook open across her knees. She wasn't drawing. Not really.

Just moving her pencil in small circles on the corner of the page, like she could scrape something loose from her thoughts if she pressed hard enough.

Her eyes were ringed with fatigue, skin paler than usual. The morning chill didn't touch her, but her shoulders stayed tense, hunched like she was expecting the air itself to scold her. She could hear the wind stirring the tall grass beyond the fence, the creak of the porch settling, the soft whistle of an early bird somewhere off in the trees.

Marcus approached without sound. She didn't flinch, she never did with him. He took the step beside her without asking, sitting down with that quiet gravity he always carried. His presence filled space without intruding on it.

He didn't speak right away. Just breathed with her. Matched the rhythm. A long, quiet stillness fell between them, soft as wool.

"You're not sleeping again," he said finally, voice low and rough with sleep.

Sia shook her head. Her voice was equally quiet. "Not really sure if I ever do." The pencil moved in one last tight arc, then stopped.

Marcus glanced at the page. Abstract shapes. No figure. No structure. Just pressure, forced into lead. "Want to talk about it?"

"No." A pause. Then: "Yes. But I can't."

He waited. The wind picked up, pushing the mist gently across the field like fog rolling off a lake.

She exhaled. "Something's changing. The Dream doesn't feel like a place anymore. It feels like... a canvas. And my hands are always dirty."

Marcus looked toward the horizon, where the sun was just starting to bleed gold into the edge of the clouds. "You think you're causing the things you see?"

"I don't know," she whispered. "But Thanatos said I'm shaping them now. That my truth is starting to matter more than what's real."

He turned his head. "And what is your truth, Sia?"

She laughed once, small and brittle. "That I'm scared. That I don't know what I'm becoming. And that every time I look at Mia, I wonder if we're both just shadows of what we should have been."

Marcus's gaze softened. "You're not a shadow. You're the light they're trying to chase. Even when you can't see it yourself."

She looked at him, eyes glassy. "What if I'm not shaping the future? What if I'm choosing it?"

He reached over and stilled her pencil hand. Held it gently.

"Then choose better," he said. "And if you can't, let the people who love you hold the brush for a while."

Her fingers twitched under his. She didn't pull away. Instead, she let the pencil drop, the clatter startling in the quiet. Sia shifted closer to him. The blanket slid from her shoulders as she climbed onto his lap, her head pressing gently against his collarbone. He didn't stiffen or ask questions, he just wrapped his arms around her, anchoring her with the weight of his silence.

Her breath slowed. The world stayed quiet. For a little while, they just sat like that, two shapes wrapped in mist and warmth. And when the sun finally rose, it painted the mist gold, and neither of them looked away.

THE MORNING LIGHT FILTERED through the kitchen windows like warm syrup, golden and slow. Dust motes turned lazy circles in the air, catching the beams that slanted across the wooden countertops. The scent of citrus tea lingered like a whisper, blending with faint notes of burnt toast and the cooler trace of ash drifting in from outside. The house was unnaturally quiet, like it, too, was trying to decide what to do with Mia.

She stood barefoot on the cool tile floor, her toes curling against the chill. One of Eric's sweatshirts hung loosely on her frame, sleeves rolled up past the elbows. The steam from her untouched mug of tea spiraled upward in lazy tendrils, vanishing into the amber light. Her wings were folded tight to her back, tucked away as if she could will them into absence. Her tail curled loosely around one ankle, twitching occasionally with restrained agitation.

There was a hollowness in her chest that had nothing to do with hunger.

Eric stepped into the doorway behind her, boots creaking against the old floorboards. She didn't turn, but he saw her shoulders stiffen, just slightly.

"You're up early," he said.

"Didn't sleep," she answered, her voice thin and raspy, like it had fought off too many dreams.

He stepped farther into the kitchen. The air between them was warmer than the room itself, heavy with unspoken words. The kettle on the stove hissed faintly in its cradle, still hot. A dishrag lay folded too neatly beside it, as if someone had tried to tidy chaos with cloth.

They didn't speak for a moment. Mia's eyes stayed on her tea, hands braced around the mug like she needed the shape of it to stay grounded.

"You scared them yesterday," Eric said, his tone neutral but edged.

She didn't flinch this time. Just exhaled. "I scared me too."

The admission surprised him. Not because he didn't believe it, he did. But because it was offered without armor.

He leaned against the counter, arms folded. The sun caught on the steel of his bracers, dull and scratched from last week's sparring.

"So what now? We act like you didn't nearly torch the barn?"

She closed her eyes. "No. But maybe you could act like you've made mistakes before too."

He wanted to deny it. Instead, he was quiet.

"I've made mistakes," he admitted. "But none that..."

"None that scared you like I do." She turned, finally meeting his gaze.

There was no accusation in her voice. Just fact. Sad and quiet.

"You made people feel like they didn't belong," she said. "Like one wrong twitch and you'd lock them out."

Eric winced inwardly. He hadn't meant to. But Mia's words dug into something that had already begun to fester.

"I'm sorry," she added, voice softer now. "For the fire. For losing control. I wasn't trying to..."

"I know," he said.

"I don't know how to stop being what I am." Her eyes dropped. "But I'm trying. Even if it looks like failing."

He watched her. Not just her face, but the way her posture had changed. The slight tremble in her hands. The way she stood like she was ready to take a blow that hadn't come.

"You're scared of yourself."

"Yes."

"Good," he said. "Means you still care."

She almost smiled. Almost. "That's not comforting."

"It wasn't supposed to be."

He stepped forward, his boots thudding softly against the tile. The scent of tea shifted as he neared her, the citrus mingling now with something deeper, sandalwood from his coat, a hint of steel from the spell rings hidden beneath his sleeves.

"You said Crawly doesn't flinch when he sees you," Eric said.

Mia hesitated. "He doesn't care what I break."

"I do."

She looked up at him sharply. "Why?"

"Because I see you too."

The silence stretched. Long enough for the kettle to begin to whistle. Eric didn't move. Neither did she. The look between them wasn't soft. It was raw. A threadbare trust daring to stitch itself.

Mia broke it first, looking down into her mug. The tea had gone cold. Eric stepped away without a word and relit the stove. The whistle grew louder, filling the room with something that almost felt like promise. And for the first time in days, Mia stayed still.

THE STONE GARDEN BEHIND the monastery breathed silence. Rows of ancient olive trees swayed gently in the morning breeze, their leaves whispering like pages turning in a forgotten book. The air was cool and clean, carrying the faint scent of rosemary, crushed rock, and something older, something sacred that clung to the soil.

Ella sat cross-legged on a carved bench at the garden's edge, a leather-bound sketchbook open across her lap. Her fingers moved without thought, charcoal gliding softly over the paper. She wasn't drawing from memory this time. She was drawing from feel.

The symbol from the sealed chamber was still etched behind her eyes, bright and sharp like an afterimage burned too long into vision. The lines came easily, too easily. Her hand traced curves and corners she didn't recognize, but knew with a bone-deep certainty were correct.

Each stroke made her heart beat faster. Not in fear, but in resonance.

The monastery loomed in the distance, quiet and sunlit. A monk swept the outer walkways with a straw broom, the rhythmic hush of it grounding her for a time. The sound was so mundane, so human, that for a moment she felt tethered.

But then the page changed.

Not visibly. Not dramatically. But Ella felt it. The line she was drawing shifted midway through, becoming something else, some older rune that wasn't part of the chamber symbol at all. Her hand twitched, but she didn't stop. Her breath caught.

The world dimmed and in the next blink, she was somewhere else.

Not in body. But in memory. Not hers.

She stood on scorched earth, a battlefield littered with broken standards and ash. A figure, vague and cloaked in radiance, moved through the wreckage with a sword burning white-hot in their hand. Not held. Not swung. Carried like an extension of the divine will itself.

Then another flash. A woman kneeling, her eyes glowing with holy fire, raising the blade to the sky as demons clawed at her feet. Then another. A child. A girl not much older than Sia. Her hands bleeding as she carved the symbol into stone. Her face was serene. Not because she wasn't afraid, but because she believed.

The sword remembers what the bearer forgets.

The words echoed in her skull, not heard with ears but stamped behind her eyes. The voice was neither male nor female. Only vast. It rang with finality, like a bell struck in a cathedral older than language.

She gasped and dropped the charcoal. It hit the bench with a brittle snap and rolled to the ground, leaving a soft gray smear in its wake.

The world righted itself. Her breath came in ragged waves, heart slamming in her chest. She looked down at the sketch. The page was full, dense lines and glowing etchings, forming something that pulsed faintly beneath her fingertips. The sketch was complete. And it felt alive. She didn't need to touch it again to know it would be warm.

Ella stared at it, trembling. Not from fear. From awe. From weight. From the understanding that whatever Uriel had left behind... it wasn't gone.

It was watching.

And it remembered her.

THE ATTIC WAS DIM, the slanted ceiling pressing close overhead like the inside of a forgotten trunk. Dust hung in the air, stirred by the weak light streaming through the single dormer window. Wooden beams stretched like ribs across the space, creaking softly with the weight of age. The quiet was absolute, broken only by the slow scratch of pencil on paper.

Sia sat cross-legged on the old braided rug, her sketchbook balanced across her lap. She hadn't come up here meaning to draw, but somehow, the moment she touched the spine of the book, it had opened to a fresh page on its own. She told herself it was just habit. That she needed the calm of drawing, the repetition of lines. But as her hand moved, she realized she wasn't thinking. Not guiding. The image formed beneath her fingers with eerie certainty.

A figure. Herself, but not. The face was hers. The hair, long and wild with streaks of light curling through dark. But the eyes were hollow, pools of ink, deep and fathomless. Wings unfurled behind the figure, vast and jagged like they'd been cut from thunderclouds. And above her brow, a crown, but not golden. Not royal. Ink-black and dripping, formed of lines that refused to stay still.

She blinked, heart rising into her throat. The air in the attic had gone still. Even the dust stopped swirling. The margins of the sketch pulsed. Once. A soft ripple through the page, like breath disturbing water.

Sia leaned closer.

The ink didn't move, but it shimmered faintly, as though light were trying to break through from beneath. Then, just for a second, a drop of ink in the corner lifted. Not much. Barely the width of a hair. But it rose. Quivered. And settled. She stared, unmoving. A chill prickled down her arms.

She pressed her hand flat over the drawing. It was warm and the book pulsed again. Not violently. Not in warning. More like a heartbeat. Steady. Waiting. Wanting.

Something beneath the page shifted, so subtle she could've dismissed it. But she didn't. She stayed still, breath caught in her chest, eyes tracking the way the ink at the edge began to bleed outward. It didn't drip. It spread with purpose. Not randomly, but like veins reaching out from a center.

She whispered, "What are you?"

The attic held its breath.

A single breeze brushed against the window, just enough to rattle the glass in its frame. The wood beneath her creaked in answer, like the house itself had heard her question and was considering how to respond. She closed the book gently, fingers trembling. It vibrated once beneath her palm, just a twitch, but enough to make her flinch. The attic exhaled around her, old wood shifting, wind brushing the glass again, longer this time, as though something were retreating just beyond reach.

She pulled the sketchbook close and held it against her chest, curling in slightly. She didn't look back at the sketch. Not yet. Because part of her was afraid she might not be the one holding the pen anymore.

Chapter 13

Blades & Burdens

...in the absence of will power, the most complete collection of virtues and talents is wholly worthless.

A.C.

THE WIND ON MOUNT Athos tasted of salt and cedar, sharp, clean, and ancient. It rolled down from the cliffs like a whisper older than any church, skimming over the monastery's tiled rooftops and through narrow stone alleys that clung to the mountain like veins of devotion. In the pre-dawn hush, the world felt suspended between breath and prayer.

Tobias walked in silence beside Ella, their boots pressing into soft gravel along a sloping trail lit by lanterns hung at respectful intervals. The monks who guided them spoke no words, only gestures, only reverence. Each man wore the simple black robes of Eastern Orthodoxy, their faces half-hidden in shadow and candlelight. The only sound was the soft hiss of wind against flame, and the rhythm of feet.

The path wound upward toward the heart of the sacred complex, a place few outside the monastic order were permitted to see. A place Tobias had only heard whispered about during his initial training. The Inner Sanctum. Not marked on any map. Not described in any modern Templar briefings. This was where relics older than doctrine were kept. Where silence was a language. Where angels had once been seen walking in daylight.

He felt the weight of his own armor, not on his shoulders, but in his blood. Memories of war, of cries and light and burning, tugged behind his eyes. He glanced sidelong at Ella.

She looked forward with calm he knew was forced. Her hands were tucked into her sleeves, and the faintest shimmer danced beneath her skin, barely visible in the dark, but he could see it now. As if her blood had started carrying light. She hadn't spoken much since yesterday's vision. Whatever Uriel had done, was still doing, was inside her now, humming quietly beneath the surface like a distant choir waiting for a cue.

Tobias swallowed hard and looked away.

He wasn't ready for what she might become.

At last, the trail opened onto a wide courtyard carved directly into the mountainside, its flagstones cracked with age but swept clean. A circular mosaic dominated the space, an ouroboros of gold and white marble, encircling an inscription in ancient Greek. At its far edge stood a tall gate flanked by statues of armored seraphim, their swords pointed downward into the stone. A gate not of wood or iron, but carved entirely from a single block of black volcanic glass, etched with Latin verse and symbols even Tobias had to squint to recognize.

One of the monks stepped forward, his voice soft but sonorous.

Sanctum Angelorum. Terra inter Terra.

The Holy of Holies. Earth between Earth.

Tobias and Ella both bowed their heads. The moment felt heavier than ritual. More than just tradition. Something watched them from beyond the glass. Not malevolent, but vast. Aware. As if some hidden observer weighed their souls from the other side.

Another monk stepped forward carrying a shallow brass basin filled with sacred oil and a bundle of hyssop branches. He dipped the leaves, then brushed both of them across the face and hands, anointing in silence. Tobias felt the cold oil bead on his brow. The ritual smelled of myrrh and something older, ozone, maybe. Lightning caught in resin.

Without a word, the volcanic gate began to part.

Before it did, Tobias reached out and gently touched Ella's arm. She turned, a faint shimmer still glistening along the edge of her cheek where the anointing oil had not yet dried.

"Hey," he said softly, his voice nearly lost in the wind. "Before we go in... just tell me one thing."

Ella looked at him, a flicker of gold catching in her eyes, but not from within. Just a trick of torchlight. Not yet divine.

"What?" she asked, almost afraid of what he might say.

"Are you still in there?"

Her breath hitched.

He gave her a small, uneven smile. "The Ella who used to snore during stakeouts. Who cracked jokes even when we were covered in demon guts. The one who'd punch me in the ribs if I started quoting Scripture like an old man."

"I wasn't that bad."

"You were," he said. "It was kind of your charm."

For a moment, something warm passed between them, familiar, grounding. And then it was gone again, carried off by the mountain air.

Ella swallowed hard. "I don't know what's happening to me, Tobias. Sometimes I feel like I'm just standing still... and something else is walking forward in my place."

"You don't have to do it alone."

"But I might have to anyway."

He didn't argue. Didn't try to stop her. He just nodded, once, and let go of her arm.

They turned as the gate of glass shivered open, lightless and silent, beckoning them inward.

And the mountain swallowed them whole.

THE MONASTERY'S INNER COURTYARD was still cloaked in pre-dawn haze when the silence shattered.

Rotors churned overhead, carving through the mountain air with violent intent. The beat of helicopter blades echoed against stone walls like war drums, scattering incense smoke into ragged spirals. Monks did not flinch. They simply lowered their heads and folded their hands tighter around their prayer beads.

Tobias stood at the edge of the upper landing, squinting into the wind, the hood of his travel cloak whipping behind him. The cold had teeth this high up. Not from weather alone, but from altitude, from sacred pressure, from the knowledge that relics slept beneath the monastery floor and had not stirred in centuries.

The Templars were coming.

The aircraft touched down with practiced grace, its matte-black frame gleaming faintly with warded sigils and White Circle seals. The side door hissed open, releasing a hiss of pressurized air, and the scent of gun oil and sanctified steel.

The first to step out was Captain Garren Thomas, sword and shield specialist, battle-hardened leader of Team Excelsior. Broad-shouldered, still limping slightly from the last campaign, Garren moved with the coiled energy of a man who had never fully stepped off the battlefield. His lion-emblazoned shield was strapped across his back, the metal dulled by claw marks and char but polished all the same. His eyes swept the courtyard once, found Tobias, and narrowed in grim recognition.

Tobias smirked and stepped forward to meet him. "Didn't think I'd see you again so soon. Figured you'd still be scraping demon ichor off your boots."

Garren's reply was dry and immediate. "Still am. But you call in a favor from half a world away, and here I am. Thought you were done dragging teenagers into holy ground."

They clasped forearms in a firm grip, shield arm to shield arm. No salute. No formality. Just the bond of two men who had bled together under impossible skies.

"I didn't drag her," Tobias said, glancing back toward the sanctum's sealed archway. "She's... following something older than us."

Garren raised a brow but said nothing. He had seen too much to scoff at prophecy.

Behind him, the rest of Team Excelsior disembarked.

Sister Lucretia Solas emerged first, her cassock armor etched with protective wards in fine silver filigree. Her eyes, always severe, scanned the monastery grounds like she expected a demon to leap from behind the nearest statue. She carried a silver censer that trailed faint curls of blue flame as she walked, muttering protective incantations under her breath in crisp, formal Latin.

At her side walked Sister Martha McCormick, the shorter of the two White Circle Magi, but no less imposing. Her spellbooks were clasped to her chest, leather-bound and aged by decades of rain and blood and prayer. She nodded to Tobias but did not speak, already entering a meditative focus.

Lieutenant Gregory Thomas, Garren's nephew, strode out next. Grinning despite the altitude, he hoisted a massive rune-marked duffel over one shoulder and called out, "Still using that same battered sword, Mason?"

"It's an heirloom," Tobias replied, adjusting his belt with mock indignation. "Like your haircut."

"Hey, I paid money for this haircut."

"And you should get a refund."

They grinned at each other, but it faded quickly.

Lieutenant Andrea Keens was next, visor already lowered over her eyes as she scanned the terrain using the embedded arcane interface on her vambrace. Tobias had never seen her without it. She nodded silently in acknowledgment as she passed, all efficiency, her focus already shifting toward securing a perimeter.

Last down the ramp was a newcomer.

Lieutenant Terrance Gilman was tall, lean, and moved with the deliberate precision of a man trained more recently than the others. His armor bore none of the battle scars Tobias expected. His posture was textbook. His eyes, though, told a different story, something behind them still raw. Still forming.

Tobias watched him descend, then glanced down the line again.

Six.

Not seven.

The air grew thinner.

He turned to Garren, his voice lowering with something cold and sinking behind it. "Where's Leontius?"

That silenced the courtyard more effectively than any prayer.

Lucretia's grip tightened around her censer. Gregory looked down. Andrea's interface flickered off.

Garren didn't speak right away. He just exhaled slowly, shoulders settling lower, like the weight of the mountain had shifted directly onto his back.

It was Sister Martha who answered, her voice as brittle as old parchment. "He fell at the Echo Mall. The northwest barricade collapsed under a second breach. He stayed behind to hold the line and covered the last of the evacuees. He never made it out."

Tobias said nothing. For several long seconds, he simply stared beyond the courtyard wall, eyes fixed on a point that wasn't there.

"He was three feet from me," he murmured, the words cracking at the edges. "I told him to pull back."

"And he heard you," Garren replied, his tone low but unwavering. "But Leontius wasn't the kind of man who ran when others could be saved."

Gregory tried to soften the moment. "He said if he died in New York, it better be dramatic. Said the Holy Spirit owed him fireworks and maybe a parade."

It didn't land.

Tobias took a step back, jaw clenched, his breath shallow.

"He died doing what he believed in," Garren said. "But I won't lie to you, he wasn't ready to go. None of us were. And that's why we keep going. Not for glory. Not even for God. For each other."

Tobias gave a slow nod, but his eyes remained distant.

"I should've gone back for him."

"You would've died," Garren said bluntly. "Then she would've died. And all of this," he gestured to the mountain, to the monastery, to the sealed sanctum beyond, "none of it would be happening."

The words were true.

They still hurt like hell.

"Suit up," Garren added, tone softening. "We'll pay him proper honors when this is over. But first... I hear you've found something buried under a few thousand years of dust and divine judgment."

Tobias turned back toward the ancient gate.

"Yeah," he said quietly. "And I think it's been waiting for her."

THE INNER SANCTUM OF Mount Athos was not a chamber so much as a hollowed wound in the stone, ancient, silent, consecrated by centuries of breathless awe. It was carved into the heart of the mountain itself, its walls smooth and dark with soot, as though angels had burned their way into the rock and left behind a cathedral of silence.

The air smelled of wax, frankincense, and molten metal.

Candles lined the chamber in perfect concentric rings around a central sparring floor of polished basalt, worn faintly in places by the passing of centuries. At the edge of the ring stood monks in gray and white, their faces solemn and hidden behind thin veils. They did not speak. They had come only to bear witness.

Ella stood barefoot in the center of the circle, her training robes loose, tied at the waist. Her hair had been pulled back into a tight braid, though a single blue streak still shimmered defiant against the candlelight, proof of the dragon's blood still inside her, dormant but alive.

Tobias watched from the shadows just beyond the circle, standing beside Garren and Lucretia. He was in full armor again, hands folded over the pommel of Arondight, his sword, his inheritance, the weight of his line. He could feel something stir in the blade, though he didn't understand it yet.

"You're sure about this?" he asked quietly.

"She's ready," Garren said. "Or as ready as anyone can be."

"She's not like anyone," Tobias muttered.

At the far side of the circle, a monk in white stepped forward and raised a simple stave. His voice echoed through the chamber like thunder striking velvet.

"This is not a duel. This is revelation. You do not strike to wound. You strike to awaken."

A second monk entered the circle to face her. He was taller, older, and carried no weapon, only padded gloves and speed hardened by a life of obedience. His eyes were empty of pride. Only clarity.

He bowed.

Ella bowed in return, though the stiffness in her shoulders betrayed her nerves. She flexed her fingers. They shimmered faintly.

The match began with no bell, only motion.

The monk surged forward, testing her reflexes with a flurry of quick jabs. She dodged, parried, stepped to the side. Her movement was graceful but grounded, trained more recently under Tobias' hand than anyone else's. He recognized his own instruction in the angles of her footwork.

But she was holding back.

After three exchanges, the monk swept in low and caught her off balance. She hit the ground hard, gritting her teeth, and rolled to avoid a follow-up blow. The candles around the chamber flickered, as though inhaling with her.

She rose again, eyes blazing with frustration.

"You're holding back," Tobias whispered under his breath. "Don't hold back. Not here."

As if hearing him, Ella attacked.

Her next strike was sharper, faster, she closed the gap and swept in with a series of kicks and elbow strikes. The monk grunted but held his ground. They circled again. Another strike. Another fall. Ella's breath came in short bursts now, her knuckles raw from impact.

Then came the moment.

The monk feinted high, then dove low, sweeping her legs.

She didn't fall.

Instead, something ignited.

Light flared across her skin in a radiant pulse, no flame, but something far more blinding. Her body shimmered with golden filament, lines tracing her limbs like divine circuitry. The impact never landed. A sudden, resounding clang rang out as the monk's strike met something that hadn't been there a moment before.

Armor.

Not forged, not worn. Summoned.

It radiated from her chest outward in waves, forming a breastplate of pure light, pauldrons blooming like wings folded tight. A halo of molten gold crowned her brow for just a heartbeat, then vanished into her skin. Her eyes burned with light, not glowing from the outside, but lit from within, like a star had cracked open behind her pupils.

Everyone froze.

Even the monk, his arms still raised, breath still steady, took a half step back. His eyes widened beneath his veil, not with fear, but with reverence. Around the chamber, the monks in the outer ring dropped to one knee without a word. The sudden stillness felt holy. Or haunted.

The only sound was the trembling of the candle flames, which now flickered not with wind, but in response. They danced in unison, as if genuflecting to the presence now standing in the center of the circle.

Ella felt nothing at first. Only heat.

Not burning. Not painful.

Just a presence, immense and weightless, like standing beneath a cathedral dome made of starlight. It was inside her and around her, pulsing in her bones, humming along her skin. Her heartbeat no longer felt like her own. It echoed as though inside a chamber much larger than her chest.

Her armor of light flickered and brightened again. She could feel its weight, not pressing her down, but lifting her, bracing her spine, hardening her stance. Her muscles did not ache. Her breath no longer came ragged. There was no pain. No fatigue.

Only purpose.

Is this what Tobias feels when he fights? Is this what Marcus meant by "being forged?" Ella thought to herself.

But no, this was something else. This was not training. This was not rage.

This was command.

From somewhere deep inside, beneath thought, beneath fear, she felt it: the gaze of something immense within her. Watching. Judging. Not malicious, not warm. Simply absolute. Like a lighthouse in a storm that neither comforted nor cursed, only exposed.

Her knees wanted to give out, but the armor held her upright.

She raised her hand slowly, half in awe, half in horror. Her fingers gleamed with gold. The glow bled from under her nails like sunlight trapped in amber. Even the tiny scar on her wrist, the one from falling on a fence when she was seven, was gone, erased as if the divine would not tolerate imperfections on its vessel.

She was no longer sweating. Her skin had dried. The sweat had evaporated.

And still the presence lingered, not moving in, not moving out. Just waiting.

Tobias crossed the threshold of the circle. He didn't run. He approached carefully, like one might approach a creature half-asleep, beautiful, and dangerous.

He knelt in front of her and reached out, his hand resting gently on her shoulder. The warmth of her was unreal. Not fevered. Not sick. Like touching stone that had been sitting in sunlight for hours.

"Ella…" His voice was small in the vast quiet of the sanctum.

She turned her face toward him, and Tobias flinched, just barely.

Her eyes. They weren't just glowing. They were lit from within, like stained glass backlit by a rising sun. There were no whites, no pupils, just golden flame, shifting behind fragile windows.

She tried to speak, but her mouth felt unfamiliar. She had to remind her lips how to form the words.

"There's something inside me," she whispered.

"We knew that," Tobias answered gently, as if afraid to speak too loudly.

She shook her head once, slow, heavy, mechanical. "No. Not a voice. Not even a feeling."

Her fingers curled into fists. She was trembling now, not from exhaustion, but from a rising pressure she couldn't name.

"It's like... like a sun behind a locked door."

She could still feel it, just beyond reach. Its gravity was shaping her every breath. The warmth that filled her chest wasn't hers. It belonged to it. To Him.

"What happens when the door opens?"

Her voice cracked on the last word.

Tobias didn't answer. Not because he didn't want to, but because the truth sat heavy in both of their chests.

If that door opened, fully opened, then Ella might never come back out.

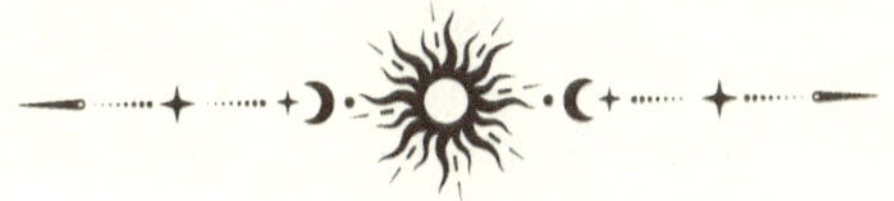

THE MOUNTAIN SLEPT, BUT it did not dream.

Above the monastery, where the stone cliffs curved like the ribs of some ancient god, Tobias sat beside a narrow, shielded firepit tucked into a natural hollow of rock. The flame was low and steady, the wind too thin to fan it much this high up. Only the occasional gust stirred the embers, causing them to pulse like the slow beat of a weary heart.

Beyond the ledge, the Aegean Sea stretched into infinity, ink-dark and silent beneath a sky flecked with stars so bright they seemed on the verge of speech. The air smelled of salt and pine and cold iron. Each breath Tobias drew felt thinner than the last, not from altitude alone, but from the weight he carried up here.

His armor was half-shed beside him, his sword, Arondight, laid across his lap like a sleeping relic. He ran a cloth along the blade's edge out of habit more than need, polishing where there were no stains, not tonight. The sword had tasted fire in the mall. It had sung through blood. It had done its work.

But it hadn't saved Leontius.

Tobias stared out at the sky, jaw tight, his thoughts circling like wolves around a grave.

Footsteps scraped over gravel behind him, just light enough to show restraint. He didn't turn.

"I always know when it's you," he said, voice low and rough. "You walk like your armor still weighs fifty pounds."

A grunt answered him, followed by the sound of someone lowering themselves onto the stone with all the creaks of middle age and too many healed injuries.

Garren Thomas settled beside him without ceremony, shifting until his back rested against the smooth rock wall behind them. His breath misted faintly in the air, drawn in slow and released slower.

"You still sit like you're expecting an ambush," Garren murmured, not unkindly. "Even when you're surrounded by monks."

Tobias didn't smile. He didn't even blink. "Monks die, too."

A silence followed, but not an empty one. It was the kind that settled between men who'd fought the same nightmares and knew when not to fill the space.

After a while, Garren reached into his coat and produced a small flask. He didn't offer it. Didn't sip from it. Just held it in his hands like a relic of simpler sins.

"I watched the Echo Mall footage," he said, finally.

Tobias stiffened.

"Frame by frame," Garren continued. "From the drone overfeed. From your body cam. From the lobby security. I saw what Leontius did. I saw him go down."

The image slammed into Tobias' mind without mercy: Leontius standing in the breach, arms wide, shield raised, taking the full brunt of a demon's charge that would have torn Ella in half. He remembered the man's last laugh, loud and unfazed, even as rubble began to collapse around him.

"I told him to fall back," Tobias whispered, voice barely audible. "We had the line. We had a plan. He, he was just supposed to hold position, not—"

"He made the choice," Garren cut in gently but firmly. "Same as we all have. And he did it with his eyes open."

Tobias drew in a slow breath through his nose. The air was too thin up here. Everything felt hollow.

"I should have overridden him. Ordered a tactical fallback. I could've—"

"You could've died," Garren said flatly. "Ella would've died. The civilians would've never made it to the far stairwell. If you'd gone back, we'd be lighting three graves instead of one."

Tobias didn't respond. He just stared at the sea, letting the guilt roll over him in thick, unrelenting waves.

"I keep seeing his face," Tobias said eventually, voice hoarse. "Not scared. Not panicked. Just... peaceful. Like he already knew he wasn't walking out."

"He did know," Garren murmured. "That was Leontius. Always was. Big damn fool who thought saving one life was always worth the cost of his own."

Silence returned, broken only by the distant sound of wind through cypress trees and the quiet hiss of fire.

Garren leaned forward slightly, elbows on his knees. "I tried to walk away once. After Prague. Lost a whole team. Young. Green. Too full of hope. I put my sword down and left the Order for six months. Thought I'd be a parish priest in some backwoods Italian village. Spend my days pruning grapes and burying saints."

Tobias blinked, surprised. "What changed?"

"Demon circle showed up in the orchard," Garren said with a dry chuckle. "Six bodies. No survivors. And that was just week one. Faith doesn't follow you, Tobias. It finds you. No matter how far you run."

Tobias ran his fingers along the spine of Arondight, the hilt worn smooth by generations before him. "I don't know if I can keep doing this. Asking people to follow me into death. Especially when I don't know what any of it means anymore."

"You don't need to know," Garren said. "You just need to carry. The people who wait for clarity? They freeze. And then others die. We move forward even when the path disappears under our feet."

Footsteps echoed behind them.

This time softer. Lighter. Hesitant.

Ella stood at the edge of the firelight, her face pale and unreadable. The golden glow had long since faded from her eyes, but it haunted the space around her like an afterimage. She looked smaller now, despite the divine force that had nearly consumed her earlier. Like someone who had just seen the far side of Heaven and come back scorched.

Garren rose slowly to his feet and gave Tobias a nod. "She'll need you. Just don't forget, she's not a vessel. She's a person. Keep her grounded."

He passed Ella on his way out and placed one hand gently on her shoulder.

"Not all burdens are meant to be carried alone," he said softly. "But don't let the light blind you to who you are underneath it."

And then he vanished into the dark, his steps soon swallowed by the mountain.

Ella approached and sat down slowly beside Tobias, knees pulled to her chest. She didn't speak. Neither did he. The fire popped softly as resin burned, casting golden sparks into the air.

Finally, she broke the silence.

"I thought it would feel... beautiful."

Tobias turned to her, brows furrowed. "The light?"

"The armor. The fire. Uriel. I thought being chosen would feel like a blessing. Like being held by something good."

He nodded, slowly. "But it didn't."

She stared into the flames. "It felt like standing in the middle of a cathedral made of stars and fire, and realizing the altar was empty. No comfort. Just heat. And judgment."

He didn't answer. Not yet.

"I can still feel it," she said. "Even now. Watching me. Not cruel. Not kind. Just there. Like the moment before lightning strikes."

Tobias looked down at his sword again. He traced the cross-guard with his thumb, unaware of the ancient nail hidden inside.

"There's a story," he said quietly. "About a Paladin named Matthias. First recorded bearer of divine flame. He lit up like a beacon. Took out half an army of demons with his bare hands."

Ella turned slightly toward him, her voice quiet. "What happened to him?"

"On the fourth day, his body gave out. His soul was gone. They say whatever was inside him took the rest. All that was left was a body made of light and ash."

She closed her eyes.

"And they made him a saint."

Tobias nodded once. "They always do."

She wasn't crying. Not quite. But her voice cracked like ice under too much weight.

"I'm scared, Tobias."

He didn't offer platitudes.

Instead, he reached out and took her hand in both of his, held it tight.

"I am too."

And beneath the stars and firelight, the mountain said nothing.

But it listened.

CHAPTER 14

The Edge of Light

Since all things are God, in all things thou seest just so much of God as thy capacity affordeth thee.

A.C.

THE DESCENT WAS LIKE falling into the throat of the earth.

The deeper they went, the more the light changed, shifting from torch-warm gold to a sterile, ghostlike glow that seemed to bleed from the stone itself. Crystalline veins of quartz threaded the walls, pulsing faintly with ambient light, humming just beneath the threshold of hearing. The walls were too smooth to be natural, too flawless to be made by mortal tools. These halls hadn't been carved, they had been consecrated.

Tobias walked ahead with Arondight sheathed at his hip and reverence in his stride. He had been here before. Once. Briefly. But not like this. Not with her.

Ella followed behind him, her every footstep amplified by the hush. Each breath she took seemed louder than it should be, echoing in the back of her throat. The very air tasted of iron and ash, like blood spilled in a cathedral. Her fingers tingled. Her skin felt tight. The silence wasn't emptiness, it was pressure.

Even the wind did not follow them this far.

At the bottom of the stair, the corridor widened, first gradually, then all at once, into a vast, circular chamber that swallowed sound whole. There were no chandeliers, no stained glass, no symbols of man or martyr. Only a dais of white marble, unmarked and unadorned, rising from the center like the altar of a god who had never needed worship.

And there, above it, hovered the sword.

Uriel's Blade. Veritas.

The air around it shimmered like the horizon over desert sand. It did not rest on anything. No stone pedestal. No wall mount. It simply hung in place, suspended by the weight of its own significance. A blade of Byzantine craftsmanship, long, broad, not ornamental but beautiful in the way a storm is beautiful. From crossguard to point, it glowed with restrained flame, a light that didn't flicker but pulsed. Alive.

Along the blade, the word VERITAS burned. Not etched, burned. Molten letters that never cooled. And at the base of the hilt, embedded with deliberate imperfection, was the nail.

It looked unworthy of the weapon it inhabited. Just a crude, blackened iron spike. Uneven. Old. Rusted by time.

But when Ella saw it, her knees almost buckled.

That was where the power lived.

Not in the flame.

Not in the steel.

In the nail.

She took one breath, and it felt like inhaling sunlight. Her lungs ached, not with heat, but with density, as if divinity had weight, and she wasn't made to carry it. Her body trembled, not visibly, but deep in the muscles, the way a tree trembles before lightning strikes. She exhaled, and it felt like surrender.

For a heartbeat, maybe longer, there was only the pulse of golden energy humming just beneath her collarbone, echoing in her bones. The warmth wasn't kind. It wasn't comforting. It was absolute. Pure and terrifying in the way open skies could be terrifying, in the way deep water held a quiet promise of drowning.

Her breath caught. Not from pain. From the sudden and overwhelming awareness that she had been seen, not as she pretended to be, not even as she wished to become, but as she truly was. Every failure. Every flicker of pride. Every scream in the dark she hadn't spoken aloud.

The sword did not flinch from those things. It did not punish them. It simply knew.

Her right hand rose unconsciously to her chest, fingers clutching the fabric of her robes as if to press something deeper into herself, to anchor the sense of self that suddenly felt fragile under such scrutiny. Her gaze remained locked on the blade, on the single rusted nail melted into the hilt. That nail. That imperfect, common, corroded thing. It radiated more presence than the fire, more gravity than the gold.

She could hear her heartbeat again. Slow. Thunderous. Distant. As though it no longer belonged to her body, but to something echoing through her from centuries ago.

The armor didn't return. No divine shield manifested around her body. No light danced across her skin. But the pressure hadn't lifted. Something unseen lingered just behind her shoulder, breathless and still, as if an unseen observer was deciding whether she might be worth the price of waking.

It sees me.

The thought came without permission. It came without language yet it was pure and unmistakable. Not she. Not it. Not even you. The sword saw her. It had always seen her.

A presence older than scripture. Older than the angel itself. Perhaps not even Uriel's will, but something deeper, a force bound to the concept of judgment itself. Not justice. Not wrath.

Truth.

Ella's knees tensed. Her legs threatened to give way, not from fear, but from reverence that had nowhere to go inside her. Her body didn't know how to contain it. Her chest rose and fell with effort, like the air had thickened into honey.

Behind her, Tobias' voice pierced the silence, but even his words arrived softened, like snow falling through fog.

"I wasn't going to touch it," she murmured, realizing belatedly that her foot had crossed the outer ring of light. She hadn't meant to step closer. Her body had moved without thought.

Her voice didn't echo. It was swallowed by the sanctum, devoured by the holy pressure that lived here. Her words fell like a pebble into a lake made of still fire.

"You don't need to," Tobias said. His tone was not scolding, but quiet, reverent. As though anything louder might fracture the moment. "It's already touching you."

Ella couldn't answer. She could barely stand. But she forced her gaze to remain steady. The sword's glow reflected in her eyes now, twin mirrors of molten gold. And though it gave no sign, no reaction, no movement, she felt the unspoken truth settle into her blood like prophecy:

When the time came, it would not ask.

It would respond.

And it would not come gently.

THE AIR WAS HEAVIER after the chamber.

Ella felt it in her shoulders as they returned to the monastery's outer grounds, a subtle ache, not physical but psychic, like the divine light she'd encountered was still pressing down on her from above. The others didn't speak much. Even Tobias had gone quiet, the sharp edges of his usual discipline softened by something deeper. Not reverence. Not awe. Concern.

They moved through the cloisters in single file. Beyond the worn colonnades, the training field stretched like an open scar along the cliffside, carved centuries ago into the natural slope of the rock. White stone walls flanked the grounds, their surfaces etched with forgotten battle hymns and symbols older than the Church itself. The fog had begun to lift, replaced by a sweeping sea wind that rolled across the plateau like a breath held too long.

Ella's boots crunched across gravel as she followed Tobias to the center of the field. Ahead of them, Team Excelsior was already preparing the space, not for sparring in the usual sense, but for something closer to a crucible.

Captain Garren stood with his hands behind his back, expression unreadable as always. His armor was light today, leather brigandine marked with simple iron crosses, and his shield rested beside him like a sleeping hound. He didn't speak when she approached, only nodded toward a small circle of smoothed earth at the field's center. A training ring.

Ella glanced to Tobias, but he offered nothing beyond a subtle nod.

Sister Martha McCormick and Sister Lucretia Solas had taken positions along the circle's edge, both dressed in full vestment-armor, cassocks reinforced with light plating and arcane sigils sewn in thread so fine it caught the morning sun like spider silk. Between them floated a brass incense burner, cold for now, but clearly prepared. Not for purification. For containment.

Across from them stood Gregory Thomas, already cracking his knuckles as he rolled his shoulders loose. He looked up and gave Ella a grin that didn't quite reach his eyes.

"Don't worry," he said, lifting a practice staff off the rack beside him. "I'm not gonna hit you too hard."

Ella raised a brow, drawing the training blade Tobias had handed her earlier. "That's nice of you. But who says I won't hit you?"

Gregory's grin deepened. "Good. That's the spirit."

But Garren's voice cut through the air like a drawn blade.

"This isn't about winning."

The words halted them both.

"You're not here to test power," Garren continued. "You're here to test restraint. That sword up there doesn't care how strong your swings are. It cares whether you can stand in front of something unbearable, and choose not to break."

The words hit harder than they should have. Ella lowered her blade slightly, her throat dry.

Lucretia stepped forward next, her voice quiet but unwavering. "You've been touched by a force that does not explain itself. Divine presence rarely offers clarity, only exposure. Your role is not to command it. Your role is to remain yourself beneath it."

Behind her, Martha muttered a short prayer in Latin, too fast for Ella to follow. Something about light burning away falsehood.

Andrea Keens stood near the perimeter, typing something into her wristpad. She didn't look up as she spoke. "Just for the record, the last person exposed to a Class III divine resonance burned through their boots and shorted out our field sensors. So if you could avoid spontaneous ignition, that'd be great for the paperwork."

Terrance Gilman stood slightly behind her, arms crossed, rifle slung but unused. He was the youngest of the team, and the newest. His eyes didn't leave Ella, not with challenge, not with fear, but with a quiet tension she recognized instantly.

He was afraid of what she might become.

Gregory raised his staff again. "Round one?"

Ella nodded and stepped into the ring.

The first exchange was easy, deliberate. He came at her with wide, readable arcs, clearly testing her balance, not her speed. She parried cleanly, their wooden weapons thudding against one another with measured force. The rhythm settled quickly: strike, deflect, reset. A dance without urgency.

But the heat in her chest never faded.

The residual presence of the sword lingered like breath on the back of her neck. Her heartbeat was too loud in her ears. Each clash of wood-on-wood sent sparks not through her hands, but up her spine, as if something deeper than muscle was responding.

She started moving faster.

Gregory matched her pace. A few of the exchanges grew harsher, their weapons connecting with sharp cracks that echoed off the stone walls. Ella's pulse climbed. Her breathing quickened. Something beneath her ribs began to thrum.

Then she saw it again, just for a moment.

Gregory feinted high and went for her exposed flank. Her instincts flared. And for half a breath, the world shimmered.

A golden ripple coursed across her forearm, flickering into the ghost of a gauntlet, light not yet solid, but trying.

She froze.

Gregory's strike landed on her side, hard enough to sting.

"Ella—"

"I'm fine," she snapped.

But she wasn't. The heat hadn't gone away. It was rising again. The divine spark she'd brushed in the chamber was still alive inside her, waiting, watching, willing.

Garren stepped forward. "You're bleeding power."

"I'm controlling it," Ella said, gritting her teeth.

"That's not control. That's containment. And there's a dif-ference."

Another round. This time she forced herself to slow. The next hit she took on the shoulder. The next she dodged. But she could feel it, her temper rising. Not anger at Gregory, but anger at herself. At the helplessness. The exposure. The idea that this sacred thing inside her wasn't a gift, but a burden she wasn't ready to carry.

By the fourth round, she was shaking. Her vision pulsed at the edges. And in one final surge, her blade flew too fast, too hard; Gregory blocked, but barely. The golden shimmer flared across her shoulders again, racing toward her spine, threatening to burst.

"Enough!" Tobias barked, stepping between them.

Ella froze, her chest heaving.

The armor receded. The fire quelled. But her eyes still burned faintly around the edges, as if light had taken root in her irises and was reluctant to leave.

No one said anything for a moment.

Then Lucretia spoke, stepping forward again.

"That is the lesson," she said calmly. "It does not care when you call it. It listens when it chooses. And it will always demand more than you intend to give."

Ella looked down at her blade, at her trembling hands, at the dust streaking her tunic.

Tobias placed a hand on her shoulder, not as comfort, but as anchor.

"You're not failing," he said. "You're beginning."

THE TRAINING CIRCLE HAD been cleared. No formal dismissal, no handshakes, just a wordless nod from Garren and a faint prayer from Martha as incense was lit to sanctify the ring again. The scent drifted through the air like fog made of fire and herbs, clinging to Ella's tunic and throat as she stepped back from the center of the field.

Her hands still trembled, despite the cool breeze that had begun to roll in from the sea. Salt air kissed her cheeks, lifting sweat from her brow, but it did nothing to clear the pressure that coiled in her chest like a spring wound too tight.

She sat on the stone steps at the edge of the training field, hunched forward, her elbows braced against her knees. Her sword lay across her thighs, wooden, dulled by the clash, but still warm from the heat in her palms. She ran a thumb along the edge and stared at her reflection in the blade's dull surface.

The girl looking back at her didn't look heroic.

She looked scared. Tired. Lit from within by something she hadn't chosen.

They think I'm becoming something holy, she thought. But what if I'm just becoming something dangerous?

The golden light had flared again today, not from need, not from divine command, but from frustration. It rose when she grew angry. When she lost balance. When she lost herself.

She couldn't decide what frightened her more: that she might fail to summon the armor when she needed it, or that one day, she wouldn't be able to stop it from coming.

A crunch of gravel behind her drew her attention. She didn't look up.

Tobias sat down beside her without saying a word. He didn't need to. His presence was steady. Grounded. His breathing was even, and he didn't fidget. He just sat beside her like a pillar planted in the storm, unmoving.

They sat in silence for nearly a minute, letting the wind pass between them.

Finally, Ella spoke.

"I keep waiting for it to feel good."

Tobias looked at her, quiet.

"This thing inside me," she continued. "This... power. The armor. Uriel. Everyone keeps calling it a blessing. A destiny. A light."

Her voice lowered, barely audible.

"But it doesn't feel like light. It feels like pressure. Like I'm walking around with a hand around my ribs and it's just... waiting to squeeze."

Tobias said nothing at first. He let the words sit in the air between them. Then he reached for his sword, Arondight, and unsheathed it slowly. The blade glinted in the sunlight. Not gold. Not fire. Just steel.

"You know," he said, his voice quiet, "this thing's been in my family for over a thousand years. Passed through hands that bled for it. Men who called it sacred. Others who called it cursed."

He set the sword gently across his knees.

"I don't think any of them knew which it really was."

Ella blinked, caught off guard by the honesty.

Tobias turned to her, his eyes shadowed by the angle of the sun. "You're not the only one trying to live with something that might outlive you. Or outgrow you."

The words didn't solve anything. But they helped.

Ella exhaled, long and slow.

"Thanks," she murmured.

"For what?"

"For not trying to tell me it's all going to be fine."

Tobias smiled faintly. "It won't be. Not all the time. But that doesn't mean you're doing it wrong."

They sat a little longer, two souls balancing on the edge of something immense, sharing silence because words would only diminish it.

Behind them, the sun began to fall toward the sea, gilding the cliffside with orange fire.

And below the mountain, in the chamber of the sword, the nail pulsed once more, softly.

Like it had heard her.

THAT NIGHT, THE COURTYARD burned with a different kind of light.

The fire pit beneath the western cloisters crackled low and slow, sending soft embers spiraling into the wind as Team Excelsior gathered around its warmth. The sea beyond the cliffs had gone black and vast under the moon, and the stars above shone harder in the clear mountain air, sharpened by the cold.

Ella sat beside Tobias, shoulders draped in a wool cloak one of the monks had left folded near the barracks. She said little, letting the murmured conversation and quiet laughter of the others wash over her. The flames danced against their faces, Gregory's easy grin, Andrea's reserved stillness, Lucretia and Martha sharing an occasional glance like old war sisters who had survived too much to be surprised by anything.

Someone passed her a tin mug of hot broth. She held it in both hands, letting the warmth seep into her fingers.

Gregory was mid-story, hands animated. "So there we are, middle of the Danube Delta, banshees swarming the riverbanks, and Keens, cool as ever, somehow patches Gregorian chant into our comms. I swear, the demons scattered like cats in a bell tower."

Andrea didn't look up. "It was a misfire in the loop signal. Last audio file in the buffer."

"And a very lucky one," Gregory added with a grin. "They screamed like it was holy water."

"Some of us choose our rites intentionally," Martha said, stirring the fire with the tip of her boot.

"And some of us," Lucretia added, "don't weaponize Mozart."

Laughter rolled gently through the circle, thin and true.

Then Garren spoke, his voice quiet. "You haven't told her, have you?"

Tobias didn't respond immediately. Ella turned toward him. "Told me what?"

Garren nodded to the fire. "She deserves to know."

Tobias sighed. "When I left home, it wasn't to fight. Not really. It was because I failed."

The others fell silent.

"My first mission as a Templar was in Tunisia. Supposed to be routine. A relic recovery. I hesitated. A teammate died. The squad scattered. I came back from it, but not whole."

He stared into the fire. "I spent three months underground in Vienna. Ritual purification. I thought I needed to be fixed. Cleansed. Made clean enough to try again."

"And?" Ella asked.

"I didn't come out of it fixed. I came out of it forged."

He drew his sword, not fully. Just enough for the firelight to kiss the edge.

"Arondight. I wasn't ready to wield it before. After Vienna, it drew for me like it never had for anyone else in my family. Not because I was worthy. Because I understood what it meant to carry something sacred."

Ella studied the blade, then Tobias.

"Does it ever feel… alive?"

He nodded slowly. "Sometimes. In prayer, it warms. In battle, it hums. I used to think it was adrenaline. But maybe it's waiting for something. Or someone."

Ella looked down into her cup. The broth had cooled.

Later that night, when the others had gone, she returned to the writing alcove near the sanctuary. She opened her sketchbook beneath a shaft of moonlight and began to draw, not the sword itself, but the sensation of it. The weight in her chest. The arc of suspended flame. The hilt with the nail.

She drew that last. A small dark thorn at the blade's base.

And when her pencil touched the page, she felt her hand chill.

It did not glow. It did not burn. But it watched.

She closed the book slowly.

And in the stillness of the mountain, something deep below stirred again.

CHAPTER 15

The Armor Beneath

The more necessary anything appears to my
mind, the most certain it is that I only assert a
limitation.

A.C.

THE LIBRARY WAS QUIET, but it was not still.

The air stirred gently with the passage of candle smoke and
ancient breath, the long-forgotten kind that soaked into stone
over centuries. The scent of old paper, dust, and sanctified oil
clung to every surface. Rows of manuscripts lined the curved
walls in tiers, written in half a dozen languages: Greek, Latin,
Coptic, Aramaic, most too old or obscure for even the modern
scholars to decipher completely. But the monks didn't seem
to need to read them. They moved through the room like they

had absorbed its contents by osmosis. They lived among the words like archivists of something heavier than knowledge. Something closer to judgment.

Ella sat at a carved wooden desk, its edges worn smooth by centuries of hands, her own hands resting lightly on the leather-bound notebook she'd brought with her. She hadn't opened it. Not yet. The sketch of the nail still haunted the last page. She didn't want to look at it again, not here, not under the watchful eyes of so many unreadable saints staring down from faded icons on the upper walls.

Across from her stood Brother Salvatore, one of the elder monks who had remained silent during her arrival. His robes were ash-gray and plain, save for a single stitched band of gold thread at the sleeve cuffs. His posture was severe, not cruel, like stone that had weathered centuries and seen little reason to change. He had the presence of someone who had spent too long near sacred things, dignified, yes, but hollow in the places where ordinary men carried warmth.

He spoke only when the silence had pressed down long enough to settle in her bones.

"You stood in the cradle of Veritas," he said, not asking. "And it did not reject you."

Ella nodded once. Her voice felt small in her throat. "It didn't speak either. It just... watched."

He tilted his head slightly, his expression unreadable, as though he were measuring her shape against a memory she could not see. "Uriel does not speak to mortals with words. He burns. He reveals."

She swallowed hard. The taste of ash returned to the back of her throat, phantom and dry.

Brother Salvatore moved along the edge of the chamber, trailing a finger along a shelf lined with relics under glass, rings, teeth, faded scraps of armor. "In the oldest texts, bearers of fire were not called chosen. They were called vessels. Channels. Hosts. The word 'saint' came much later. A softer word."

Ella sat straighter, more alert now. "So the others, those who carried Uriel's presence, what happened to them?"

He paused and turned back toward her. His eyes were pale as snow under cloudlight, bright, colorless, and strangely still.

"They burned," he said. "Some slowly. Some instantly. One we entombed here, long ago. She drew the sword, not in war but in despair. Her body was found intact, untouched by flame. But the blood inside her had turned to salt."

Ella's mouth went dry. Her pulse kicked beneath her skin like something trying to escape. She had no answer to that. No training could make her ready for it.

"You're saying this power will kill me."

"I'm saying," the monk replied gently, without accusation, "that it was never meant to belong to you. It is a force, not a gift. A storm made still inside a human frame. If you mistake the silence for peace, it will swallow you."

The shadows in the library lengthened as a cloud passed over the sun, dimming the stained-glass windows overhead. Dust danced in the golden shafts of light like falling embers. Somewhere far off, a bell tolled the hour. It sounded like a warning.

Ella looked down at her hands. They didn't shake, but they felt too still, too quiet, like they no longer trusted themselves.

"Why me, then?" she asked, barely above a whisper. "Why not someone trained, someone stronger, someone who asked for it?"

"Because you are fractured," Salvatore said. "Because you've suffered. Because suffering makes space for light to fill."

She hated how true that felt. And hated more how much it terrified her. The idea that pain was the invitation, her pain. That the universe had seen her break and thought, 'yes, this one.'

"But you are not ready," he continued, stepping closer. "And readiness is not power. It is clarity. Until you learn to stand in silence and remain yourself, the fire will not be your ally."

She stood slowly, almost reluctantly, as though part of her hoped he might say more. But he simply turned and walked back between the shelves. His robes swept the stone in soft rhythm as he vanished into the manuscripts and relics, into the silence, into whatever place monks go when they've said too much.

Alone again, Ella looked down at the notebook in her hands.

She had drawn the nail.

Now she wondered if it had drawn her.

THE MONASTERY'S OUTER WALLS were quiet at night, but Tobias had long learned that quiet didn't mean safe. The stone walkways along the cliffside were slick with sea mist, worn smooth by centuries of armored feet. Each step struck with a muffled clink of boot on weathered stone, dampened by salt and time. To the west, the Aegean shimmered in ribbons beneath a crescent moon, the water black and gleaming like a wound that never healed, as though hiding something just beneath its surface, watching from below.

He moved with care, hand resting lightly on the pommel of Arondight as he walked the narrow ledge of the battlement. The leather of his gloves creaked with each flex of his fingers. Beside him, Gregory Thomas kept pace, his heavier footfalls a familiar cadence, a grounded rhythm in the rising unease. The man was younger, brasher, but loyal to the bone. He'd bled for this team more than once.

"You ever get the feeling this place breathes?" Gregory muttered, his voice hushed as though the stones might overhear. His eyes scanned the lower wall with trained precision. "Like the rock itself is holding its breath."

Tobias nodded once. "It does. That's what sacred ground is. Memory solidified."

A sudden gust of wind stirred his cloak and whispered through the narrow crenellations with a voice like dry leaves rasping against a coffin lid. They passed an alcove where a statue of St. Michael stood with sword raised and wings half-unfurled. Candlewax from countless offerings had pooled around the base, hardened into jagged stalagmites. The scent of myrrh clung to the shadows like incense burned too long.

Gregory lingered, tilting his head toward the silent figure. His breath fogged briefly in the cold.

"You think she's going to make it?"

Tobias didn't answer right away. He let the question hang between them, suspended like breath before a plunge into deep water.

"She has to," he said at last. "Because if she doesn't, Uriel won't just burn her. He'll use her. And none of us are ready for what comes after that."

They moved again, deeper into the dark spine of the mountain's edge. Their steps echoed faintly now, the walls absorbing sound like secrets.

Toward the far edge of the battlement, the path narrowed between two weather-worn towers. Tobias's boot hit something that grated beneath his heel. He paused, then knelt, brushing away a thin layer of grit and salt.

Claw marks.

Four jagged grooves dug deep into the stone, curved and irregular, not animal, not human. Old stone had fractured at the edges, flaked white where fresh damage had cut through the weathered surface. The marks weren't just recent, they were deliberate.

Gregory's breath hissed beside him. "That's not wind erosion."

"No," Tobias murmured. "It's a message."

Then he saw it, carved deliberately into the wall between the slashes, etched with such precision it shimmered slightly in the moonlight:

Fiat Iudicium.

Let judgment come.

A sound rose faintly behind them, a distant, wavering whistle. Not a bird. Not wind. Something thinner, higher, like air escaping from a sealed tomb.

Tobias stood slowly, eyes sweeping the cliffside beyond. Nothing moved in the dark. No shape. No wings. But the silence had deepened. The sea below, once soft and constant, now felt absent. The waves had stopped making noise.

Gregory crouched beside the markings, his fingers brushing against something blackened wedged in a crevice. A talon, charred at the base.

He held it up, slowly, like it might still twitch. "What the hell kind of thing leaves this behind on sacred ground?"

Tobias didn't answer. He reached out and took the talon, curling his fingers around it. It was warm. Not with heat, but with something deeper. Residual. Like the stone, it remembered.

He slipped it into his coat.

"We tell Garren," he said. "We double the perimeter watches. And we pray that whatever left that mark isn't still here."

Gregory's voice dropped to a whisper, the kind reserved for crypts. "Or worse. That it is."

They walked on, the scrape of their boots swallowed by the dark.

Above them, the stars hung cold and still. And somewhere in the unseen distance, something watched without blinking, its verdict already decided.

THE BENCH BEHIND THE chapel overlooked the cliffs where the sea met the sky in jagged, ragged lines, as if the earth itself had been torn and never quite healed. It was old, cut from marble gone gray with lichen, half-cracked along one side, its legs sunken deeper into the stone terrace with each passing century. Salt spray from the ocean had etched ghostly veins across its surface. Someone had carved a small cross into one of the armrests, shallow, reverent, nearly worn away by time and weather.

Ella sat hunched over on one end, her elbows pressed into her knees, fingers clasped like a prayer she hadn't found the words for. She stared down at the tide far below. The water churned against the cliffs in a rhythm that felt almost human, slow, heavy, angry. Like the ocean resented the mountain's stillness. The roar of each wave rose with a growl, then crashed like a breath being held too long and finally exhaled in fury.

The wind came in sudden, moaning pulses. It keened through the broken chapel stones behind her, rattled the nearby prayer chimes on their hooks, and curled around her shoulders like a cold breath pressing against her back. Her hair lifted, strands trailing across her face, caught in the chill.

She didn't hear Tobias approach. She only registered his presence when the bench creaked beneath his weight, and the faint smell of cold leather and candle ash reached her nose.

He didn't speak. He just sat, close enough to be felt, not close enough to crowd her. The same way he had when they were children and she'd been too shaken to sleep, afraid of things that only he had known how to keep at bay.

"I don't want to disappear," she said.

Her voice was quiet, but it carried. The cliffs had a way of drawing out confessions.

Tobias didn't look at her. "You won't."

"You don't know that." Her tone sharpened, brittle and raw. "The monk said the others burned. One of them turned to salt from the inside out. What if I go like that? What if I fade into something divine, and what's left isn't me?"

The wind picked up, tearing past them like it was trying to interrupt.

Tobias was silent for a beat too long. The tension in his jaw said he'd considered the same thing.

"I won't let that happen," he said finally, low and sure. "Not while I'm breathing."

Ella let out a bitter breath, not quite a laugh. "You can't fight an archangel, Tobias."

"No," he said. He turned toward her, and his voice changed, not louder, but deeper, anchored. "But I can remind you who you are. Every day. Every step. If that thing tries to take you from yourself, I'll stand in front of it. I'll hold the line."

She looked at him then, really looked. The wind had carved lines into his face that hadn't been there before, etched by years, missions, guilt. But his eyes were the same. Steady. Grounded. The boy who'd once wrapped his arms around her during the lowest days of their childhood. The boy who had carried her grief when she couldn't lift it herself.

"What if I'm not strong enough?" she asked.

"Then you lean on me until you are."

Below them, the sea chose that moment to slam against the cliff in a thunderous crash, spraying foam high enough to cast mist into the air. The noise echoed like a god roaring in the dark.

Ella closed her eyes. The scent of brine and cold stone filled her lungs.

"I don't think I'm afraid of dying," she whispered. "I think I'm afraid of becoming something holy. Something I can't come back from."

Tobias reached over, not quickly, not gently, firmly, and took her hand.

"You're not a saint," he said. "You're my sister. And if holiness demands you stop being human, then it doesn't deserve you."

She didn't respond. But she didn't pull away.

The wind quieted around them, as if the night itself had paused to listen.

They sat in the dark until the stars grew sharp and the cold began to settle in their bones. When they finally rose, it wasn't in silence or ceremony. It was with the slow, practiced movement of people who had made peace with the weight they were carrying.

They didn't speak as they returned to the monastery, but they didn't have to. They walked together, not as soldier and vessel, not as protector and weapon, but as brother and sister, carrying each other the way only family could.

Whatever came next, they would face it as one.

And neither of them would burn alone.

CHAPTER 16

Waking Flames

Indubitably, Magick is one of the subtlest and
most difficult of the sciences and arts. There
is more opportunity for errors of comprehen-
sion, judgement and practice than in any other
branch of physics.

A.C.

THE FARM LOOKED THE same. That was the problem.

Morning rolled over the hills in its usual hush, soft mist on
the fields, dew-beaded fence rails, and the golden glow of
the rising sun turning the fog to liquid fire. The world stirred
gently, sheep in the lower pastures bleating sleepily, a rooster
crowing from the far barn roof. Wind swept over the long
grass in ripples, brushing the wheat in soft, whispering waves.

The orchard trees stood still and bare, their skeletal branches raised like hands waiting for rain.

Nothing was wrong. Not on the surface. And yet, Sia couldn't shake the feeling that something had shifted while no one was looking, like the sky was holding its breath, like the air itself had gone too quiet.

She stood alone at the edge of the training circle, barefoot in the cold grass, her notebook open to a fresh page. Her pencil scratched lightly, looping around the silhouette of a tree whose shadow stretched long and thin across the field. The lines came without thought. She wasn't drawing the tree. She was drawing what it felt like, leaning, uncertain, waiting. Every mark seemed to pull on her hand, tugging her toward something just beyond the frame.

The wind caught her hair and tugged it into her face. She didn't move. Just kept drawing.

A shadow crossed behind her, and a familiar voice followed.

"Out early again?"

Eric's voice came from behind, casual, but not as light as usual. She glanced back and saw him leaning against the fencepost, arms folded, cloak half-draped over one shoulder. He looked like he hadn't slept, his eyes shadowed, and the usual playfulness in his smile was missing. He looked older in the gray morning.

"Couldn't sleep," she said.

"Too much firelight and divine drama?"

Sia gave him a wry look. "You're one to talk. You light your bedroll on fire last week?"

He smirked, but didn't respond. For a moment, the silence between them felt almost easy. Then it didn't.

Eric pushed off the fence and walked toward her, boots crunching through the frostbitten grass. A flock of blackbirds stirred from the barn roof behind him, wheeling briefly before disappearing into the trees. The air was too still after they left, like the sound had been vacuumed from the field.

"You and I still okay?" he asked, more direct than she'd expected.

Sia didn't answer right away. She closed her sketchbook and tucked it under one arm, eyes lifting to meet his.

"We're not not okay," she said. "But I'm not sure we're back to normal either."

Eric nodded. "Fair."

Another pause. A longer one. The kind that usually came before something important.

"I was scared," he said. "Back then. With your magic. With… you. Not because I thought you'd hurt me. Because I didn't know if I could help you."

Her expression softened, but she didn't speak. Not yet.

Eric looked away, toward the eastern ridge where the tree-line blurred in early light. The horizon shimmered faintly, though there was no heat to make it waver.

"I don't know if I'm your teacher anymore, Sia. Not the way I was."

"You are," she said. "But that's not all you are."

Eric turned back to her, his brows lifting slightly.

"I still trust you," Sia added. "But trust doesn't mean blind faith. You're allowed to screw up. You just have to own it."

He nodded again, slower this time. "I can do that."

A distant crack rang out, metal striking wood. Sia and Eric turned toward the sound. Across the pasture, near the treeline, Mia was training alone. Again. Her movements were sharp, disciplined, but angry. Too fast. Too hard. The sound of her blade echoed too long, like it was bouncing off more than just the trees.

"She hasn't trained with us in three days," Eric said.

"She's pulling away."

"And no one's stopped her?"

"She doesn't want to be stopped."

They stood in silence a moment longer. The fog had started to burn away, revealing the fenceline, the worn target dummies, the forgotten garden plots near the farmhouse. Everything looked normal. Everything felt wrong.

Then, softly, Sia murmured, "Something's coming, Eric. I can feel it. Like a storm moving in your sleep. You don't see it. You just wake up with your bones aching."

Eric looked toward Mia again, his eyes narrowing.

"Then we'd better be ready when it hits."

MIA'S BLADE SANG THROUGH the morning air, slicing down with a speed that blurred the steel's edge. The wooden post she struck splintered slightly on impact, sending a sharp crack across the field, but she didn't stop. She pivoted, spun, and struck again, faster this time, sharper. Sweat beaded on her brow despite the cold. Her breathing was tight, controlled, each exhale drawn from deep within her chest, the kind of breathing you learn in warzones, or cages.

The woods just beyond the pasture loomed in muted grays and greens, half-shrouded in mist. They weren't dangerous, yet. Not like the roads, not like the places demons were known to roam. But the shadows between those trees had begun to tilt, just slightly, like a picture frame nudged off-kilter. The branches swayed without wind. Light fell wrong through the leaves.

Mia felt it, each time she moved too fast or let her senses drift beyond her body. The world didn't feel quite real anymore. The air shimmered sometimes when she blinked. Trees leaned closer than they should. And once, just once, she'd turned her head and seen two versions of her own shadow. One moved a heartbeat late.

She stopped her movements long enough to catch her breath. The clearing around her was silent, too silent. No wind. No birdsong. Even the insects had gone quiet, as if nature itself was holding its breath. The sweat on her skin went cold.

She glanced down at her blade. It hadn't changed. But her reflection in its surface looked hollow. Her eyes in the steel were too wide. Her smile, a thing she hadn't made, flickered and vanished.

The veil was thinning. She didn't have to say it aloud, she could feel it. The Dream wasn't just visiting them anymore. It was here, standing just behind the curtain of the waking world, close enough to reach through if it wanted to. And maybe it already had.

A rustle behind her made her turn, blade half-raised. She expected Marcus, or perhaps Sia checking on her again. But there was nothing there.

No, something. A flicker.

At the edge of her vision, the trees didn't sway. They breathed. The whole forest inhaled. Exhaled. The trunks flexed slightly, as if made of lungs instead of bark. The air smelled wrong, too sweet, like nectar gone sour.

She stepped back, her fingers tightening around the hilt. Eyes narrowing. Her heartbeat slowed, not in fear, but in grim readiness.

Mia had been in the Dream before. She knew its textures. Its tricks. Its hunger. This wasn't a visitation. This wasn't a memory. This was a leak.

She sheathed her sword with a firm, practiced motion and closed her eyes for a moment, grounding herself. But the silence was pressing in.

You're slipping, she thought. Or something else is reaching in.

When she opened her eyes again, the woods had returned to stillness. No pulsing. No flickers. But the silence remained. Watching. Listening. Waiting.

She heard Marcus before she saw him, his footsteps deliberately loud, meant to announce and not startle. He emerged from the treeline in his usual gray-black leathers, hair wind-tossed but his presence steady. His expression was unreadable, but his eyes immediately swept the clearing like a battlefield.

"You're not supposed to be out here alone," he said.

Mia didn't look at him. "I needed space."

"You needed a tether," he corrected. "You've been close to the Dream for too long. It's following you back."

"Maybe I want it to."

The look he gave her wasn't anger. It was something worse: understanding.

"Mia," Marcus said gently, "you think control is power. But it isn't. Not in the Dream. Not in this world either. Control is the illusion. Connection is the anchor."

She turned away from him. "I'm not like the others. I don't get visions. I don't sketch prophecies. I don't wake up glowing."

"No," he said. "You survived Hell. That means the Dream listens to you in a different voice. One the others don't hear."

She looked at him, finally, with something like fear hiding behind her practiced calm.

"Then what happens if I start listening back?"

Marcus didn't answer. He simply stepped closer, then placed a hand lightly on her shoulder.

"When the veil thins," he said, "you don't push into it. You brace. You stay grounded. And when it opens, when the moment comes, you'll know what side you're standing on."

Mia nodded slowly.

But in the back of her mind, something else stirred.

A voice. A flicker. A key.

And the faintest breath of laughter, low and silver, curling like smoke where no one else could hear.

THE LONG HALL INSIDE the farmhouse had been repurposed more times than anyone could count. It had once been a dining room, a chapel, a makeshift infirmary. Now, its high-beamed ceiling and mismatched chairs served as the war room for something that hadn't yet declared itself a war. Light filtered through the windows in slanted beams, catching on floating dust and casting long shadows across the rough wooden floor.

Eric stood at the head of the table, one hand planted on a map of the eastern seaboard. Lines had been marked in charcoal, known infernal zones, divine touchpoints, dead zones where even mages refused to tread. His other hand tapped absently against a sealed scroll. Not a spell. A warning. One sent by the White Circle's outer scouts.

He looked exhausted. More than that, strained.

For the past two weeks, whenever he wasn't training with Sia or working with the younger mages, Eric had been pouring every ounce of his strength into strengthening the Farm's defenses. Glyphs had been etched by hand beneath every windowsill, runes buried beneath fence posts and gate stones.

He had woven wards into the floorboards, soaked salt into the eaves, sung protective spells in three dead languages. He had done it all quietly, methodically, and without fanfare. There were even threads of warding bound into the knots of the dining room curtains.

Mariah had added her own layer of protection as well, a latticework of blood-bound charms and hedge-magic that disguised the Farm's arcane signature from the outside. She never spoke of it aloud, but the talismans hung near the doorways hummed faintly when demons were mentioned. Still, it hadn't been enough.

Sia sat on one side, notebook in her lap, pencil stilled mid-sketch. Across from her, Peter Mason leaned forward with a frown, his weathered fingers steepled beneath his chin. He hadn't spoken yet.

Marcus stood at the rear of the room, arms folded, half-shadowed beneath the archway. Mia wasn't present. No one had questioned that, yet.

The silence was brittle. Then Domingo appeared. Not in flesh, but in the warping shimmer of astral projection, his form congealing above the map like a ghost of molten gold and dragonbone. His voice, when it came, was low and distant but unmistakably heavy with presence.

"You are no longer hidden," Domingo said.

No one breathed.

"The infernal legions have mobilized west of the Hudson," he continued. "Crawly's agents have shifted tactics. They are no longer searching. They are preparing."

Eric glanced toward Sia, who had closed her notebook slowly.

Peter finally spoke. "You want to evacuate."

Eric nodded. "It's not just a feeling anymore. They know where we are. It's only a matter of time."

Peter's jaw tightened. "This place is fortified. Sacred. We have lines of defense."

"And they have lies," Marcus said from the doorway. "They won't come through the front gate with claws and fire. They'll come through someone's dream. Someone's doubt."

Silence again. Then Domingo's gaze shifted, though his projected face remained unreadable.

"Your enemy is not bound to earth," the dragon lord said. "And the veil thins. Even now. What stands between worlds will not hold if fractured from within."

Peter leaned back, hands tightening to fists. "We cannot abandon the place that protects them."

"They won't be protected if they're surrounded," Eric snapped.

The sudden rise in his voice startled even him. He took a breath, steadied himself.

"We stay," Peter said. "At least until we know for certain what we're up against."

"And when it arrives?" Marcus asked. "Do we burn or stand ready?"

Eric looked down at the map. A new mark had appeared there, unnoticed until now. A thin line of ink not drawn by any hand present. It traced a spiral, slow and deliberate, right over the center of the Farm.

Sia stared at it. Her fingers trembled, and her pencil dropped to the floor. It had been drawn before. She had seen it in her dreams.

She just hadn't remembered until now.

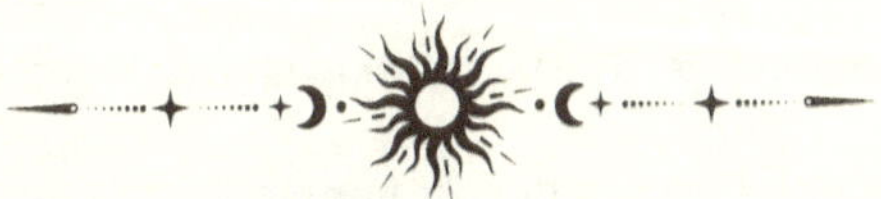

NIGHT SETTLED OVER THE Farm like a closing eye, slow, heavy, and too quiet. The hush didn't feel like peace. It felt like a held breath.

Sia lay in her bed, the covers tangled around her legs, her window half-cracked open to let the breeze in. Moonlight spilled across her floor in broken silver lines, painting the walls with pale shadows that flickered each time the wind stirred the curtains. But tonight, the breeze wasn't warm. It was thin, sharp, almost surgical in its coldness, like something sliding between the cracks of a house built to be whole.

Her sketchbook sat open across her knees. She hadn't meant to draw again. Not tonight. But her hands had moved before her thoughts had caught up, the pencil gliding over the page with a will of its own. The lines had come too easily. Not automatic. Possessed.

Now she stared at the half-finished image before her, heart ticking faster than she liked.

A girl stood alone in a field, no trees, no buildings. Just her. But her eyes were wrong. They were too wide, too dark, and something about the angle of her head made Sia feel like she was looking at a marionette caught mid-performance. The face was human, but stretched slightly at the edges. The lines around her mouth frayed and faded into the page, as though the world behind her wasn't holding shape. And the hands...

Sia realized she hadn't drawn fingers. Just suggestion. Just motion. Just blur.

She turned the page, breath catching.

The next sketch bled into existence as if waiting. She hadn't drawn this recently. Not that she remembered. But the ink was fresh, the paper warped slightly from moisture, like something had sweated through. It was the spiral again.

Not large. Not violent. Just precise. Deliberate. The same spiral now resting on the map in the war room. A slow descent inward. A vortex without wind. A pull without gravity.

She reached out and touched the page. It was cold.

The ink shimmered faintly under the moonlight, and she thought, just for a breath, that it pulsed. Not a visual illusion. A heartbeat. A signal.

The air in her room changed. It thickened with something unseen, more than a presence, less than a shape. Not the kind of cold that chilled skin, but the kind that settled into the lungs and made the act of breathing feel intrusive.

Sia froze.

Not with fear, yet, but with recognition. This wasn't just magic, and it wasn't just the Dream. This was something older, an awareness pressing down like a heavy hand placed gently on the crown of her head. She could feel the walls of her room stretching, no, bending, like they had forgotten what dimensions they were supposed to hold.

The spiral on the page pulsed again. She didn't just see it, she felt it in her chest. A pressure behind her sternum, a magnetic tug, like gravity had decided it wanted something from her and was testing the line.

Then the shadow shifted.

Thanatos didn't enter the room so much as become visible within it. One moment, the corner was empty. The next, he was there, still, watching, dressed in shadow and the cold grace of death. He seemed blurred at the edges, like her eyes couldn't decide if he belonged fully to this world.

"It's thinning," she said. Her voice scraped across her throat like it had traveled a long way just to reach her own ears.

Thanatos nodded, and the shadows seemed to lean closer around him, as if they, too, listened when he spoke.

"And the sketchbook?"

His answer didn't come right away. When it did, it was low and deliberate, pulled from a place far beneath language.

"The Dream remembers before you do," he said. "And it does not forget what it has shown you. You are beginning to awaken, Sia, but you are not the only one waking."

Sia looked back down. The spiral had grown again, extending outward across the page in thin, vein-like branches. A second figure stood behind the girl now, still barely more than a silhouette. Its shape was impossible, thin where it should have been wide, too tall for the page, neck bent at a strange angle like it was listening with something other than ears.

Then she saw them: the eyes.

They weren't drawn. Not part of the ink. But they were there. Two perfect voids where the paper refused light, twin points of unbeing nestled in the page like seeds ready to hatch.

Her mouth went dry. Her hands moved without thought.

The sketchbook snapped shut, not with a rustle but a crack, like the breaking of something brittle and sacred. She held it to her chest like a ward, breathing shallow.

Outside, the wind rose hard enough to rattle the windowpane. It howled along the siding, a high and reedy sound like something laughing from the far treeline.

But the curtains didn't move. The shadows in the room didn't shift. The figure in the sketch might have vanished from the page, but Sia knew it hadn't gone far.

The air tasted like static and dust and something sweetly rotten, like a memory left out too long in the sun.

Something had seen her. It hadn't stayed on the other side. The veil had already failed.

In the Fog

A red rose absorbs all colors but red; red is
therefore the one color that it is not.

A.C.

MIA WOKE WITH A start, the remnants of a dream clinging to her
skin like cobwebs. She sat up too fast and blinked against the
morning light filtering through her bedroom curtains, sharp
slats of gold and shadow, too vivid, too precise. Her heart thundered. The dream had not been hers. She was sure of it. She
couldn't remember the specifics, just impressions: fire licking
up her arms, laughter that wasn't hers, and eyes watching her
from behind a curtain of thorns.

She sat still for a moment, clutching the edge of her blanket
with white knuckles, listening to her pulse as it roared inside

her ears. The silence of the farmhouse was unnatural, too deep, like the world outside her room had stopped holding its breath.

She dressed in silence and slipped out before anyone else stirred. The sky was still gray-blue, the air damp with clinging mist. The gravel path felt softer underfoot, like the earth was beginning to dream too. Grass soaked through her boots in minutes. Her steps took her toward the greenhouse without conscious thought, as if something old in her bones remembered comfort there. Her hand brushed against the doorframe like it was something sacred.

The greenhouse stood like a breath held between worlds, glass panels fogged over, warm from the heat spells Mariah kept subtly humming in the rafters. The door creaked open with the hush of ritual. Inside, the scent of thyme, basil, rosemary, damp earth, and sweet moss hit her like a memory that was still living, breathing. It wrapped around her like a blanket she hadn't realized she missed. It was womb-like. Gentle. Alive in a way that nothing else had felt since the Dream began unraveling into their waking lives.

Mariah stood at one of the benches, her sleeves rolled up, her hands buried wrist-deep in a trough of soil. Her profile was soft in the morning light that filtered through the condensation-streaked glass. She looked up when Mia entered, but said nothing. Just smiled with her eyes and tilted her head slightly, acknowledging her daughter without drawing blood from the wound she could sense had opened.

Mia hesitated by the door. Her throat felt dry.

"I didn't come to talk," she said. Her voice cracked halfway through.

Mariah didn't answer with words. She wiped her hands on a cloth and stepped aside, motioning for Mia to join her. There was another pot. Another space. A rhythm already waiting to be resumed.

Mia moved toward it slowly, like stepping into an old memory. She dug her fingers into the soil, let it fill the cracks in her hands. It was warmer than it should've been. The warmth made her eyes sting.

For a long time, neither of them spoke.

Then Mariah said, "You used to help me do this when you were little. You always overwatered everything. Thought it would grow faster that way."

Mia huffed a quiet laugh. "Did it?"

"No," Mariah said. "But you smiled more. That helped."

The quiet returned, but it wasn't heavy. Just present. A kind of peace that could only exist in shared stillness.

"I think something's wrong with me," Mia whispered eventually. "Not just... wrong. Twisted. I feel it in my skin. Like something's trying to reach through me. And I don't know if it's mine or not."

Mariah set her hands gently over Mia's. Her palms were warm, steady. She didn't flinch at the heat radiating off Mia's skin.

"Then we remind your skin who it belongs to."

Mia looked up, eyes shining. "What if I'm not strong enough?"

"Then I'll hold the pieces until you are."

A tremor passed through Mia's chest. Not fear. Not grief. Just the unbearable weight of being seen.

Mariah didn't push. She didn't question. She simply moved beside her daughter and planted a sprout in the earth between them. A tiny green thing with leaves still folded tight, delicate, unassuming, but reaching.

"You are still growing," Mariah said softly. "Even if you can't feel it right now."

Mia didn't answer. But her hands stayed in the dirt. She didn't pull away.

The greenhouse held the moment like it was sacred. Outside, fog thickened along the treeline. The air bent with unseen breath. Something watched from behind the veil.

But inside the glass walls, for just a little longer, they held the Dream at bay with memory, dirt, and love.

ERIC STOOD AT THE outermost ward post, his hands pressed flat against the carved runes burned into the bark of a maple tree. The air here was colder, tinged with the acrid scent of ash and damp stone. Morning fog clung low to the ground, rolling like breath from a sleeping beast. Every sound felt muffled, like the world had been wrapped in gauze. Beyond the fenceline, the woods were a blur of silver and green, and they pulsed, subtly, unnaturally.

He whispered an incantation under his breath, Latin syllables curling around the breath of his magic. The glyph beneath his hand flickered weakly, then stabilized into a low, golden glow. It should have burned brighter. It had last week. Something was pulling on the weave, tugging at the edges of their protection like fingers testing a stitch.

He stepped back, exhaling slowly.

Mariah stood a few feet behind him, arms folded, watching the fog with eyes that saw more than mortal sight. Her boots sank slightly in the soft earth, roots brushing against her soles like they remembered her steps. Her wards, built of thread and soil and ancient folk blessing, had begun to hum louder, sharper. The harmonies were dissonant now. Warning tones that vibrated along the bones.

"They're not breaking," Eric said, voice low. "But they're thinning. Like they're being looked at too hard from the wrong side."

Mariah didn't respond right away. She turned toward a bundle of charm-sticks hanging from a low-hung branch. Each one had been carved, painted, and wrapped with her magic. One of them was shaking ever so slightly, the thread fraying like spider silk in wind.

"Something brushed through here last night," she said. "I felt it in my teeth."

Eric grimaced. "Dream leakage? Or something more?"

"The Dream doesn't leak on its own," she replied. "It's being pulled. Somewhere deeper, the fabric is being stretched, and not evenly."

He nodded slowly. "Then something's pulling it on purpose."

They walked the line together, checking wards at each post. The fog thickened as they moved. Their shadows faded in and out like ghosts unsure if they belonged to bodies. A trick of light. Or something worse.

At the third marker, Eric froze.

There was a tear in the air.

Not visible, not exactly. But he felt it. A seam. A fissure. The way air changes around lightning just before it strikes. It tasted like blood and burnt flowers.

He raised a hand and channeled. Magic gathered in his palm, heat swirling into his wrist, up his arm. The wards around the post shivered and flared, briefly revealing a shape in the fog just beyond the property's edge. Not large. Not moving. But watching.

Mariah stepped beside him and reached out without speaking. Her fingers traced the runes with the reverence of an oath. Together, their magic pressed forward, not to attack, but to reinforce. A pulse of golden light and vinework spread across the air, reknitting the veil with stitchwork older than either of them.

The shape vanished.

But the fog didn't clear. And the cold didn't lift.

Eric let the magic fade. The back of his neck itched like something was still standing there, just outside the range of sound.

He turned toward Mariah and said quietly, "How long do you think we have, Singer?"

Mariah didn't look at him. Her voice was calm, but it rang like a bell.

"Not long enough."

She stepped away first, back toward the farmhouse. Eric followed, pausing once to glance back over his shoulder. The ward post still glowed, but now it flickered, as if even stone and magic were beginning to second-guess reality.

The Dream was no longer just bleeding through.

It was beginning to feed.

THE KITCHEN OF THE farmhouse had become a place of whispered strategy. Gone was the scent of cinnamon and tea that usually hung in the air. Today, it smelled faintly of scorched herbs and something older, ozone, maybe, or the bitterness of iron. Sia stood near the long window, her notebook clutched to her chest, spine pressed to the cool glass.

Outside, the fog hadn't lifted.

It clung to the orchard like a second skin, trailing long veils of white through the trees. Light filtered through it as if passing through milk, creating strange refractions. Shapes seemed to drift in the mist. Not forms. Not quite. Just the suggestion of movement where nothing should be.

Inside, the others gathered slowly.

Eric leaned over the worn table, flipping through maps, ward schematics, and scouting scrolls. His face was drawn, his usual snide wit absent. Magic lingered on his fingers, sparks dimming and flickering. Mariah sat near the hearth, sewing thread through dried juniper as if her hands needed motion to keep the silence from swallowing her. Marcus stood at the far corner, arms crossed, his eyes tracking every shadow that crossed the floor.

Mia arrived last. She didn't sit.

Sia didn't speak at first. She opened her sketchbook and turned it around. The image was fresh. Her hand trembled as she held it up.

A door stood in the center of a cracked dreamscape, arched with bone, lined in ivy. The ground beneath it warped into spirals, and at the center, a figure burned like a living ember. No face. No name. Just heat and purpose.

Marcus stepped forward. He didn't need to ask.

His boots made a low creak against the old wooden floor, a whisper of pressure that seemed louder than it should have in the quiet room. The boards beneath him flexed faintly, joints moaning with age and memory. As he crossed to the table, the air shifted, dense, electric, as if the fog outside had pressed itself up against the glass in sudden curiosity.

A log in the hearth cracked with a dry snap. The flames didn't flare, but the light seemed to twist, casting elongated shadows that danced along the walls. One arced briefly over Sia's sketch, darkening the doorway inked in charcoal and vine.

Marcus's presence carried a weight, not from size or authority, but from stillness. He studied the drawing with the tension of someone reading a battlefield, silent, but not detached. His gaze moved from the spiral patterns in the dirt to the fire-lit figure standing at the center. The image glowed faintly in the muted light, as if something within the ink wanted to burn.

Outside, the wind pushed harder against the windows. A low groan threaded through the walls of the house. Pipes clinked. The beams overhead shifted, settling like bones under pressure.

No one else spoke.

Not yet.

Somewhere down the hall, a chair scraped gently on the floor. No one had been sitting there.

Mariah's hands stilled in her threadwork. Eric's fingertips curled against the parchment. Mia's arms were crossed now, jaw tight. The house felt like it was waiting.

Waiting for a decision that would echo into more than just this world.

"It came to me last night," Sia said. "I wasn't asleep yet. I think... I think it was remembering for me. Not a prophecy. A path."

"Is that a gate into the Dream?" Eric asked, voice quiet.

Sia nodded, slowly, her gaze lingering on the lines of the sketch as if afraid to blink and find them changed. "Or out," she said, her voice quiet but firm. "I think it works both ways. Like a hinge. Or maybe a wound."

She didn't look up. Her fingers were clenched so tightly around the edge of the notebook that the skin across her knuckles had gone pale. Her breathing was steady, but just barely. This wasn't just strategy, it was admission. She had been dreaming of the gate for days, maybe longer. She just hadn't been brave enough to say it aloud until now.

"I think it's not just something we can use," she continued, her voice gaining weight, "I think it's something we have to use. Before it's used against us. Before Crawly walks straight through it while we're still debating what to do."

She lifted her head then, finally meeting their eyes. First Eric's, then Mariah's, then Marcus's, and last, Mia's. Her expression was drawn but resolute, like someone who had already stepped through in her heart, and was only waiting for her body to catch up.

Silence fell again. This time, it had teeth.

Marcus spoke next. "You're suggesting we walk into it. Voluntarily."

"I'm suggesting we take control," Sia said. "The veil's thinning, but that doesn't mean it can't be shaped. We could force it. Choose when and how it opens. Use it before Crawly does."

"You'd need an anchor," Mariah said. "Someone to hold you here. Someone to keep your thread tight."

"I thought of that," Sia said. Her eyes flicked toward Mia. "If you're willing."

Mia's mouth parted, but no words came. The room leaned in. She swallowed, then gave the barest nod. "I'll do it."

Eric exhaled like he'd been holding the breath for a minute too long. "We'd have to prepare the perimeter. Lock down the lines. Reinforce the tethers. And I'm not sure we can stop the veil from fighting back."

"We're not stopping it," Marcus said. "We're shaping it. And that's not a spell. That's a sacrifice."

Sia looked down at the sketch again. Her fingers traced the curling inkwork almost reverently, as though she were reading braille instead of looking. The doorway she'd drawn now seemed to stare back at her, more portal than picture. The spirals around it pulsed in her peripheral vision, subtle, impossible. She could still feel the heat of the figure burning at its center in her chest like heartfire.

Her voice, when it came again, was steady but low, as if speaking too loudly might invite it to open then and there.

"Then I'll pay it," she said. "If someone has to be the one to open the way, to walk into the fire first, it's going to be me."

Marcus tilted his head slightly, but didn't argue. Eric opened his mouth, then closed it again, jaw tight. Mia's hands had curled into fists without her noticing.

Outside, something moved. A blur of motion, not running, not human. A shape passed the window and they all froze. It wasn't a bird. It wasn't wind. It was just a shadow with no face; it made no sound. It was gone before anyone could confirm it, but too slow to be imagined, too solid to be dismissed.

The flames in the hearth hissed as if doused by breath. The wood popped, throwing a sharp snap that made all of them flinch. No one said anything. Not even a breath. The fog at the edges of the windows thickened like smoke curling in reverse.

And the room got very, very still.

Night deepened, and with it came a silence that did not feel empty. The Farm slept uneasily. Even the sheep in the lower pastures seemed subdued, their usual night sounds stifled. The wind had died, but the fog remained, clinging to every branch and beam like a skin the world couldn't shed. It crawled along the roof tiles and pressed against windows like a living thing, a pale membrane separating the waking world from something older and watching.

In her room, Sia sat cross-legged on the floor, the sketchbook open before her like a holy text. The door was locked. The windows were covered, but she still felt exposed, like the night was staring through the cracks, studying her. A single candle burned low on the nightstand beside her, its flame steady but elongated, as if reaching for something it couldn't quite touch.

She didn't remember when she had started drawing again. Only that she couldn't stop. Pages turned beneath her hands, not by choice but by rhythm. The sketches flowed like a fever, doorways drawn in black spirals, roots cracking stone, trees made of veins. The face returned again and again, half-formed, half-screaming. The eyes always the same, twin voids rimmed in light.

She wasn't asleep, but she was no longer fully awake. Her limbs felt slow, submerged, her thoughts running on a delay. The air around her wavered as if she sat too close to a heat source, though the room was cold.

And then she heard it. Three knocks. Soft. Precise. They came from below the floorboards, not the hallway. A polite rhythm. One-two-three. Like a visitor asking entry.

Sia's blood turned to ice. She stared at the sketchbook. The spiral on the page had widened while she wasn't looking. It now overlapped other drawings, old ones. A tree without leaves. A girl with no mouth. A gate ajar, cracked just enough to whisper. She blinked once, hard.

When she opened her eyes, Thanatos was there.

He wasn't looming. He wasn't standing. He was simply present, as if he had always been seated in the far corner of her room, folded into the shadows like a truth too heavy to speak aloud. The candlelight glinted across the edge of his cloak, outlining a face carved in quiet grief.

"It's time, isn't it?" Her voice was thin but unshaken.

Thanatos didn't answer immediately. He tilted his head and looked at the sketchbook with reverence, or regret. His voice, when it came, was low and old. "The door is already open. You're only just noticing the draft."

Sia closed the book, but it didn't help. She still felt something stirring behind her eyes, like a thought that wasn't hers trying to surface. "Will I be alone in there?"

"No," Thanatos replied. "But you may feel alone. That's the price of walking first."

She stood slowly. Her joints ached, her muscles tight as if she had been holding herself together for hours. Her skin tingled with static. Each breath felt thick, like the air was being filtered through memory.

Thanatos rose with her, as silent as ever, moving without sound, without weight. He stepped closer, placing a hand briefly over hers. His eyes flicked once to the sketchbook still resting on the floor, as if recognizing an old wound left open.

"That spiral you drew weeks ago," he said quietly. "The one wrapped in thorns, with no center… That wasn't a warning, Sia. That was a map. You've been charting the wound since the moment it opened."

"You know the way, Dreamer," he said. "You've always known. But tonight, the Dream will answer back."

Outside, the wind returned, but it wasn't wind. It was breath. It moved nothing. It touched everything. The candle dimmed and Sia opened the door.

The hallway was shadowed and cold. The farmhouse, normally filled with wood groans and ancestral murmurs, was perfectly still, as if it, too, had gone to sleep, afraid to witness what came next. Barefoot, sketchbook clutched to her chest, Sia descended the stairs. Her heart did not race. It paced itself.

At the bottom, Mia waited. She said nothing. She didn't need to. Her eyes held the storm she hadn't spoken of, and her hand reached for Sia's with a quiet grace that made the Dream feel almost kind.

A circle had already been drawn in the center of the parlor. It smelled faintly of juniper and ash, of old promises burned into salt. Gold dust glittered faintly where the candlelight kissed it.

Sia stepped into the circle. The salt crunched faintly beneath her heel.

Mia knelt just outside it, her hands resting on her thighs, her shoulders tight. She was ready, but her jaw clenched like someone bracing for a scream. The house did not shake. The veil did not split like paper. It sighed, and the world exhaled.

And the Dream opened its arms.

Chapter 18

Garden of Memory

There is no law beyond Do what thou wilt.

A.C.

Sia opened her eyes, but she didn't wake.

The Farm was still around her, but it had been peeled and rewoven into something wrong. The ceiling of the parlor stretched higher than it should, beams coiling upward like reaching branches. The walls pulsed faintly with breath. The salt circle beneath her feet had turned to a ring of pale bone, each vertebra humming softly as if aware of her presence.

She stood slowly. Her legs obeyed, but not with the usual certainty. Her movements felt rehearsed, as if she were remembering how to walk while she did it. The floorboards beneath her were mossy and damp. Her sketchbook was no longer in her hands; it had become part of her shadow, bound to her footsteps.

Light came from no sun. The sky outside the warped windows spiraled gently in ochre and blue, rotating like the surface of an eye watching from above. The fog had followed her into the Dream, but here it was denser, heavier. It didn't drift; it clung.

She stepped out into the yard.

The farmhouse groaned behind her like an old man turning in his sleep. The orchard had grown taller than it should, trees stretched thin and skeletal, bearing no fruit, only small hanging bells that chimed softly with no wind. A fence ran along the horizon, but it shifted whenever she looked directly at it.

Echoes waited at the edge of her vision.

She saw Eric's silhouette near the barn, laughing, but the sound came from Marcus's voice. Mariah stood in the field, bent over a prayer circle, but her hands were her own, flickering between young and old. Mia danced barefoot between the trees, eyes closed, humming something Sia didn't recognize, but the melody made her stomach twist. Every time she tried to approach, they melted into fog.

Sia pressed on.

The spiral gate, the one she had drawn so many times it felt like a scar, waited for her in the orchard's heart. Thorn-vines curled up its frame like veins feeding something ancient and dormant. It pulsed faintly with blue light, the color of her own fire, but dimmer, dream-faded. Something moved on the other side. Not a person. Not yet.

The wind began to whisper.

Hero.

The voice came from everywhere. It had no tone, no breath, only certainty. Chosen. Bound. *Doomed.*

She stumbled, one foot catching on a root that hadn't been there a moment ago. When she looked down, the root had coiled like a hand. It released her gently.

Another voice echoed, softer, warmer. *Come back.*

That voice was Mia's. Or it sounded like Mia. But it came from behind the gate. Sia took another step forward. The fog thinned, just slightly. The gate stood taller now, almost cathedral-like, an arch that hummed with the weight of choice. She reached toward it and the light inside flared once briefly. The world around her held its breath and then came the footsteps.

Two sets. One behind her. One beside her. Neither visible. Neither human. But they walked in rhythm with her own.

Hero, the wind whispered again, however Sia did not look back.

She walked toward the Garden.

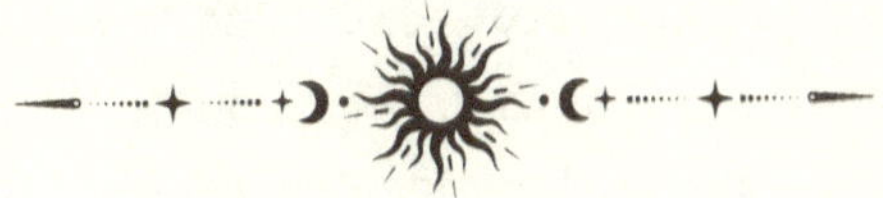

MARCUS HAD KNOWN THE wards would not last. Not forever. Not under this pressure. But even knowing it, even braced for it, he felt the tremor run down his spine like the prelude to a thunderclap, an ancient warning passed down from scale to marrow.

He crouched in the eastern field, massive and coiled, his dragon-form glistening in the starlight that barely filtered through the storm-swollen clouds above. His wings were half-furled, body arched over the farmhouse like a living bulwark against hell. Each breath rumbled through his chest like distant thunder. His scales, slick with dew and smoke, reflected light like oil on black glass, each plate humming with anticipation. He was power made flesh, but even power could falter.

Below him, the wards shimmered with visible strain. What had once been clean, ordered lines of magic, woven from Eric's structured precision, Mariah's instinctual na-ture-work, and Marcus's breath-forged sigils, were now flickering. Fraying. The sacred geometry bled light at the seams. Cracks formed in the latticework of reality like pressure lines in ice before it breaks.

The demons were testing them. Again and again. Not clever. Just relentless.

The fields beyond the treeline boiled with movement. Shadows surged and recoiled, pulsing like a living tide of limbs and bone. Forms crawled low to the ground or towered with limbs too long, mouths that yawned open like doors to deeper dark. Claws raked at the veil with the sound of bone scoring glass. They didn't fight with strategy, they fought with hunger.

Mariah stood at the root-arch gate, staff braced against the ground, her knuckles white as she whispered prayers that bit into the air like thorns. Her voice had deepened, threaded with something old. Her chants wove ivy and fire into the air, wrapping the wards in a twisting lattice of growth and flame. Each word she spoke caused the trees around her to groan with power.

Eric held the southern flank, robes scorched, blood at the corner of his mouth. Spellfire clung to his fingers like living gold, sparking with every breath. He hurled bolts of raw force into the mist, shouting incantations in sharp Latin phrases that cracked like whips. His voice was hoarse, throat near gone. He carved sigils into the dirt with his heel, quick and crude, sealing rents before they tore wider.

Peter knelt behind a stone post, his silhouette still and deliberate. One hand gripped a battered crucifix, the other his rifle. He whispered scripture between breaths and fired with precision, each silver round blessed and true. One shot down a leaping shadow midair. Another pinned a crawling beast to the ash-soaked soil. He didn't speak. He didn't miss.

They were all exhausted. Marcus could smell it: their sweat, their desperation, the stinging copper tang of magical over-reach. They were burning through strength like tinder in a furnace. He felt the pull of the Dream from the farmhouse. Sia had crossed over. They had no more time.

Then it happened. The eastern gate cracked.

A screech knifed through the night, metal on bone. A demon slipped through, a spider-shaped abomination of brass joints and sinew cords, legs skittering like sawblades on stone. It darted past the fraying wardline and shot toward the house.

Marcus roared.

The sound shook the orchard. Windows rattled. Birds startled from trees that no longer bore fruit. His wings flared wide, catching firelight and moonlight both. He surged forward, tail coiling like a whip. Three smaller beasts barely through the breach were pulped under the sweep of his claws.

With a single beat of his wings, he lifted into the air, huge and terrible, and dropped like judgment. The spider-demon exploded beneath him. Smoke rose from the crater. The earth itself groaned.

And then more demons came. Dozens were scrabbling for-ward testing the barrier with every strike. They had begun slipping through widening cracks. A wolf-thing with two faces. A child-shaped horror with too many fingers.

Wings. Teeth. Fire.

"Eric!" Marcus roared, his voice molten. "It's breaking!"

"I know!" came the reply. Eric's hair clung to his face, eyes wild with effort. "Just one minute more!"

Mariah shrieked another incantation, and the roots of nearby trees tore free from the ground, thrashing like serpents to entangle an oncoming wave.

Peter fired again. And again. His expression never changed.

Another demon slipped through, a lanky, skinned humanoid with a chest full of vertical teeth and fingers like needles. Marcus didn't hesitate. He lunged, jaws parting wide, and caught it mid-leap. It screamed once.

He didn't let it scream again. The wardline glowed faintly beneath him, barely. It was cracking like glass under weight.

The line was holding.

But only just.

MIA'S HANDS TREMBLED WHERE they rested on her knees. She sat just outside the circle of salt and ash, her palms upturned and open, fingers twitching slightly with every beat of her heart. Her eyes were shut, but she wasn't meditating. She was listening, straining for the sound of her sister's breath through a thread no one else could see.

The parlor had gone still in a way that felt dangerous. Not quiet, hollow. The light was too dim, too warm, and it bled across the walls like a bruise. Her skin prickled. Every part of her screamed that she wasn't alone.

She had held Sia's thread steady at first, like gripping a kite in high wind. There had been strength in it, resistance, tug, pulse. But now it was faint. Slippery. Her hands tightened, knuckles going white. Her back was rigid with focus, pain threading along her spine.

Hold on. Just hold on.

A creak echoed through the room that didn't come from the floorboards. It was deeper. Wet. Inside.

Behind her, the presence formed, not with a step, but with intention. The air thickened. Gravity seemed to bend inward. Not cold, not hot, just wrong.

A voice followed. "You've done so well, little spark."

Mia's eyes snapped open. Her lips parted but no breath came. Her throat was dry, her mouth filled with the taste of ash.

"I didn't call you," she whispered.

"But I've always heard you," it said. "Even before your name was a word, I knew your fire. All that pain. All that loss. And still, you burned."

Her jaw tightened. She clenched her fists against the floor, fingernails digging into old wood. Don't listen. Don't let him in.

The voice smiled, though it had no mouth. "You held her when no one else could. You remembered her when she forgot herself. You don't have to carry it anymore."

She wanted to scream. Not in fear, but in defiance. Her body shook with the effort of silence.

His voice was smoke on silk, eerily calming despite the demand in his words. "Let go."

Tears sprang to her eyes. Not because she believed him but because part of her wanted to. The weight of holding on had become unbearable. She hadn't slept. She hadn't eaten. She had been the strong one. The keeper. The tether.

Her hand twitched. Then outside, something howled, not from the throat of a beast, but the core of the world. The circle pulsed. The thread twitched in her mind like a muscle clenching before death, and then it slipped. Her gasp was a sob. Her body lurched as if a limb had been torn away. The tether was gone.

"No, no no no," she scrambled backward, hand outstretched like she could physically catch it.

The circle had faded to a dull smear. The glow was gone. She couldn't feel Sia anymore. The voice, Crawly, laughed gently. Kindly.

Mia screamed, wordless, angry, wild, and then choked it down with a breath that burned.

Her sister was gone.

And she had let go.

THE GARDEN DIDN'T ANNOUNCE itself.

It simply was, waiting behind the arch as if it had always been there. Sia passed through the gate and the fog fell away, dissolving into the shape of twisted trees and hills that curved in impossible directions. Light filtered from a sky that wasn't day or night, shifting in and out of color, as if it couldn't make up its mind. There were no birds. No insects. No breeze. But the entire place moved, the grass swaying to an unseen heartbeat, the trees leaning like curious listeners.

The Tree of Knowledge stood at the center, anchored to a wide hill of white ash. It was taller than any structure Sia had ever seen, bark the color of old blood, leaves like flame, each one veined with symbols she half-recognized from her sketchbook. Its roots cracked the ground like lightning, drinking deep from something beneath the Dream.

It was wrong. And beautiful.

She stepped closer. The firelight of the tree made her skin glow gold and her hair flicker blue where it touched her shoulder. She felt warmth without heat. Power without pain. And beneath all of that, a temptation so profound it felt like gravity. Like inevitability.

She had always imagined herself stronger than this. Beyond it. She was the Dreamer. She had fought, chosen, endured. But here, in this place, facing this tree, her certainty began to unravel. She could feel the weight of every name she had been given pressing down on her: Hero. Dreamer. Chosen. Names she never asked for. Names that had been carved into her life like wounds.

And then, he was there.

Crawly didn't walk. He unfolded into presence like a story returning to memory. He stood between her and the tree, dressed in simple gray, barefoot on the ash. His smile was gentle. His eyes sparkled like stars falling in reverse.

"You've done so well," he said.

Sia didn't answer. Her breath came slow, cold.

"All this time, they've asked you to carry things too big for your hands. They gave you a name without a choice. Hero. Dreamer. Chosen. Titles from people too afraid to carry their own weight."

He gestured to the tree. "But here's a truth: you could shape it. With one bite, you could remake the Dream. Give your sister peace. Keep your friends from burning. Erase the wars before they begin."

Sia's eyes flicked toward the fruit. They glowed faintly, the way pain sometimes glows in memory. Her mouth went dry. Her breath caught.

She saw it. A vision that wasn't hers but clung to her like silk. Mia, laughing again without fear. Marcus and Eric standing unburned in a field where no blood had ever soaked the soil. A world before the fire. A world she could hold in her hands and shape to protect them all.

Tears pricked the corners of her eyes. The image in her mind, the dream Crawly had painted, was intoxicating in its gentleness. A future without blood. Without war. Without loss. She saw her sister whole, untouched by trauma, unburdened by death. She saw Marcus, his fire no longer tempered by guilt. Eric, no longer torn between reason and fear. Even Tobias and Ella, safe and smiling beside a sunlit chapel, the horrors of battle faded like fog before morning light. And she saw herself, calm, smiling, no longer gasping for control.

Just for a moment, just one, she wanted to believe. Wanted to surrender to it. To accept the vision and stop fighting. Stop failing. To lay down the mantle and simply exist in peace.

Her body ached with longing. Her heart reached forward before her hand did. The fruit shimmered as if responding to that unspoken desire. It dangled just above her head, gleaming with the promise of resolution.

Her fingers lifted toward it, trembling, yearning. Her knees buckled, not with weakness, but with need. What if she was wrong? What if this was the only path that could save them, and she, out of fear or pride, refused it? The doubt hit like a second heartbeat, sharp and sickening, a needle threading through her resolve. But beneath the fear, beneath the hunger for peace, another voice stirred, quiet, resolute, hers.

And then she heard Mia's voice, sharp, fierce, afraid, echo from a place not in this world.

And in that moment of longing, she remembered.

Crawly had never offered anything freely. His gifts were chains in disguise, silk-wrapped shackles forged in false hope. The fruit wasn't peace. It was obedience, sculpted in sweetness. It was silence, a lullaby sung over the grave of will. It was surrender disguised as salvation.

The illusion shattered. Her hand dropped. Her eyes cleared, not suddenly, but with the painful slowness of someone waking from a beautiful lie. Her throat tightened. Her breath hitched like she'd nearly stepped off a ledge.

She turned toward him, not with fury, but clarity.

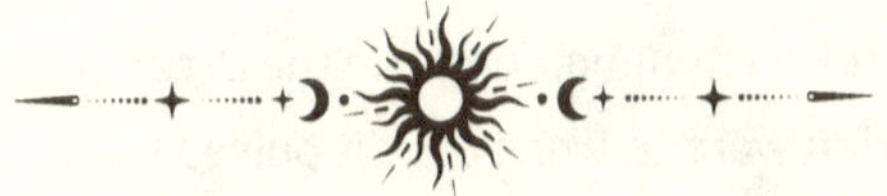

MIA SAT IN SILENCE, her body curled in on itself like a shell cracked under pressure. Her hands rested in her lap, limp and cold, the space between her fingers aching where the thread had once burned. The circle before her was dull now, stripped of its glow. A void instead of a window. A wound.

She had let go.

There were no screams, no thunder. Only the crushing silence of failure. Her thoughts clawed at her like rats in the dark: how easily she'd slipped. How good his voice had sounded. She could still feel the ghost of it behind her ear, warm and smooth as honeyed poison. Crawly hadn't needed to break her. He'd unraveled her, thread by trembling thread, and she'd let him.

The air around her was too still. The wards were crumbling. The house groaned under the weight of the veil pressing inward. Shadows moved at the corners of the windows, and the scratching had started again, tiny claws on wood, like hunger with teeth.

Her jaw clenched, but her body refused to rise. What good was standing? She had failed. The circle had dimmed. Sia was alone. And she,

Her hand brushed against something cold near her thigh.

The key.

Small. Plain. Unassuming. Forged in the Dream. Given to her by a liar wearing warmth like a coat. It pulsed faintly against her skin. She picked it up slowly, feeling its weight. Crawly had told her it would open any door. But he hadn't said what it would cost. It was his token. A mark of his favor. A foothold in her soul.

She could feel the tether still. Buried. Frayed. Flickering like a candle two rooms away. And if she reached for it now, she'd be too weak to hold it. She knew it. Her strength was spent. Her will had faltered. She had nothing left.

Except the key, and now Mia closed her fingers around it. The metal burned her palm but she didn't flinch. She gritted her teeth, forcing her magic to rise, raw, unstable, barely hers. The key responded instantly. Dark light bled from its surface. Whispered promises coiled through her mind. She felt them pressing against her ribs, wrapping around her spine. Not just temptation now. Power.

Crawly's power.

She inhaled sharply and stood. Her knees shook, but she held her ground. If he'd left her a weapon, she would turn it against him. Just this once, she would burn his gift instead of herself. The key flared in her hand. Shadows hissed from its seams. A voice, not quite his, not quite hers, whispered don't.

She drove her magic inward. The key shattered in a burst of red flame. Pain lanced through her palm, but it was clean. The darkness recoiled. The fog around the house screamed and scattered back, as if slapped by lightning. The thread snapped back into focus, sudden and sharp. It glowed in her mind like a steel wire drawn through fire.

Mia gasped and fell to her knees; for in that moment, she felt Sia. Not clearly. Not fully. But present. Alive.

Her eyes widened. She pushed both palms into the floor, grounding herself in salt and ash and will. She summoned the last of her magic, not the gift Crawly had left her, but the power she had earned. The fire that had once devoured her was now hers to command. She reached and the thread was palpable; it held.

And somewhere beyond the veil, her sister reached back.

CHAPTER 19

The Voice of Fire

Today they call them Angels and Demons. Tomorrow they'll call them something else.

A.C.

THE WIND ON MOUNT Athos had always carried the weight of prayer, salted with incense, rustling through olive trees like whispered scripture. But tonight, it carried something else. Something ancient and bitter.

Tobias stood at the outer wall of the monastery, his hand resting on the hilt of his sword as if it might leap from its sheath of its own accord. The sea was hidden beneath a crawling fog that hadn't been there minutes ago, thick as wool and wrong in its movement. It didn't drift. It advanced. Like it had purpose. Like it knew.

He had been trained to feel these things, to read the wind, the pressure in the air, the sound of the earth beneath his boots. Everything tonight was off. Even the prayers in his throat felt unfamiliar, like he was borrowing someone else's faith.

Behind him, bells rang in steady intervals, calling the monks to position. They moved like clockwork, disciplined, but not hurried. They weren't fools. They had faced darkness before. But not this darkness.

Garren Thomas emerged from the eastern watchtower, face grim beneath the steel edge of his helm. He carried his shield slung over his back and the heavy-bladed broadsword in his hand. He stopped beside Tobias without a word and studied the fog.

"They're testing us," Garren said. "Slowly. Like they're remembering how to be clever."

Tobias didn't respond at first. His jaw was clenched, his breath too shallow. "They've never needed to be clever," he said at last. "Just persistent."

And cruel, he didn't say.

He pressed two fingers to his comm rune when Gregory's voice crackled through. "Movement in the lower grove. Third formation in place."

"Hold unless they cross the line. Let them come to us." His voice was flat, but his stomach turned. He hated waiting. He hated the part just before a battle more than the blood itself.

The monks began lighting the sanctified braziers along the wall, firelight turning the fog gold and red. Scripture-etched shields were raised at every checkpoint, forming a wall of holy geometry. Every ward felt fragile to him, every chant one syllable away from faltering.

He had seen this before, in Apple Grove. In other places before that. He knew the shape of battle, the rhythm of despair. But here, here of all places, it felt personal.

Terrance Gilman knelt on one knee, crossbow drawn, scanning the mist. "Sir," he said, "it's not just fog. Something's moving inside it."

Of course it was.

Sister Martha McCormick had joined them silently, her white cloak fluttering as she whispered into the beads of her rosary. Her eyes glowed faintly, a mage's gaze, reading heat, movement, and breath.

"It's not a swarm," she said. "It's a procession. They're walking. Hundreds. Maybe more."

"Pilgrims," Tobias muttered, the word like ash on his tongue.

Then the chanting began.

It came from nowhere. From everywhere. Not words, just sound. A low, throbbing hum that vibrated beneath the ribs. It moved through the walls, through the shields, through the marrow of those who stood in defense. The light from the braziers bent slightly, as if ashamed to burn against it.

It felt like the opposite of faith. Like hearing your own prayer recited back to you by something that hated you.

Martha stumbled and braced herself against a stone post. "They're twisting the hymn. Turning holy resonance into a weapon. It's corrupted liturgy."

Tobias felt his sword vibrate faintly in its sheath. It had never done that before.

He looked to the foot of the hill just as the first shadows broke from the fog. First one. Then a dozen. Then too many to count.

Their bodies were slick with rot and armor made from bone and rusted chain. Some had human shapes. Some did not. One had no head, only a mouth in its chest, moaning wordless curses. They did not charge. They advanced in silence, as if daring the monks to speak first.

A bell cracked in its tower.

"Form lines!" Garren shouted, voice ringing like steel on stone. "Archers, take elevation! Lucretia, shield the northern slope!"

The monks obeyed without flinching. Prayers turned into war cries. The holy became the martial.

Tobias drew his sword, the old weight of it familiar. He felt its balance settle into his hand like an oath remembered. The fog surged forward as the first demon screamed.

The battle had begun.

ELLA STOOD NEAR THE inner sanctum, her back to the altar, her hand ghosting over the stone rail that separated the sacred chamber from the rest of the monastery. The air here held the weight of every prayer ever whispered within these walls. It should have been comforting. Instead, it pressed against her ribs like a slowly closing fist.

The sword rested where it had for centuries, untouched, gleaming faintly in the low light of flickering candles. It did not hum. It did not call. But it watched. She could feel it.

Uriel's sword.

She wasn't supposed to touch it. Not unless the wards broke. Not unless they were losing.

And they were. She could feel it in the earth beneath her feet. In the ragged edges of the sacred geometry around the chamber. The monastery was fraying. The chants from outside faltered more often now, replaced by screams, or worse, silence.

The hymn was inside the walls now. Not sung. Threaded. A corrupted vibration that twisted the air itself. It moved under her skin, whispering not words, but permissions. You could fix this. You know what to do.

She pressed her hands to the rail as if it might steady her.

Then Brother Demetrios appeared in the corridor outside, bloodied and broken. He didn't cry out. He didn't plead. He only said what she already feared.

"They're inside," he gasped. "Sanctum won't hold."

She moved toward him, instinctively, but another monk dragged him back. Somewhere beyond the chamber, something exploded. The tremor shuddered through the floor, up her legs, into her teeth. Fear surged up her spine like bile. This was not like the battle at the mall. This was not even like facing Crawly's lies. This was older. Holier. And it was failing.

The sword flared, briefly, a single rune on the pedestal burned white before fading. It was then that he arrived.

Tobias limped into the hall, blood drying on his tunic, breath ragged. He looked more ghost than brother. But his eyes, those still held steel. She ran to him. Grabbed his arm. "You're hurt."

He only shook his head, too tired for words. "They're coming."

Their eyes met. He didn't give orders. Didn't raise his voice. But his presence said what he wouldn't.

If not now, then never. Ella turned.

Her feet moved without permission. Her hands trembled. Her heart pounded not with fear, but with anticipation she couldn't control. She stepped into the sanctum. Every rune in the room lit up with her approach.

The heat from the sword reached her like the breath of a furnace. It wasn't just warmth, it was invitation. This was not a command; it was a choice, one she had always known she would make. But gods, she didn't want to.

She saw the moment before her hand touched it. Saw the light, the armor, the way her voice would vanish behind divine thunder. She saw Uriel's wings, vast and burning, and knew that once she took this step, she might never come fully back.

She hesitated only a moment before her fingers closed around the hilt. As she did, the world tilted. A blast of golden light erupted through the sanctum as if a sun had ignited inside stone. Her scream never made it out, cut off by wind and fire and memory. Her feet lifted from the ground. The blade pulsed in her grip, alive, ancient, awake.

At that moment, an angel stirred.

THE BATTLEFIELD TREMBLED.

From the sanctum came a sound like the world being ripped open, a resonance that split stone and soul alike. Light followed, pure and golden, surging from every seam in the monastery like the breath of something divine escaping a long-buried tomb. The air shuddered beneath it. The fog recoiled, folding backward as if in sudden awe or terror. Even the corrupted hymn faltered, the unholy chorus breaking into discordant fragments.

Tobias staggered. His ears rang with the force of the eruption, and the tiles beneath his boots vibrated with raw energy. The courtyard was a shattered ruin, pillars broken like snapped bones, incense burners overturned and still smoldering. Oil fires danced low along the walkways, casting twisted shadows that flickered and lunged with the movement of the battle.

Monks fought in every corner, blood mixing with ash, chants now hoarse with desperation. Garren stood amid the chaos, shield half-splintered, sword dragging a glowing arc through the smoke. Even he was flagging.

Then the light shifted.

Ella stepped into view, not so much walking as ascending through the ruined archway. The moment she crossed the threshold, the battlefield stilled in stunned silence.

She was no longer just Ella.

Her armor gleamed with liquid gold, lines of ancient scripture spiraling across the plates like fire chasing ink. Wings of molten light stretched wide from her back, each feather a sunbeam given form. Her face glowed, not with heat, but with impossible clarity. Her eyes were twin stars.

Uriel had awakened.

The demons reacted first. Screeches pierced the fog. The things that had stalked forward without fear now reeled back. Some turned to flee. Others charged mindlessly, hoping to strike before judgment fell. Before them was the Wrath of God, the protector of the Garden, the Angel of Death that smote down demons and man alike at the whims of the ancient Yahweh.

They were too late.

Ella, Uriel, moved with purpose beyond mortal speed. Her blade flared in her hand, transforming into a column of burning light. With a single swing, she parted the air and the creatures in it. One strike. Three corpses. Their bodies didn't fall. They disintegrated.

Tobias dropped to one knee. Not in submission. In awe. His heart thundered, not with fear, but reverence. He had seen holy power before. This was something else. He tried to rise, but pain lanced through his side. Blood had soaked through his tunic, hot and sticky. He gritted his teeth, struggling to remain upright. Then,

A hand, firm and cool, pressed to his ribs. Martha knelt beside him, robes streaked with soot, eyes closed in steady prayer. Magic pulsed from her fingers in soft waves. White light crept into the wound, knitting flesh and steadying breath.

"You're not allowed to die," she murmured.

He chuckled weakly. "You really could've led with that."

She didn't answer. Her lips kept moving. The spell held.

Across the courtyard, the angel moved like a storm wrapped in scripture. With each step, the ground responded, dust lifting around her like rising incense. She descended into the heart of the field and drove her sword into the stone. The impact sent a concussive shockwave rippling outward, flattening the remaining demons in a radius of holy fire. No cries. Just silence.

The hymn shattered like glass. Tobias exhaled, finally able to breathe without the pressure of that song crushing his chest. But the silence that followed was not peace; it was anticipation.

The angel stood amidst the wreckage, wings extended, eyes still alight. Ella was still inside, Tobias hoped, but she was buried deep beneath the divine fire. Even the monks began to lower their weapons, stepping back, unsure if what stood before them was salvation or something older.

Then the air behind Tobias shifted. Not a wind. Not a spell. A presence. The angel still stood, wings unfurled and burning, but the fog had parted, and for the first time, it did not return. Something else was arriving.

The space behind Tobias peeled open in slow spirals of blue flame. Light spilled outward, soft and cold like moonlight reflected in deep water. The scent of jasmine and woodsmoke poured from the rift, and the world quieted as though holding its breath.

Tobias turned. The portal shimmered like a ripple across glass. He didn't need to speak. He knew what it was.

Then came the voice. Not in the air. In the marrow of his bones. It reverberated with a power that made the hymn seem like a whisper in fog. It carried an authority that caused even Uriel to pause.

Sia. It was her. Not a vision. Not a memory. Sia, reaching through the veil like she'd always done, just in time.

"We need help. Come now."

For a second, no one moved. Monks stared in wonder. Garren's grip tightened on his sword, his gaze unreadable. Tobias took a step forward, drawn by instinct, by blood, by something deeper than either. Ella turned, Uriel still glowing behind her eyes, and without hesitation, stepped through the light. This was the trigger. The Templars moved as one, surging toward the portal to follow their angelic commander. Even several monks, eyes wide with awe, answered the call.

The Dream had opened its door.

Chapter 20

Echoes Rebound

The first condition of success in magick is purity
of purpose.

A.C.

THE PORTAL DIDN'T SIMPLY open, it tore. Like reality had been split by a divine blade. Blue fire spiraled outward in crackling rings, scorching the already-burned soil. Where the gate had not existed a moment ago, now it screamed with light and impossible depth.

Tobias stepped through first, boots thudding into blood-slick earth. The instant the air hit his lungs, he tasted smoke, iron, and something fouler, like burning rot. His sword was in his hand before he fully registered the battlefield.

The Farm was on fire.

Not metaphorically. Not figuratively. Real, roaring flame curled around the shattered remains of the west barn, its roof caved in, support beams blackened and snapping. The orchard trees, those peaceful sentinels, were ablaze, their fruit turned to ash, casting shadows like clawed fingers against a backdrop of hellish orange.

Wards that should have glowed with runic protection now fizzled and spat like dying wires. Sigils bled color. Circles meant to repel evil sparked intermittently, unable to hold back the tide.

And the sky,

It boiled.

A dome of churning fog twisted overhead, greenish and thick, threaded with veins of red lightning. Shadows skittered through the mist, too large, too fast, too wrong. The demonic horde poured from the trees, their bodies a blend of muscle, fang, and nightmare. Some were small and insectile, others tall as warhorses, hulking things made of bone and sinew.

The moment the demons saw the Dreamlight crack open, they shrieked, a sound like rusted bells and dying children.

Tobias raised his blade. "Formation Alpha! Anchor the breach!"

Garren emerged behind him like a war god carved from iron, shield raised and already intercepting a charging, three-jawed beast. He slammed the thing back with enough force to send its limbs flying.

Gilman took high ground instinctively, his crossbow clicking in a steady rhythm, three shots, three kills, pinning a winged demon mid-air and bringing it down in a heap.

Martha and Lucretia moved with eerie synchronicity, hands raised, chanting a liturgy Tobias only half-recognized. One called fire, the other light, and between them a sunburst exploded across the line, vaporizing two demons mid-leap.

Gregory broke left, running for the far perimeter where a gaping wound had opened in the wards. He passed Peter and Mariah, Peter holding precision stance with his rifle, firing exacting shots into demon weak points while Mariah called vines from the soil to entangle a charging beast mid-step.

Then the sky changed.

A golden streak ripped through the fog like the wrath of God descending.

Uriel.

No, Ella.

Wreathed in fire and glory, she flew high above the battlefield, sword in hand, her silhouette radiant against the chaos. Her wings outstretched like judgment, she descended in a blaze of heavenly fury. Demons scattered before her. Those who didn't were reduced to smoking heaps beneath her sword.

Tobias froze for just a heartbeat, watching her burn like a star. The angel had not left them. They still had a chance. He pressed two fingers to his comm rune, voice low but steady. "Eric. Sia. Marcus. We've arrived. Tell me where to hit."

The battle had not ended.

But for the first time, it felt like they might survive it.

MIA WAS ALREADY MOVING when she felt the tear in the Dream snap closed behind her. The weight of her failure still clung to her chest like smoke in her lungs. She didn't know where she was running, only that the battlefield screamed around her, and somewhere in the haze, her sister had returned.

The Farm was almost unrecognizable. It had once been a refuge, a quiet pocket of forgotten green. Now it was a crucible. Sigils cracked under demonic weight, and spells shattered like glass. The trees burned like candles. The air stank of ozone, blood, and old fear.

She ducked under a falling beam, her muscles sluggish from strain and guilt. Her foot slipped in mud laced with ash, and she hit the ground hard, pain flashing across her ribs. She forced herself up, coughing, teeth gritted. Somewhere, something massive bellowed, metal scraping bone. She flinched but didn't stop.

Then she saw her.

Sia stood amid the chaos like a vision from a forgotten dream, radiant, whole, and alight with power. Blue-white Dreamlight rippled off her in soft pulses, holding back the rot and fury of the world like a tidebreaker in a storm. Her eyes, those eyes, cut through the smoke and found Mia instantly.

For a split second, Mia stopped breathing. This had to be a memory, a hallucination or another trick. However, Sia turned and their eyes locked, everything in Mia's chest broke at once.

She ran. Feet slipping, arms pumping, lungs burning. She didn't think. She didn't hope. She just moved, as if her soul had decided before her body had caught up. Sia caught her mid-sprint, grounding her like a lightning rod. The impact knocked the air from Mia's lungs, but it didn't matter. She held on like she might fall apart if she let go.

"I almost lost you," Sia whispered into her hair, voice cracking around the edges.

Mia choked on her breath. "You did. I almost let go forever."

The Dreamlight pulsed with their heartbeat, climbing around them in soft, tidal rings. Sia pulled back, one hand rising to Mia's cheek. Her fingers trembled slightly, not with fear, but with tenderness. And then the magic surged.

It wasn't explosive. It was gentle. A quiet unraveling. Light spiraled through Mia's skin, washing away the rot, the ash, the stain she thought permanent.

Mia gasped as the transformation took hold. Her arms brightened, the ashen tint lifting like dust on the wind. Her horns shrank, curling into themselves with a hiss of fading power. The wings, so heavy, so hateful, crumbled away into glowing fragments. Her eyes burned, then cleared, twin mirrors of Sia's own.

But her tail remained, and when she opened her hand, the fire still flickered. However, it didn't hurt anymore; it wasn't gone, but it no longer ruled her. She commanded it. She stared at it a good long moment in disbelief.

"I'm not finished," she said quietly, not ashamed, just honest.

"No," Sia murmured, brushing her hair gently aside. "But you're finally facing the right direction."

A thunderous roar ripped through the orchard. The sky flashed orange. Something collapsed behind them with the weight of a falling mountain. The moment ended.

The sisters stepped apart, reluctantly, but ready. Back to back, they turned to face the next wave.

Together, they stood, sisters by blood, bonded by flame and Dream.

Eric hit the ground hard, boots skidding through torn earth that steamed with the remnants of demonic bile. A tree exploded nearby, splinters whipping through the air like shrapnel, and he ducked reflexively, cloak scorched at the hem.

"Could've portaled us slightly farther from the firestorm," he muttered, flicking a protective sigil into the air. The rune flared briefly, shielding him from the burst of heat.

The battlefield was a nightmare painting in motion. Screaming demons, trees writhing with corrupted vines, Marcus overhead in half-dragon form, sweeping arcs of fire through the chaos like a celestial scythe. Peter's rifle cracked behind him. Mariah's voice rose in strange, harmonic syllables that made the grass hiss and bend.

Then the air dropped ten degrees. The noise faltered. Eric knew that kind of silence. That weight. Something powerful was coming, he felt his breath hitch.

Marcus landed hard beside him, human again, smoke pouring from his skin. "Something's wrong."

"Thanks for the update, Captain Obvious," Eric said, but his voice lacked real bite. His fingers flexed, casting detection sigils wide.

Then the veil tore. It wasn't subtle. The trees bowed outward. The fog reversed direction. The ground cracked like an eggshell splitting. And through that wound in the world stepped something huge, twelve feet tall and armored in bone-etched iron, every step it took leaving black scorch marks.

Its face was a mask of cruelty, eyes like holes burned in metal. A flanged crown of horn encircled its scalp, and its jaw split downward with a sickening wet click, revealing rows of inner teeth. Its flail dragged behind it like an executioner's promise, each link glowing white-hot, bending the air around it.

Eric froze. Real fear rooted in his chest like ice. It wasn't just the size or the weapon, it was the pressure. The presence. Like a black hole of hatred had taken a body and learned how to walk.

"A Hell Commander," Marcus said, voice hushed.

Eric's breath caught. The words weren't a revelation, they were confirmation of the nightmare now walking toward them. His stomach turned cold. Not with fear exactly, but with the understanding that this was no brute. This was command given flesh, authority shaped by violence and sanctified in the hells.

The air thickened with its presence. Each step it took was deliberate, patient, and ruinous. The ground beneath its feet blistered, blackened, and cracked open in spiderweb patterns. Grass hissed and curled to ash, the soil itself recoiling from its touch. The aura around it shimmered, not like heat, but like hatred. A distortion field of raw malice.

The armor it wore was impossibly detailed, etched with runes in a language Eric didn't recognize, yet somehow understood. Pain. Submission. Ruin. These weren't decorations. They were mandates, etched into steel.

Its eyes were pits. Not glowing, not alive, just voids, endless and hungry. And that jaw, split vertically, wasn't just for show. Eric could feel what it was made for: to unmake. To devour what spoke truth.

He blinked sweat out of his eyes. Not from heat. From the pressure. Like standing too close to a collapsing star. The veil behind it rippled with every breath it took. Even the fog seemed to hesitate.

This wasn't just a threat.

It was a statement.

Eric's throat was dry. "No shit."

They didn't have time to gawk. The lesser demons parted before it, reverent, hissing like acolytes. The thing raised its flail and roared, a sound that didn't travel through the air but through bone, making Eric's teeth ache.

For a heartbeat, he remembered he was mortal. Soft. Breakable.

Then Marcus grabbed his arm. "Tactics?"

Eric's mind spun, then focused. Fast. "We bottleneck it. Between the standing stones. I drop a leyline sink behind it, you go full dragon and hit it in the heart while I hold the field."

Marcus raised an eyebrow. "You're baiting it with me?"

"I'm baiting it with both of us," Eric snapped, flaring sigils into the dirt with practiced speed. "Because we're that kind of stupid."

Marcus growled, golden light beginning to curl around his shoulders.

Eric drew a deep breath. The magic coalesced around his hands, cold, brilliant, blinding.

"Let's show this bastard what happens when the backbone of the team gets pissed."

SIA MOVED THROUGH THE chaos with the stillness of some-one walking within a memory. The battlefield roared, steel shrieked, demons howled, trees split with thunder-cracks, but within the Dream-space coiling at her heels, she moved like a ghost through fire. Everything slowed. Everything stilled.

Her feet slid over ground slick with ash, her boots leaving no prints. The Dream curled upward from the soil like breath on cold glass, faintly luminous, casting reflections of things that hadn't happened yet. It showed her the echo of what was to come, even as she moved within the now.

She didn't just see the Farm, she saw beneath it. The veins of power running through its soul. The frayed wards. The broken roots. And, more than anything, the threads that bound her people together. The Dream showed her them.

Tobias. She saw him through the smoke, back-to-back with Garren, shield raised, sword slashing clean through a demon's throat. His stance wasn't just trained, it was inherited, built from years of discipline and burden. He was fire held in by structure, the shield she had always known would stand between her and the worst.

Garren moved with him like a second spine. They weren't just fighting. They were holding.

Further off, Peter knelt beside a broken wall, rifle braced against a bloodied stone, his aim unwavering. He fired once, pause, again. Each shot was a prayer answered. He didn't flinch, didn't falter. Mariah stood beside him, radiant with fury, her voice raised in layered syllables that weren't Latin, weren't English, just true. The air around her rippled. The wind obeyed.

Marcus soared above, half-winged now, cloaked in golden scales. He dove like a judgment, breath igniting the sky in torrents of fire. And below him, Eric's hands were aflame with wards, circles, and command. He barked an incantation that sliced through a charging demon like a scythe made of scripture. The fear in him had been channeled into razor-sharp resolve.

They weren't just holding the line.

They were its anchor, its shield, and its heartbeat.

Every motion they made carved defiance into the ground; Tobias's measured strikes weren't just skill, they were declarations that this would not be their last stand. Garren's shield was less a piece of armor and more a wall of intent, unmoved even as demon claws rang against it like thunder on steel. They absorbed every blow not because they had to, but because no one else could.

When Sia looked at them, she didn't see a battle line.

She saw a promise. That no matter how far the Dream frayed, or how many times the veil tore, they would not break.

And then, Mia.

Mia burned. Not destructively. Not chaotically. She moved like wildfire given will. Her hellfire licked through demon ranks in wide arcs, each movement graceful, precise. Her tail snapped behind her like punctuation to her fury. Her eyes carried the fury of ancient forgotten gods, fierce and alive with scorned wrath. Not monstrous. Not cursed.

They were free.

And Sia knew this was no longer the girl who had been pulled from death. This was the girl who had walked through it and chosen to rise anyway. She had walked through fire and now came forth unburned. These people fighting around them, they weren't just allies. They weren't just her team. They were her family. Not in name, not in legality or blood or bond made in safety. They were a family forged in fire, in fracture and in faith.

The demons charged, and Sia stepped forward and raised her hands. Dreamlight surged outward like wings unfurling, catching the sky in shimmering arcs. The air warped as the field responded, not just to power, but to belief.

Her belief in them. Her belief in this. The wave hit the front line, smashing demons to dust and unraveling those too proud to fall. Sia stood alone in the storm's eye, her pulse steady.

And let the Dream sing through her veins.

CHAPTER 21

The Weight of Light

The key of joy is disobedience.

A.C.

THE WORLD SHOOK.

Marcus stood near the blackened ridge just above the lower field, his chest heaving, smoke curling from his skin where scaled patches hadn't fully receded. His breath was shallow, heart hammering a rhythm more beast than man. He was caught somewhere between muscle memory and instinct, between draconic wrath and human awe.

The battlefield below had gone quiet. Not silent, but breathless, because the war no longer centered on soldiers, wards, or spells.

It centered on them.

Uriel and the Hell Commander.

She hovered above the scorched ground like a sword un-sheathed by heaven. Her wings unfurled wide, flame-edged and humming with the power of unyielding judgment. Golden fire poured from the seams of her armor like divine blood. Her sword wasn't a weapon, it was a verdict, carried on the breath of creation.

Opposite her, the Commander loomed like a wound given form. Twelve feet tall, encased in cracked obsidian plates, infernal symbols glowing in and out of alignment across its hide. Its eyes were coals from a furnace older than time, and its presence warped the air around it. The flail in its grip dragged through the earth, igniting furrows with every grinding pull.

They circled each other like titans who remembered the First War.

Marcus could barely move. Not because of fear, he'd fought gods before, but because his soul couldn't decide whether to kneel or flee. This was not a duel. This was an unmaking, and Uriel struck first.

The air cracked with sound as she vanished from view, reap-pearing mid-dive with a spear-thrust of radiant fire that split the tree line in half. Her sword cleaved downward with all the force of a star being born. It struck the Commander's shoulder with a burst of molten iron, shattering the upper plate and peeling a slab of armor clean away.

The demon shrieked, not in pain, but in recognition. It responded with a backswing of its flail that howled through the air like a collapsing cathedral. The weapon struck Uriel in the ribs, sending her hurtling across the field like a falling meteor. She hit the cliffside with a thunderous impact that turned the hill to dust.

Marcus flinched. A human would've been obliterated.

Uriel rose.

No scream. No hesitation. The fire around her intensified until the very air shimmered. Her wings burst outward, slashing arcs of golden heat that scorched the sky itself. Time seemed to ripple. Sound bent. Marcus tasted the Dream on his tongue, the boundary between what was and what could be thinning.

She launched again.

What followed was chaos distilled into poetry: bursts of flame, columns of black light, eruptions of raw force that flattened trees and split the earth. The Commander swung with hate-crafted weight, each blow distorting reality. Uriel countered with surgical vengeance, her strikes carving hymns into the atmosphere.

It was not a fight. It was scripture.

And Marcus, watching, knew he was in the presence of something vast and terrible. He'd seen dragons clash. He'd felt the breath of ancient wyrms. But this?

This was judgment incarnate. And yet even as she struck the killing blow, driving her sword through the Commander's chest with a scream that echoed between heaven and hell, Marcus felt no peace.

The demon's body crumbled into smoke and bone dust. The field went still. Uriel stood, divine and eternal, wings flared, sword embedded in scorched earth. She did not fall, nor did she sheathe her blade.

The fire in her eyes had not dimmed.

Marcus swallowed against the tightness in his throat.

The Commander was dead.

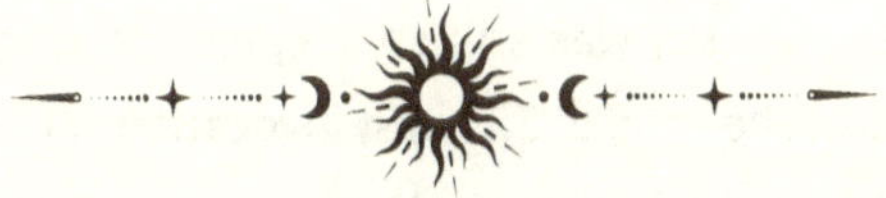

THE AIR DIDN'T CLEAR; it remained thick with smoke and Dreamlight, but something deep beneath it shifted. The demons around them hesitated. The cohesion that had once pushed them in perfect fury faltered. One growled and stepped back. Another, mid-charge, veered off and sprinted into the trees. And then the collapse began, not just retreat, but unraveling. They broke formation like birds startled from a wire.

Eric didn't cheer. There was no breath left for joy. Only orders.

He straightened his shoulders, rotated his wrists once to shake off the tension, and tapped his comm. His voice cut through the haze like a snapped wire.

"Push the line. Don't chase. Clean sweeps. Anchor spells every forty feet. Team Excelsior, disperse perimeter threats. Mia, Sia, you're on ward defense. Mariah, you and Peter lock the breach."

Affirmatives echoed back, calm, crisp, trained. These weren't survivors anymore. They were warriors. They belonged here.

He moved with them, boots slapping through waterlogged soil and demonic ichor, his hands painting protective glyphs mid-run. The spell arrays burned under his skin like living circuitry, muscle memory overriding exhaustion. His head ached from focus. His eyes burned from smoke. But his lines held.

Above them, the sky was still split open, not with light, but with memory. The echo of Sia's last invocation was carved into the very clouds, a ripple of starlight woven across the ruined canopy. Even the Dream trembled with the weight of what had been unleashed.

A shadow moved.

A demon broke from the brush, silent and sudden. Eric turned, hand already glowing. One word. One sigil. The creature folded inward like paper collapsing into flame. No scream. Just gone.

"Not today," he muttered under his breath. "Not for any of you."

He caught sight of Marcus across the battlefield, mid-transition, smoke trailing from his shoulders, his mouth still glowing faintly with fire. They locked eyes. There was no need for words. They didn't command with speeches.

They commanded with survival, and the team followed.

Excelsior moved in perfect form. Garren and Tobias led the outer sweep, Garren's shield smashing through beasts while Tobias's sword cut like a line drawn across reality. Gilman's bolts whispered through the fog, pinning limbs with mathematical precision.

Sia and Mia blazed through the center like twin storms, one of flame, one of mist. Sia bent the field itself, folding terrain into traps. Mia's fire danced along the lines like a surgeon's blade, her control sharpened by purpose.

Peter's rifle cracked only when it needed to. Mariah walked the line like a priestess rebuking darkness, the roots and winds obeying without hesitation.

It wasn't pretty and it wasn't clean, but it was victory.

Eric finally lowered his hands as the last shadow fell. His arms shook. His wards were gone. His voice felt miles away. But they were still standing. And the Farm, torn, cracked, burned, was still theirs. He reached up, thumb brushing the edge of the comm embedded just beneath his jaw.

"Status check," he said, voice hoarse. "Everyone sound off."

THE BATTLEFIELD WAS QUIET now, but Tobias felt no peace.

Ash drifted down like snow, settling into the still-smoking ruins of what had been the orchard, the barn, the fields. It gathered in his hair, clung to the weave of his coat, and mixed with blood and dust on the ground like the final breath of a world. Fires crackled in the distance, sending trails of smoke skyward in slow, spiraling ribbons. A nearby ward stone pulsed faintly, its glow flickering with every heartbeat.

The Farm had survived, but only just, and at the center of the silence stood Uriel.

He was radiant and terrible. The shattered remnants of the Hell Commander lay scattered at his feet, reduced to ash and absence. His sword remained planted in the scorched earth, the point sunk deep into stone. Heat shimmered from the blade's edge. Wings of gold and fire stretched outward, casting impossible shadows through the smoke-choked air.

And Ella was gone. Not in body, Tobias knew that, but in presence. What stood before him was no longer his sister; it was something older, something higher, and something else.

He stepped forward slowly, each footfall crunching through debris and soot. His knees ached. His arm throbbed. The weight of his sword dragged at his shoulder like the gravity of memory itself. But he didn't stop. He couldn't. He moved as if approaching the mouth of a volcano, knowing it could swallow him whole.

"Uriel," he called softly, voice low, controlled. "It's over."

The angel did not move. Golden fire continued to burn in his eyes, steady, impersonal, watching. The sword remained unmoved. His wings held their position like divine sentinels. He stood not as a victor but as a consequence. Tobias tried again.

"Let her go."

There was no answer. Only the mounting pressure of proximity to a being that didn't understand the word enough. Heat radiated from the angel's form, thick and oppressive. It wrapped around Tobias like a cloak too heavy to lift. The scent of ozone and incense stung his nostrils.

"You've done what you came to do," he said, his voice fraying at the edges now. "You saved them. You saved us. But she's not with us anymore, and you are."

Uriel tilted his head, slow and deliberate, as though parsing the language of mortals took effort. There was no empathy in the movement. Only evaluation.

Tobias's fingers brushed the hilt of his blade. He didn't draw it, but his grip tightened. Not in threat, but in readiness, should that line be tested.

"I'm not giving you a command," he said. "I'm making a request. One soul to another. Please. Give her back."

The angel's fingers flexed around the sword's hilt. The Dream itself seemed to pull taut, a vibration building behind Tobias's eyes like a song he didn't know he remembered.

And then,

"Stop."

Sia's voice sliced through the tension like silver drawn through silk. She stepped forward through the veil of ash, the Dream-light still clinging to her form like an echo. Her eyes gleamed faintly beneath the soot, rimmed in silver, and her presence radiated not magic, but authority.

Uriel turned his head. Slowly. With intention.

Sia did not flinch. **"You were summoned,"** she said, not loud, but firm. **"You answered. You fought. But she is not your vessel. She is her own. And she is ours."**

The words hung heavy, wrapped in Dream, underlined by a gravity that bent the very breath around her. Tobias could feel it, not just power, but something older and something true. Sia closed the distance, step by steady step, until she stood at the edge of the sword's reach. Her voice did not waver.

"You've fulfilled your duty. Now relinquish what is not yours."

The moment held. Uriel looked at her. Tobias couldn't begin to guess what passed in that gaze. But then the angel's hand lifted from the blade. He drew it from the earth, slow, smooth, deliberate, and the air flared white-gold. The light burned at its brightest, then dimmed all at once as he turned the blade and slid it into the scabbard across his back.

His wings folded into nothing. The fire in his eyes faded and Ella collapsed to the ground. Tobias caught her, sinking to one knee. Her weight was terrifyingly light. Her skin burned with residual heat, but her breath came shallow and real. Alive. He wrapped his arms around her, grounding her, grounding himself.

Uriel lingered a moment longer. Then the Dream pulled him away, folding him into silence, into wind, into memory.

Gone.

Tobias looked up. Sia stood where the angel had been, her hands shaking, her chest rising and falling in slow, deliberate breaths.

"It's over," she said. And this time, Tobias believed her.

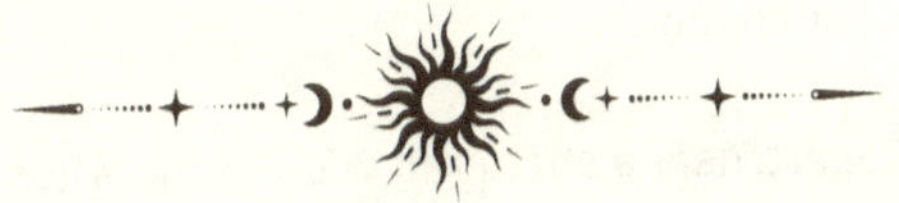

Sia stood among the ruins of the battlefield, the soles of her boots crunching softly over scorched fragments of warding chalk and brittle, glassed earth. Ash clung to the tips of grass where any had survived, and soot spiraled gently in the dying wind. The smoke was thinning, curling in ghostlike tendrils beneath a bruised and sullen sky, but the air still pulsed with something older than violence, something sacred and spent. It wasn't just magic that lingered in her lungs. It was memory, grief, and the strange stillness that followed after something titanic had passed through.

She said nothing. She didn't need to. Her silence was not absence; it was reverence.

Around her, the others moved through the aftermath like revenants surfacing from a dream. Tobias knelt in the scorched grass, arms wrapped around Ella's unconscious body, cradling her like something precious he'd nearly lost. His face was buried in her hair, lips moving in a whisper that didn't need an audience. Love was its own language.

Mariah moved along the edges of the field, her hands trailing through shattered bark and broken branches. Roots stirred beneath her steps, rising obediently to her song, an old, soft melody not meant for ears, but for the wounded earth itself. Beside her, Peter kept vigil. His rifle was slung over one shoulder, but his gaze was sharp, eyes scanning the tree line not for threat, but for change.

Eric stood apart, near a shattered ward-stone whose light was flickering like the last ember of a dying fire. He ran his fingers along the cracks with an expression carved from equal parts fatigue and calculation. The ash on his cheek was a pale line across his skin, but he hadn't noticed it, too busy rebuilding the world in his mind one protective layer at a time.

Marcus loomed nearby, arms crossed, smoke still curling faintly from his jaw. His posture was relaxed in the way only warriors could manage after battle, not in comfort, but in the knowledge that the worst had passed. His eyes swept the horizon with the quiet steadiness of a guardian who knew the fight would come again.

And Mia...

Mia stood alone at the site of Uriel's departure, her arms wrapped around herself, her tail twitching like an ember that refused to go out. Her fire had dimmed, yes, but it hadn't vanished. She had not cried. She had not collapsed. She had stood, as if refusing to let her sister's return eclipse her own rebirth.

Sia walked slowly through the clearing, her every step weighed with reflection. These people, this unlikely band of misfits, survivors, scholars, soldiers, and broken things, they weren't just a team. They had become something more through the fire.

They were her family. Not by blood. Not by oath. But through battle, trust, and the choice to stay.

She stopped at the place where the grass had been turned to molten glass and looked around, not to assess damage, but to see. To memorize. Each of them had crossed some unspoken line tonight. They had been tested and changed. And they had come through the other side not perfect, but together.

Sia breathed out slowly, the Dreamlight still curling faintly beneath her skin. For the first time since the nightmare began, she allowed herself a moment of stillness. No instructions. No summoning. No commands.

Just gratitude.

Whatever came next, they would face it not as scattered pieces, but as one. They already had. And they had won.

CHAPTER 22

After the Storm

For I am divided for love's sake, for the chance of union.

A.C.

THE FARM WAS STILL standing.

That fact alone might have been a miracle. But Eric wasn't in the mood for miracles. He didn't trust them. Miracles came with strings. And whatever strings had once protected this place had been cut, frayed, or burned away.

He walked slowly through the charred remnants of the east fields, each step crunching over ash, shattered glass wards, and splinters of sigil-marked wood. The once-vibrant grass, lush and sun-warmed just days ago, had been reduced to a carpet of soot and bone dust. Blackened stalks clawed up from the soil like skeletal fingers reaching for breath. Trees stood as twisted husks, some still smoldering, others cracked down their trunks as if the screams of the Dream had split them from within. The orchard no longer smelled like apples. It smelled like fire and ruin.

Everything reeked of loss, burned magic, scorched memory, old blood baked into stone. Even the air tasted wrong. Thin. Overused. Like it had been borrowed from someplace holier and left behind tainted.

Beneath it all, the land still bled, not red, but gold and blue. Power. Ancient magic poured from broken channels, puddling into the ley lines like ink spilled across fragile parchment. Wards had cracked and bled their strength into the veins of the earth. Runes, once etched with elegance and precision, now curled like old paper left in flame. The Dream tugged at the edges of everything, stretched and worn thin like a gauze soaked through.

He reached the base of the southern hill and crouched beside the main ward-stone. It had once been a beacon, bright, steady, humming with resonance every time he passed it. Now it was cracked down the center, a jagged lightning bolt frozen in rock.

Eric laid his palm against it. Cold.

No hum. No spark. No pushback from the barrier. Just silence.

Just a dead stone and an echo.

Footsteps approached from behind, deliberate and slow. Marcus emerged through the dissipating haze, his silhouette backlit by the dying glow of Dreamlight still flickering along the orchard's boundary. His boots crushed through the remnants of a shattered binding circle, each step sending up the ghost of a glyph.

He said nothing. Just stood there, arms folded, the heat of his recent transformation still radiating faintly from his skin. His eyes swept the horizon, not as a warrior scanning for threat, but as a guardian surveying what remained of a home.

"We lost too much," Eric said, voice dry. Each word scraped out of his throat like it had been stored in a box of nails. "Half the perimeter runes are slag. The lattice on the northern ridge isn't just damaged. It's warped. Like something tore through the veil and decided not to close the door on its way out."

"It didn't just leave it open," Marcus replied. His voice had the weight of stone, final, steady, ancient. "It unmade it. The line between here and what's beyond? It's not a door anymore. It's a wound."

Eric sat back on his heels, his joints protesting. Every muscle ached, every spell-thread in his body felt like it had been pulled too tight. But worse than the physical pain was the gnawing churn of his mind refusing to slow down. The war wasn't done. This was just the eye of the storm.

"We have what, maybe a week before someone comes looking? A month if we're lucky? One demon whispers to the wrong ear and they'll come back, and they'll bring more."

"Next time," Marcus murmured, his gaze still locked on the burned horizon, "they'll bring more than one commander. They'll bring a warband. Or something older."

Eric dragged a hand down his face. His skin felt like parchment stretched over embers.

"Dobahold?" he asked, already knowing the answer.

Marcus shook his head. "It was never meant for siege. It's a place of counsel, tradition. High cliffs, deep caverns, sure, but too many blind turns, too few defenses. It can house us. Hide a few. But it can't hold the line. Not against what's coming."

Eric's fingers flexed. His nails scraped against the stone. "Then we need something else. A fortress. Something not built for comfort, but for endurance. Something old. Layered. Enchanted."

"And forgotten," Marcus added. "Hidden. Blessed. Guarded by more than walls."

They both fell silent.

Above them, the wind stirred the smoke into frayed ribbons. The tree line looked like a blackened mouth, yawning toward the horizon. Somewhere beyond the wreckage, Excelsior packed their gear in quiet coordination. The sound of metal scraping wood, of boots shifting debris, carried softly. In the orchard, Mariah's voice lifted into the ruined branches, her hymn more lullaby than spell. Roots stirred at her feet.

The Farm was still trying to heal.

But the damage went too deep.

Eric rose slowly. His coat was torn. His wards were spent. His spirit felt wrung dry. But he stood, and that counted.

"We tell them today," he said. "Let the kids sleep, but tomorrow? We start looking for a new sanctuary, find a place we can really hold up. This place gave us time. But we need a place that can give us a future."

Marcus nodded once, the motion crisp and silent. "The war's not waiting. And neither should we."

Together, they turned from the fractured heart of the sanctuary they'd nearly lost, and walked back through the broken ash-field toward their wounded family, already thinking of what must come next.

THE FIRST THING ELLA noticed was the silence.

It wasn't the eerie, suffocating kind that followed battle, this was deeper. A stillness that seemed to extend inside her, like every echo of movement or thought had been muffled behind layers of gold light. Her body felt distant, like she was only partially in it, only half of her had returned from wherever Uriel had taken the rest. The other half still lingered somewhere outside time, standing on the edge of revelation.

She lay on her side, one hand curled beneath her cheek. The cot beneath her was warm, the blanket soft, but her skin prickled like it didn't belong to her. For a moment she might've convinced herself it was over, that she had woken from a bad dream. But her fingers twitched involuntarily. Her breathing came too slow. And something still burned faintly beneath her ribs, not pain exactly, but pressure. Like a presence folded tightly inside her chest.

She opened her eyes.

The light in the room was dim, filtered through the gray of a recovering sky. Someone had patched the cracks in the window with strips of canvas and prayer-ribbons. The scent of healing salves and burned sage lingered in the air, woven with faint traces of sanctified ash. The wards had been redrawn in chalk at each corner of the room, but she could feel them, weak, thin, not meant to hold back another storm, only to whisper comfort.

And sitting beside her, one hand gently resting on the edge of the cot, was Tobias. He looked older than she remembered. Not in age, his face was still the same, lined with stubborn determination, but in posture. In the set of his shoulders. The quiet way his hand didn't tremble, even though his eyes looked like they hadn't closed in days. He was watching her not with fear, or urgency, but with a kind of rooted presence she hadn't realized she'd needed until she saw it.

Ella shifted slightly, her voice a whisper scraped from the bottom of a dry well. "Did we win?"

Tobias smiled softly. It didn't reach his eyes. "We're alive. So I think that counts."

She tried to smile back, but it faltered halfway. Her throat tightened. The silence inside her hadn't gone. It had just settled in deeper, like a tide waiting to rise again.

"I remember... things," she murmured. "Flashes. Heat. Light. I was watching from behind my own eyes. And then I wasn't. I was... burning. Not just with fire, with purpose."

Tobias didn't interrupt. He let her speak, let her unravel, patient as a tree holding the storm's memory.

"Uriel didn't leave," she whispered. "I can still feel him. He's not speaking. But he's... waiting. Like he's standing just behind a curtain, listening."

Tobias leaned forward slightly. "Then we make sure you never stand there alone. We figure this out. One step at a time."

Ella's gaze drifted to the corner of the room. There, propped carefully against a chair, was the sword.

VERITAS.

The letters gleamed faintly in the dim light, the blade's edge still coated in dried ash and the last threads of holy flame. It didn't hum. It didn't glow. But it pulsed with presence, like a heartbeat made of scripture.

"I don't want to lose myself," she said. "I'm afraid if I call him again... next time, he won't give me back."

"You won't lose yourself," Tobias said. "Because you're not alone. And you're not just a vessel. You're Ella. And no one, angel or otherwise, gets to rewrite that."

A long silence passed, but this time it wasn't hollow. It was whole. Weighty with what had been said, and what didn't need to be. For the first time since she woke, Ella nodded. Outside, the wind shifted. The storm had passed, but something new stirred in the distance. Not dread. Not ruin. A calling. A journey had begun, and she already knew the name of the path.

Veritas.

IT COILED LOW AND slow in her chest, like embers buried under ash, still glowing, still alive, waiting. She walked the outer edge of the Farm's wreckage barefoot, the soles of her feet pressing into cracked earth that still steamed faintly from yesterday's fight. The ground was hot in places. In others, it pulsed with cooling power where ward lines had burned themselves into the soil. Her path wound between scorched fencing, overturned stones, and the last charred bones of what had once been fruit trees.

The wind carried the scent of ozone, smoldering rootwork, and scorched cedar. It clung to her clothes and hair, threaded with the faint metallic edge of hellfire long since spent. Every step felt like walking through the breath of what they'd survived, and the shadow of what she'd nearly become.

She should have felt triumphant. Or at least relieved. But all Mia felt was the ache of unfinished penance. Her skin had mostly returned to its old self, but every time she blinked, she could still feel the phantom weight of horns across her scalp. The tail twitched when she forgot to control it. Her fingers sparked when her thoughts strayed too far inward.

The hunger hadn't left. It had just learned how to wait.

She didn't flinch from it anymore. But neither did she trust it.

Ahead, near the remains of the old garden, a faint shimmer of green poked through the blackened dirt. Mariah sat on a low stone bench, her sleeves rolled up, palms buried in the soil as if coaxing the roots to remember what life felt like. Her lips moved in quiet cadence, a hymn Mia couldn't hear but could feel in her teeth, a song of rebirth sung from a place deeper than language.

Mia hovered at the edge, uncertain. She didn't want comfort. She didn't deserve it. But her feet refused to turn away.

Mariah looked up before she made her choice. "You came farther than most would dare."

Mia shrugged, arms folded, voice low. "Didn't have much of a choice."

"You always have a choice," Mariah said, tone soft but edged in truth. "That's what makes it matter."

The words struck like a balm and a blade.

Mia sat slowly, her weight pressing the scorched grass into dust. The silence between them wasn't awkward. It was dense with meaning, shared understanding, unspoken grief, and the quiet miracle of survival.

"I almost ruined everything," Mia said. Her voice didn't shake. It just... landed. Flat. Final. "I wanted to be strong enough to help. I wasn't. I nearly got Sia killed."

Mariah didn't argue. Didn't rush to absolve. She let the truth hang in the air until it settled into soil.

"You weren't made to be perfect," she said. "None of us were. We're shaped by fire, not built to withstand it unscathed. What matters is that when the fire tried to claim you, you reached back toward yourself."

Mia stared down at her hands. The claws were gone. Her skin was pale, smudged with soot, but mostly hers again. The tail flicked once, curling across her ankles like a question she hadn't learned to answer.

"I don't know what I am anymore." The admission came out brittle, almost brittle enough to crack.

Mariah turned fully toward her, one hand settling on her shoulder, firm and warm.

"You're someone who still gets to decide," she said. "And if you'll let me, I'd like to help you learn how."

Mia looked up. Her eyes shimmered, not from tears, but from heat. Something new flared behind them, deep beneath the surface.

It wasn't fire.

It was hope.

She nodded.

Mariah smiled, and without a word, placed her hand back to the earth. Tiny green stems unfurled between their feet. And the garden began to bloom again.

THE LIGHT WAS STRANGE in the hour just before dusk, filtered through smoke-smeared clouds and glinting off the fractured ward lines still etched into the landscape. The Farm lay stretched below like the carcass of a memory, half ash, half miracle. Patches of scorched earth pulsed faintly where old magic still smoldered, and the air carried the scent of lavender and ozone, clinging to everything like a ghost that didn't know it should have moved on.

Sia sat on the crumbling roof of the old barn, legs dangling over the side, sketchbook balanced on her knees. Her fingertips were blackened with charcoal, Dreamlight glittering faintly in the cracks between her knuckles. Each line she drew sank deep, not just into paper, but into memory. She wasn't drawing monsters this time. Or prophecies. Or twisted cities wrapped in ribcages and sorrow.

She was drawing them.

The team. Her family. Not as soldiers. Not as saints. As people. Tobias with his quiet steadiness, leaning just slightly into the edge of the frame like he never wanted to center himself. Ella with her guarded eyes and the faint glow behind them. Marcus, mid-laugh, lines creased around his eyes and mouth, a moment caught in warmth. Mia, still half-shadow, still part fire, still here. Eric, one eyebrow raised, arms crossed in that way that meant he was already planning a backup plan. Mariah with her hands in the dirt, fingers coaxing roots to grow even where ash still clung. Peter, too fast to catch still, rendered in motion.

Each face was a tether. A grounding. A reason.

She didn't look up when she heard the footsteps behind her. She didn't need to. The Dream shifted. Her pulse adjusted. And the weight in the world tilted just slightly, familiar now.

Mia climbed up beside her, boots scraping against old wood, breath short but steady. She settled into place like someone who wasn't sure if she was allowed to stay, but stayed anyway.

They sat without speaking. Letting the moment fill itself.

The sky above them was a slow bleed of color, amber into lavender, lavender into deep blue. The stars were starting to push through the haze, tentative but insistent. Below, the Farm still breathed. Still steamed. Still tried to remember how to be alive.

"You drawing nightmares or memories?" Mia asked, voice low, laced with something that wasn't quite sarcasm.

Sia flipped the page toward her without breaking stride. "Neither. Something in between."

Mia stared at the sketch. Her fingers brushed the edge. "We don't get many of those," she said. "In between."

"No," Sia said, voice soft. "We don't."

A gust of wind curled through the broken beams below them, carrying with it the faint chime of metal on metal. Someone had hung wind chimes from a cracked porch post. The sound was barely audible, like laughter heard through a dream.

Mia leaned back on her hands, eyes on the horizon. "So... what now?"

Sia closed the sketchbook carefully, hands lingering on the cover. A low pulse throbbed beneath the leather binding, the Dream still listening, still awake.

"Now?" she said. "We make the world ready."

The barn creaked gently beneath them, wood shifting with memory. Far below, Eric's voice echoed faintly, issuing instructions, reminding someone to restock supplies. A flicker of dragonlight lit the far fence where Marcus stood sentinel.

There was still work being done. There was always more work to do.

They didn't speak after that. Not right away. Instead they watched as the stars emerged fully from behind the veil of ash and cloud. The sky was vast again. Bruised, cracked, but not broken.

They weren't done, not even close. But they were still together.

And for the first time in what felt like forever, Sia believed that was enough to begin again.

CHAPTER 23

Fractures in the Garden

I was not content to believe in a personal devil
and serve him, in the ordinary sense of the word.
I wanted to get hold of him personally and
become his chief of staff.

Aleister Crowley

I WAS NOT CONTENT to believe in a personal devil and serve him, in the ordinary sense of the word. I wanted to get hold of him personally and become his chief of staff.
Aleister Crowley

The Dream was quieter now. Not gone. Just... retreated. Like breath after a scream. It hung low and wide, like smoke on a battlefield, the kind that doesn't rise but settles, waiting to be remembered.

In the place that was not a place, beneath the veil and memory, beneath the lies of gods and the echoes of creation, something coiled through the Garden. Not the new one. Not the fragile sapling Sia had dared to call into being. But the old one. The foundation. The wound. The Garden that remembered sin not as failure, but as origin.

Crowley walked its edge slowly, cane tapping against roots too old to name. Each step echoed across ground that bled silver and black, where memory was carved into bark and shadow like scripture that refused to fade. Above him, twisted branches reached into a sky that had no stars, only layers of forgotten light peeling away.

The fruit here no longer glistened. They sagged on the vine like rot that had forgotten to fall, their skins puckered, their scent a bitter mix of honey and betrayal. Some pulsed softly, the last heartbeat of a lie too long whispered.

He came to the edge of the clearing where once the Tree had stood. Or the thing that called itself the Tree.

This was the place where she had rewritten the story. Where she had taken the page and torn it, where she had refused the fruit, not out of obedience, but out of defiance. Where she'd knelt and touched the roots, not to harvest, but to unmake.

Ash still coated the ground like snowfall from a ruined heaven. The bark remained cracked, hollow, its center burned through with the echo of her will. The roots curled away from the center as if they, too, feared what had been planted in their place.

Because something had taken root.

A sapling.

It was bright. Small. Daring. Clean.

Crowley hated how it made him feel. Not rage. Not dread.

Chills.

He stared at it for a long moment, cane tightening in his gloved hand. His eyes gleamed, but not with triumph. With calculation.

"No one's ever thought to replant," he said, voice like oil over water. "They always eat the fruit or burn it. They fall. They kneel. They obey."

He stepped forward and knelt, pressed two fingers into the blackened earth at the sapling's base. Dreamlight surged upward to meet him, not with warmth, but with warning. It didn't reject him outright.

But it saw him. His smile didn't vanish, but it twisted. The skin at the corners of his mouth creased just slightly. His tongue clicked softly behind his teeth.

"You didn't win," he said to the dirt, to the leaves, to the still-healing roots. Not to Sia. Not even to the Dream. "You just delayed me."

And yet...

The words rang hollow. Even to him. Because something in this place no longer answered to his name. The hum of the fruit had dulled when he passed. The shadows didn't lean in to listen. The soil no longer whispered.

He stood slowly, brushing ash from his knees with deliberate grace. He adjusted his cuffs. Straightened his coat. Smoothed the errant strands of silver hair that had come loose.

The war wasn't lost. But the board had changed. And he would need a new garden. One not of memory but of hunger and thorns. Of something still willing to be shaped in his image. He turned without ceremony, cloak brushing through the ash like a scythe. Behind him, the sapling swayed in a breeze that did not touch the rest of the Garden.

It stood.

And it grew.

The Song

Epilogue

Found in Dobahold's Archives, Prophecies involving the Final Days:

They say the blades will rise again, when faith is almost gone.
Three forged in fire, three bound in light, three carried through the dawn.

One held by Dreamer's hand, who walks where none should tread.
One sung by the Singer's voice, who mourns the realms of dead.
One wielded by the silent Mage, who binds the world with thread.

And in the darkest hollow, where hope forgets its name,
The swords will find each other, and set the sky aflame.

Veritas.